Terra Firma Angelicus

Earth Angels

Mary Ann Gillispie

Order this book online at www.trafford.com
or email orders@trafford.com

Most Trafford titles are also available at major online book retailers.

*The cover was designed
by David Nettles, Chesapeake, Virginia*

Printed in Victoria, BC, Canada.

ISBN: 978-1-4269-3306-6 (sc)

Our mission is to efficiently provide the world's finest, most comprehensive book publishing service, enabling every author to experience success. To find out how to publish your book, your way, and have it available worldwide, visit us online at www.trafford.com

Trafford rev. 10/01/2010

www.trafford.com

North America & international
toll-free: 1 888 232 4444 (USA & Canada)
phone: 250 383 6864 • fax: 812 355 4082

CONTENTS

PROLOGUE

Have you ever had a hunch? Did you wonder how that hunch came to your mind? We go about our daily lives taking for granted the intuitions, hunches, and premonitions, rarely questioning their origin, yet many of our decisions are persuaded by this unseen guidance.

Have you heard a newscast reporting on a murder, especially the serial type, where the criminal declares he heard voices in his head tell him to kill another human? He says, "God told me to kill them." Sadly, law enforcement believes this statement as plausible.

On the other side of the coin, a murderer may declare that, "Satan told me to kill them." This murderer is mocked and ridiculed because law enforcement declares that there is no such being as Satan...*oh, yeah, the devil made you do it.* They declare the criminal to be a psycho, refusing to take responsibility for his crime, looking for someone to blame besides himself.

Is it time we ask ourselves, "Does anyone live in the invisible realm? If so, do these unseen beings have any influence on me?"

People ask every day, "Who causes all evil: injustice, hatred, revenge, murder, unforgiveness, humiliation, arrogance, lies, fears, jealousy, envy, abuse of children, famine, sexual perversion, tyranny, chaos, anarchy and war? If there really is a God, why doesn't he stop the evil?"

From the beginning of human life on the earth, history has recorded that angels (good and bad) occupy this invisible realm. Lucifer (light bearer) was an important cherub in the service of God, the Creator of the universe. History reveals that Lucifer attempted to usurp the throne of his Creator. God had no choice but to remove Lucifer from his powerful position, because he had already influenced millions of cherubim to disavow their Creator.

It was at this time that Hell was created by God…a place of eternal punishment for Lucifer and his followers. After Lucifer lost his honorable position with God, he became known as Satan (adversary/accuser), roaming the earth, seeking whom he may devour. Satan's followers are called demons…wicked…devious…depraved. Satan directs them to terrorize men on the earth, persuading them to blame and curse (disavow) their Creator.

We also find residing in this ethereal realm, God's pure and holy angelic beings. As the Apostle Paul explained in his historic writings, he visited the third heaven (Paradise) of the invisible realm, the home of God. After the death and resurrection of Jesus Christ, the Holy Spirit was sent to the earth to testify of His works, as well as comfort, teach and guide mankind on his earth journey so he will successfully arrive in Heaven.

Though fictional, Terra Firma Angelicus is based on historical documentation, and attempts to reveal the activities of the spiritual beings in the invisible realm influencing the affairs of mankind on the earth. The names I have chosen for these invisible characters are allegorical derived from either the Latin, Greek or Hebrew language…a name that best depicts their expertise. The

Glossary of Characters will name each of the invisible characters and explain their expertise.

You will meet two twenty-first century families in their personal struggles, who are also caught up in espionage, nation takeover schemes, and media propaganda (tool of tyranny), attempting to implement a New World Order that will enslave all the toadies of the world, while systematically and strategically removing any semblance of the name of Jesus Christ (Anointed One) and His Bible from the public consciousness. These global rulers know that Jesus Christ is the only enemy that must be defeated before they can obtain total control of the mind of every human being.

Graphically portrayed, you will see the daily involvement of the angelic and demonic entities of the invisible realm in the lives of all human beings on planet Earth.

Hopefully, this story will not simply acquaint you, but also educate you regarding the "real" power source of our everyday earthly life. Are you really in control of your own life...or...is someone else?

GLOSSARY OF CHARACTERS

Infinite One	God
Reconciler	Jesus Christ
Illuminator	Holy Spirit
Sacred Script	Bible
Believers	Christians
People of the Book	Christians/Jews
Abbadon	Satan/Lucifer
Land of Perpetuity	Heaven
Gehinnom Land of Abandon	Hell/Lake of Fire

Demons from Gehinnom

Land of Abandon................. Expertise

Demon	Expertise
Anomos	Anarchy/lawless
Apisteo	Unbelief
Aporeo	Hopeless/despair
Apostasia	Falling away
Chamas	Violence
Deos	Nefarious
Haga	Terror
Hema	Fury
Katara	Accuse/curse
Kazab	Lying spirit
Krina & Rasa	Condemn
Pheno	Murder
Phobos	Fear
Porneia	Sexual perversion/porn
Pyra	Fire
Remira	Deception
Seol	Grave
Thano	Spirit of death
Typhoo	Pride/arrogance

Angels from the

Land of Perpetuity .... Expertise

Eleusis .... Advent
Charis.................................. Forgiveness/gracious
Chrestos.. Kindness
Doxes .... Glory
Dunamis .... Power
Gasar & Therizo .... Reaper
Harpazo & Eleeo .... Take to oneself/seize
Karmel .... Fruitful
Kletos .... Called Ones
Hanan & Kapar .... Mercy
Phileo .... Brotherly love
Pestos.. Believe
Shalom .... Peace
Shiman............................... Messenger/ambassador
Stephanos... Crown
Teleo & Ahar .... End of things
Zelos .... Fervent

Chapter 1

Explosion

Two International Intelligence Agents (IIA) are on assignment in a tribal land of the East...the city of Afgar. The international rulers of the world are the Sinister Seven...architects of the New World Order. They have been successful in inciting all-out war on four continents. The citizens of these four continents have been ruthlessly forced into submission to Umma, by an audacious, arrogant false religious cult, whom they claim is the one true god. Their murder and mayhem is brutal and seems unending to the peaceful families, who have no one to help them against this frenzied onslaught of evil. All must submit to Dawaism or die...there is no other choice. This continual chaos is bathed with the tears and grief of their victims.

The two major continents of the industrialized West have been covertly planted with tens of thousands of terrorists in the guise of religious peacemakers. They appear pious on the outside, professing they are a religion of peace, but their religious guide book commands them to take over the governments of every nation on Earth, killing all the infidels who refuse to follow Umma.

In the city of Afgar a revolution is taking place. Hatred, violence, bombing and bloodshed is a daily occurrence. Each of the rebels have been incited to riot by infiltrated spies from the IIA, causing an insurrection against the leadership of their country. There is a clandestine Plan by the IIA to topple a peaceful president, who is resisting the New World Order, and put in place a president who will bow to the rule of the Sinister Seven. The Sinister Seven, the wealthy ruling elite, represent one family dynasty in charge of each of the seven continents on Earth. They are a powerful, malevolent, and ruthless banking cartel... self-appointed Planetary Dictators...who believe the stupid toadies of the world are incapable of governing themselves.

E-ooh, e-ooh, e-ooh shrieked the siren piercing the night with its bone-chilling sound, red lights flashing, people scampering to make way for the ambulance valiantly inching its way toward the nearest hospital with its bloody bombing victim. Actually, only one survivor was on board because the others were blown to smithereens in this violent van-bombing.

The driver of the ambulance, Joe Goldman, is not a native, but you would never guess, because his bone structure, skin tone, and deportment allowed him to fit in naturally. But he is an International Intelligence Agent (IIA) on a covert operation in this land of the chaotic East. In Afgar Joe is known only as Abrim by the locals.

An eerie calm surrounded the forlorn, terrified onlookers, as the mile-high debris from the bombing returned to the ground in slow motion like a misty fog rolling in from the ocean, depositing silt over several blocks.

But in the invisible realm laughter rang out. The rioters, who planted the IED exploding the van, were possessed by the unseen powerful forces of evil...demons. The captain of these demon spirits is named Chamas. He is on assignment in Afgar sent from Gehinnom Land of Abandon, a city in the heart of Earth that is ruled by Abbadon the arch-enemy of the Infinite One. For aeons, Abbadon has been at war with the Infinite One, scandalizing, subduing and possessing mankind, dragging them to his abode in the Land of Abandon.

If you were able to see Chamas with your eyes you would find him repulsive. His brown leather-like skin is wrinkly. He has one large horn in the middle of his forehead sitting between two deep-set beady eyes of fire. He is one big, scary dude. He had been assigned to Afgar over three years ago, bringing with him thousands of his most evil minions to take possession of the populous, stirring up riots, producing mayhem and death. Of course, death of the rebellious haters enlarges the kingdom of Gehinnom in the invisible realm. Abbadon rejoices in his victory.

Chamas brought with him a cohort named Haga. He is a scary looking creep, resembling a fire-breathing dragon with sharp ridges on his long tail. When he possesses a human being, terror reigns where that human lives, causing strife, turmoil and dread. Haga has dozens of sharp teeth, flashing them proudly when he roars and snaps wildly after his prey.

After the successful van-bombing spewed body parts over many blocks, Chamas and Haga could be seen sitting on the ledge of a three-story building adjacent the devastation their minions have created in the streets of Afgar. Gleefully Chamas watched his handiwork unfold into total anarchy, congratulating Haga and his many demons for their victory...mission accomplished.

With much joviality, slapping each other on the back and clapping their hands, Chamas and Haga deliciously observed their achievement. They are quite aware that humans do not believe in evil spirits, so they experience no resistance when they enter and take possession of their lives.

While relishing the chaos and death in the streets of Afgar, a disturbing scene unfolds right before their eyes, causing spine-chilling consternation for Chamas and Haga, vaporizing their exhilaration in a flash. The slow-moving ambulance caught the attention of Chamas and Haga, because they suddenly saw the Illuminator appear beside the unaware, severely injured occupant. Despite the fact their cohort Thano, vampire spirit of death with blood dripping from his fangs, has his hand on the neck of the dying bombing victim, these invisible captains of war cringed and cowered at the sight of the illustrious Illuminator, who had come to the aid of one of His own. In a flash, out of nowhere, the ambulance was surrounded by dozens of majestic angels on assignment from the Land of Perpetuity. Their countenance was not only bright as the sun, each scabbard held a glistening sword. Their divine, dazzling, presence caused the power of Chamas and Haga to become inert. They hated becoming powerless, subject to the Infinite One.

Life was hanging by a thread for one IIA agent languishing in the ambulance. His real name is John Gillingham, called Gilly by family and friends. Although, while exercising his covert operation in the city of Afgar, he is known by the locals as Ahmir...a goat herder living just across the border from Afgar.

Joe and Gilly finally had their covertly trained rebels strategically placed in important positions in the current government of Afgar for a successful coup d'atat. In a matter of days, Muamond, the leader of the militants, would begin to run the government of President Yassa. President Yassa would soon be gunned down, along with his administration. It will be a bloodbath...but worth it to accomplish the Plan for the Sinister Seven. One more nation would be forced to submit to the New World Order.

But the carefully implemented plans of Joe and Gilly faced a sudden and definitely unexpected glitch...Gilly was blown up by an IED. He had painstakingly trained these rebels how to construct dangerous bombs...now he was the victim...and the coup d'etat aborted.

Chamas believes he has the right to the life of Gilly, so quickly concocted a plan to delay the ambulance, so he had time to die. Abbadon sent Chamas another captain to help him complete his mission successfully. Phobos (fear) was suddenly on the ledge of the building with Chamas. Phobos was small in stature with black slimy skin...totally hideous. His slanting eyes are filled with flashing fire, while his lips are contorted into a wicked grin.

Chamas frantically yelled to Haga and Phobos, "Dismantle that ambulance!" He had to give Thano a chance to snatch Gilly the moment he died. Abbadon had demanded that Gilly be brought to Gehinnom stat.

Haga and Phobos immediately left the building ledge and slipped under the hood of the ambulance to dismantle the engine, which came to an abrupt halt...sputter... sputter...clunk!

Chamas arrived in time to be part of the fun. Furious, yet fearful, Joe jumped out of his rig to take a look under the hood, mumbling complaints under his breath. He distressfully murmured...revealing unresolved conflict, "This can't be happening...why does trouble always find me...can I do nothing right?"

Though his cover for the covert/ops in this nation is an ambulance driver, Joe also doubles as the hospitals' mechanic in a vehicle repair shop they own adjacent their facility. The hospital has the military contract which is especially convenient, because it gives Joe the opportunity to extract inside information, gleaned from off-the-cuff conversations with military subordinates.

Gilly is barely clinging to life, so time is of the essence, but Joe is confident in his mechanical expertise.

When the three demon captains came out from under the hood, they came face-to-face with Hema who showed up unexpectedly. He was laughing his head off as he escorted Joe out of the ambulance to help him raise the hood. He was exceptionally tall and spindly with one large eye in the middle of his forehead. Curses flowed continually from his mouth. When a human being fusses, fumes, complains bitterly, continually finding fault, while blaming others, the strife that is created brings delight to Hema. He knows he has been successful in his expertise, when he hears curses flow from the mouth of the humans.

Of course, Joe can't see his demonic helpers, but the fear and dread they personify, grip his mind tightly as he cautiously gets out of his rig. He stops abruptly… sensing something lurking in the darkness. He tentatively looks all around this forsaken wasteland noticing an eerie chill run down his spine. Standing still as a stone, except for his head, which slowly moved from left to right, eyes probing ears listening for an enemy hiding in the forbidding darkness. But…nothing was there except his invisible tormentors, so he went right to work. Joe quickly spotted the problem and implemented a swift repair of the broken wire with his trusty black tape.

"Whew, I'm glad that is all it was," said a relieved Joe to himself as he jumps into his rig and turns on the key. "Boy…that is a good sound. It purrs like a kitten."

Quickly he turned his head toward the back of the ambulance bellowing, "Gilly…hey big guy, wake up, wake up! We're only ten miles from the hospital." There was only silence.

Wild thoughts pushed their way into Joe's mind demanding attention. Joe is remembering how he and Gilly have worked together for three years undercover in Afgar, creating rebellious riots in the streets, while training the nationals to overthrow their government...all to accomplish the Plan...but now...they have failed in their assignment. His mind was troubled, as he considered their fate after the CFS finds out.

Joe and Gilly have so much in common...drugs, alcohol, women and pornography. "Man," Joe thought desperately, "I can't lose my partner in porn!"

Perusing the Internet for tantalizing sex on their laptops was the highlight of their evenings, after all day enduring the local radicals spewing venom against the West. During their covert activities they found that these religious bigots had a voracious sexual appetite, but cloaked their devious behavior behind the veneer of piety! The wicked demons of darkness Porneia (fornication) and Remira (deception) had taken possession of these religious bigots, forcing them to express their demonic perversion against the innocent, especially women, who were considered chattel. In Afgar, rape was a common humiliation by these pious pigs, which incensed Joe and Gilly, who could not help the victims. Welcome to Dawaism...the second largest religion on Earth

Porneia is a very successful slime-ball in modern-day society...worldwide. His minions of sexual perversion do not lack someone to possess in this degenerate society, because the unprincipled men and women in power have placed their stamp of approval on immorality, proven by the corrupt laws they pass.

The sensual Porneia has the appearance of a human being, with a pale and gaunt sunken-in face, while ooze seeps from follicles embedded in his hairless body. He is as sickening to look at, as is his disgusting deviance that he foists upon the humans he possesses. He is constantly rubbing his long bony fingers all over his evil companions, who must constantly kick him away in disgust…but he can't help himself…he is driven by his voracious sexual appetite…like the humans he possesses.

Now Remira…that invisible scum-bag beguiles with charm. He persuades men to reason by their five senses, rather than trust in their Creator, by faith. He is giddy with delight when he persuades a human to trust only in his intellect. Remira speaks with a soft soothing voice in order to mask his deception, which causes some humans to misinterpret his voice as that of the Illuminator.

Joe and Gilly, citizens of the free world, often discuss with each other how grateful they are to have been born in the West. But…since they are loyal Servers, they have bought the lie, the propaganda of the Council of Foreign Servers (CFS), who have assured them they are bringing freedom to the citizens of the East, by deposing leaders opposed to the Plan. Joe and Gilly, though, don't know the "real" Plan, they only know what they have been brainwashed to know and believe through their IIA training. A lying spirit named Kazab had possessed their minds since their university days, dragging them into submission to the whims and will of the Sinister Seven.

Kazab can only be described as slithery…a slimy serpent with many stubby legs. He leers through bulging beady eyes, sporting a grisly grin of barbed teeth…sharp as shark teeth. His lies are very believable, because he has led millions of humans away from their loving Creator into false religions. What a price men pay for their ignorance of the powerful demon spirits who live in the invisible realm… who actually run the affairs of men. Kazab has been a most successful servant of Abbadon.

How did John Gillingham, born in a sovereign nation where freedom of speech and religion is protected by law, find himself systematically eliminating the sovereignty (freedom) of other nations?

Thirty years ago as a teenager, Gilly attended Camp Halo, a religious summer camp. During the worship service, prompted by the invisible Illuminator, he became acutely aware of his sinfulness. That night Gilly accepted the Savior into his life, by repenting of his sins to begin his life anew.

Full of eagerness to develop his career in criminology, Gilly was eventually off to the university, where he met Joe. It didn't take long for Gilly to become putty in the hands of his atheistic professors. It brought sinister delight to the heart of his philosophy professor (and others) to lure Gilly into a conversation about his faith, simply by asking, "How did the world come into existence?"

Gilly answered, "The Infinite One created the whole universe including man." To the professor this answer was like a delicious fly caught in a web with the spider hastening to inject poison into its victim.

"Surely Gil," the stern-faced professor with his syrupy-sweet, condescending voice demanded, "you can scientifically prove your lofty idea?"

The university was inundated with millions of demonic spirits, who drove the professors they possessed to believe they have a mandate to expunge the Sacred Script and its author from the planet. These out-of-control demon spirits also have an iron-fisted grip on the curriculum taught at Gilly's university, corrupting its content. They find idealistic youth so easy to possess and drive into immorality...like a harsh task-master with a whip.

Knowing young Gilly would have no answers, because of his budding faith, the professor was able to strip to shreds his child-like faith, chiding and degrading him in front of his snickering peers. Gilly had never heard anyone so violently opposed to the Infinite One, until his red-faced professor, pointing a bony index finger in his face, sneeringly proclaimed, "Your religion is mythical nonsense. You are totally stupid to believe in what you cannot see. When you die you are just dead!" This humiliation caused doubt and unbelief to seize Gilly's mind like a vise.

At the end of his first year of college, low grades, continual demeaning confrontations from professors, and the earnest persuasion of his peers, convinced Gilly that he was foolish to believe in unseen beings in the invisible realm, good or evil, so he eventually disregarded his experience with the Reconciler. He threw off his new-found faith like a soiled coat.

Gleefully Apisteo, the invisible demon of unbelief, entered Gilly's mind taking charge of his life from that day forward. Apisteo has the appearance of a misty outline of a giant gorilla-like ten foot monster. His ghostly pale demeanor could hardly be detected visually by his cohorts in the invisible world, yet he is one of the most dangerous ghouls in Abbadon's arsenal of exterminators. Apisteo was not content being alone in Gilly's mind and body, so he yelled to his wicked friends Typhoo and Kazab. Typhoo portrayed the shape of a man. He is twelve feet tall, handsome and spooky at the same time. When he walks into the presence of the other demon spirits, confident and grinning from ear to ear, they all part a wide swath, because of their fear of him.

"Come join me," beckoned Apisteo to his sinister friends. "John Gillingham has corrupted himself, giving us permission to oppress his mind and force him to fulfill our passion against other ignorant fools in this degenerate society." Apisteo snickered as he watched these goons from the nether world slip into Gilly, forcing their evil thoughts and passions into his mind.

"It certainly is to our advantage that these stupid humans refuse to believe that we are real. Ignorance eliminates any hindrance to the defilement we accomplish in and through their lives," declared Typhoo confidently. Then out of their taunting mouths rang a hearty guffaw, echoing throughout the limitless invisible realm.

Soon Gilly's university life was out of control. His moral defenses were removed through viewing pornography, while whacked-out on drugs and alcohol. His degenerate behavior gave Porneia permission to enter and oppress his mind and body, relentlessly forcing him on a path of sexual promiscuity.

"Tee hee hee," snickered Porneia, gyrating his body with a lustful gesture, making sport in front of his demonic friends, "we're gonna have fun tonight!" Stripped of his faith, the only morals Gilly had left were the situational ethics, taught and embraced by humanist teachers in the government schools he had attended most of his life. No God...no morals...no integrity...no conscience.

All of these demons clamored for dominance, creating a severe inner struggle for Gilly, who never understood his bouts with depression and thoughts of suicide. He had no idea his whole being was infested with demon spirits, suppressing his real personality, while their personalities became strong enough to overpower his.

When Gilly sought medical help, they simply gave him pills, saying he had a stressful job. No one ever told him there were invisible demonic spirits, bent on invading and possessing the lives of all human beings, to perform through them every kind of evil that has ever been imagined.

Gilly really felt he was all alone...his life felt out of control...but no expert had any solution for him. So Gilly simply suffered in silence in his attempt to hold onto his sanity. He could never explain why he got such gratification from the death of dissidents in the foreign lands, where he was on assignment

Gilly was no longer able to make choices for himself, because he had unwittingly submitted his mind to the rule of these unseen evil entities, those who live in the darkness of the invisible nether world. These demon spirits direct their human slaves by voices in their minds. All the evil entities in control of Gilly's life were laughing their heads off, boasting to each other, "If we can persuade him to do evil by our voices in his mind, the Infinite One will be blamed for all the calamity that we bring upon him."

If Gilly had only read the Sacred Script, he would have found out he has authority in the name of the Reconciler to cast these demons far from him. Without this knowledge, he was a prisoner of the wicked demons...forced to do their will.

These evil "voices" possessing the minds of billions of human beings across the planet, cause all the hatred, revenge, child abuse, violence, murder, mayhem, and war that is escalating in every nation of the world. Demonic voices are commandeering their human captives into chaos, producing calamity and death.

Abbadon, ruler of the invisible kingdom of Gehinnom Land of Abandon, is maneuvering all leaders of every nation into anarchy, because his minions are now in possession of every leader of every nation on Earth. Leaders filled with pride, arrogance, and aggrandizement are driven by invisible demonic spirits to enslave all toadies, so they can rule over these masses. Unknowingly, Gilly and Joe are working hand-in-hand with Abbadon to accomplish his malevolent desires against humanity.

What is interesting, Gilly heard other voices in this unseen realm. These voices whispered, soft and gentle words, assuring him that he is able to resist the evil temptations that relentlessly bombard his mind. The Infinite One sent two of his powerful angelic warriors to guard him all the days of his life on Earth. Shalom and

Chrestos, who emanated shimmering rays of brilliance in the invisible realm, always spoke softly in his ear, attempting to persuade him toward moral choices. There is no intimidation or threat from the angelic realm, no intimidation or threat from the Infinite One...only gentle persistence, wooing him toward good choices. The Illuminator convicts humans of their sins, offering the way to victory through the Reconciler. But Gilly has forgotten anything he learned about the Creator and His invisible world, which was very little, so he ignored the gentle voices of his celestial angelic messengers.

By the time Gilly graduated from the university he was off to his IIA training at Prefecta. During this time Gilly became perfectly indoctrinated (brainwashed), an exemplary candidate for sabotaging the sovereignty of other nations, seducing them into the Plan of consolidating all nations into one, ruled by the megalomaniacs...the Sinister Seven. No matter how many protesting human beings had to be murdered to accomplish this lofty delusion, Gilly's government education had convinced him with the help of his Marxist, atheistic professors...that the end justifies the means. In other words...it matters not whom you harm in order to accomplish the Plan.

Gilly continued to follow the dark path.

Chapter 2

Demons of the Nether World

Thano was salivating, while blood continued to drip from his fangs, as he thought of soon having Gilly in his deathly hands, escorting him to his final resting place in the heart of the earth...the invisible city of Gehinnom Land of Abandon. E-ooh, e-ooh, e-ooh continued the ambulance as it inched its way around the boulder size pits in the bombed out road to the hospital.

"Hold on buddy, hold on," Joe shouted his anguished words into the silent, eerie darkness of the ambulance. Anxiously, he reached back fumbling back and forth attempting to touch Gilly, as if by doing so he could keep him alive. But Gilly wasn't within reach and Joe really knew it, but he had to do something...anything.

Absentmindedly Joe bent his head over the steering wheel, straining to look through the sooty window to peer at the moonlit sky on this chilly evening. While keeping an eye on the road watching for craters, he mused, "What a contrast to see these scintillating stars, so large, and hanging so low I can reach out and pluck one, yet five miles back is hatred and bloodshed...total bedlam...obscuring this beauty with fulminating body parts." A shudder ran through his body from the latter image...because of Gilly. He reached for the heater knob, cranking it on high to warm his cold hands from repairing the car.

"Joe...how can you continue to think that your allegiance to the CFS is justified, when all you can see is the hatred, violence, and war you have incited with the senseless death of millions of human beings, in order to accomplish the Plan? Isn't all human life valuable?" whispered Phileo, a dazzling, invisible, angelic warrior sent from the Infinite One, to persuade him to abandon his career with the global crime families...the Sinister Seven.

"What a novel thought," mused Joe discarding the compassionate questions almost instantly. He had been convinced by years of propaganda that many must die...for the greater good. So once again Joe successfully resisted the voice of his conscience urging him to preserve life... not destroy it.

About one mile from the hospital, Joe got excited because he knew that a competent medical staff was waiting. What he didn't know, about forty-five minutes ago Gilly lost his battle for life. Suddenly Gilly was jerked awake by someone who had gruffly grabbed him by the nape of the neck, extracting him from his physical body, leaving it limp as a rag doll on the blood-soaked cot. Struggling to free himself from the iron-fisted grip, at least to get a peak at who is violently dragging him against his will to a place unknown to him, Gilly mustered every bit of his quivering strength, but was not successful.

As Gilly was unceremoniously dragged out of the ambulance, for one brief moment a mind-boggling situation gripped his heart with sheer terror. His eyes gazed upon, and became momentarily transfixed on his blood-soaked, very still body...and..."Oh my god, I'm no longer in it," he screamed, frantically scrambling to climb back into his familiar skin.

Instantly ascending from the deep recesses of his mind, memories jolted his sensibilities. "When you die, you are simply dead forever," gushed forth the angry, life-changing words from his long forgotten university philosophy professor. This philosophy had been whole-heartedly embraced by Gilly, while casting off his own personal faith. But now this philosophy is mocking his reality.

"Liar, liar, liar," Gilly screamed at the top of his lungs to this ghostly memory. Abruptly the beasts snapped his neck into submission, preventing him from returning to his earthly body.

From his peripheral vision Gilly was barely able to glimpse two creepy ghoulish monsters, something he had only seen in monster movies. Each had one hand on the nape of his neck, preventing him from turning his head to get a better look. Stretching his eyes as far as possible to his right, he could barely see the profile of a skeleton-like creature, covered by a black filthy, coarse-fibered shroud from head to foot…the vampire Thano. After stretching his eyes as far to his left as possible, he could see that this creature was grimy-greasy beige, with prickly burs twisted into hair balls throughout the visible fur…called Deos. Now his eyes hurt from stretching, yet he still had no answers to his multiple questions.

Yelling at the top of his lungs, shrieks of fear continued to pour out of his mouth. Zillions of questions collided in his brain demanding an immediate answer, all at the same time. Why?...who?…where?…hel…lllp! Still struggling to free himself, Gilly put both of his hands up to his neck to engage all of his strength, hopefully to excise the grasp of these scary creatures. But his efforts were in vain, while his screams of terror fell on deaf ears.

Like an out of control ball bouncing off the dark dingy tunnel walls, piercing Hyena-like laughter echoed the rapturous victory of Thano and Deos for capturing another victim for the Land of Abandon. Everything was happening so fast and Gilly was valiantly attempting to clear his mind, regain his focus, and assess this horrific situation. One thing he knew for sure...he was still alive, but his body was left behind in the ambulance, still heading for the hospital with his good friend Joe at the helm!

His sense of smell was greatly enhanced in this strange, and so far, unexplained environment. The stench emitted from these two beasts was nauseating...overwhelming. Gilly wasn't sure that he had ever smelled anything so disgusting, or comparable, except maybe a rotting corpse, especially in the hot desert sun.

In his line of work as an IIA Agent, he was well acquainted with dying and death. There were many protesters attempting to prevent their sovereign government from being taken over, who were mowed down without pity. Those who got in the way of the Plan were "toast." Actually, the politically correct term is "collateral damage." But... Gilly's new experience was producing an overpowering sense of guilt...a strange new emotion for the man of steel.

Faces began appearing before his eyes, specters from his past whom he declared to be "useless eaters," those who had died resisting the Plan, involuntary sacrifices for the cause of the greater good. Never once in all of his years with the Sinister Seven had he ever experienced remorse...until now.

Flailing his arms in a desperate attempt to erase these ghostly apparitions, whom he now sees as someone's dad, maybe someone's brother or husband...is in vain... because they just keep haunting him, face after face, lost to eternity. Shivers of loathing for his contemptible behavior, shook his whole being with terrified fear of impending retribution for his crimes.

"Could the 'casualties' of the Plan have experienced what I am now experiencing when they died and left their bodies?" sobbed Gilly, overwhelmed at this revolting revelation of his crimes against humanity. Tears of anguish flowed unashamedly.

"I wouldn't wish this on my worst enemy," moaned Gilly. But he didn't know that the worst had not come...yet.

Maybe Gilly couldn't see where he was going, but he definitely was becoming aware of where he had been... how he had spent his life. The heels of his feet were hurting since he was being roughly dragged backward. The walls of this gruesome tunnel seem to be lined with creepy misshapen creatures of distorted shapes and sizes. One had a single eye in the middle of his forehead, a mouth full of sharp fangs hanging over the lower lip, and two horns on the top of the head, yet had the bulk of a bear...scary.

As Gilly was hustled through the spooky tunnel, many of these creepy creatures grabbed at him, cursing and disparaging his arrival at this place of doom and gloom. Gilly drew his arms close to his body in an effort to become a small target, recoiling from the reach of the vulgar brutes. A wave of dread rippled from his head to his toes.

One very small black, snake-skinned demon (lust/ sensual) with flashing fire behind his two beady eyes, seemed to grow right out of a crevice in the grimy tunnel wall. Slowly he extended long slithering fingers, rubbing them all over Gilly's body, uttering a perverse chortle when Gilly cringed, stiffening his body with abhorrence, as he pondered his fate.

Gilly's mind was racing for answers. It now appears very clear to him that when one dies he is not "just dead," but rather is still very much alive. He can certainly attest to this fact now. But he was perplexed, because even when he was young and devoted to the Infinite One, he was only told by his pastor about love, salvation, and someday he would be "raptured" to the Land of Perpetuity. He was told there was a place called Gehinnom Land of Abandon, but a God of love would never send His children to such a forbidding place of torment and hopelessness. Many teach that even if you are not a believer when you die, some relative (believer) can pray you into the Land of Perpetuity...which is false. Since Gilly trusted his church leaders, he never asked for more information about a place he would never have to go. Why would he?

"So who are these dreadful creatures?" pondered Gilly.

"Am I in Gehinnom? I wish I had taken the time to read what the Reconciler said about that place in the Sacred Script, rather than trust man's interpretation of prophecy... but...I really can't blame anyone but myself. I made my own choices," Gilly moaned despairingly.

This dingy and frightful tunnel has many twists and turns, gradually enlarging, on this seemingly endless journey. Before long, Gilly could see reflective light, a faint sulfureous glow on the walls of this ominous subterranean living grave. The odor of sulfur was pungent, nipping his nose as would a whiff of Limburger cheese. As the glow became slightly brighter, and the stench unbearable, he could hear in the far distance the sound of multitudes of cursing voices with screams of agony.

"What is going on? Am I entering an insane asylum?" wailed Gilly. But these raucous fiends did not answer his desperate pleas. Instead, their relentless, aggressive assault on Gilly focused on delivering their hostage to his destination. Shivers crawled up and down Gilly's spine as he plunged deeper into the abyss...against his will. A cold clamminess crept over his body, his heart pounding loudly in his ears, terror tightening his throat like a slow paralysis, causing him to gasp for breath.

Chapter 3

Troubling Reflections

Joe was frenetic by now, trying his best to get Gilly to the hospital before he died.

"How did our careful plans go awry," lamented Joe as he mentally rehashed in his mind the tried and proven scheme, that had always worked to pull down a sovereign leader and install a despot, sympathetic to the Plan of the Sinister Seven…the global banking crime cartel.

"We must have had a spy in our midst," continued the frantic, probing thoughts tramping through his brain…"but who is it?" Adrenalin was pumping wildly throughout his body causing a surge of anger and frustration.

"We're almost there, we're almost there!" cheered Joe, as if his enthusiasm could cajole Gilly from his coma.

"Just one more mile my friend and you're home free!" encouraged Joe through tears of stress and grief that he could no longer withhold.

Out of the blue, Joe was suddenly struck with the revelation, "Death is…is final! If Gilly dies, will he still be alive like my wife has always preached?" emerged the intruding question that Joe had always avoided, because he didn't have the answer.

Images of past sins danced on Joe's mind, those he had successfully buried in booze and pornography. "How can she be so stupid?" cursed Joe in the desperate darkness of the tragic moment.

"How can she think that any of that religious crap will benefit her in any way, shape or form?" he screamed out in the nothingness all around him, gesturing with sharp jabs of a pointed forefinger into the air, as if making his point to a captive audience. But...no one was there.

"Get a grip, Joe. Quit thinking on these thoughts," Joe spoke sternly to himself like a Dutch Uncle.

But the rapid-fire questions fast-tracked through his mind like a marching infantry, "Why are you drudging up this old pain that you couldn't resolve when you were home? What makes you think you can find answers in this wasteland?" were relentless torment to Joe's terrified mind.

As Joe struggled to prevent from surfacing the long buried pain in his heart, suddenly right before his eyes he had a vision of his wife, Clarissa, sitting in their cozy breakfast nook back home. He wondered how this could be. He thought he must be going crazy. Yet, he could see her as clearly as if he was there in person. He did know that this was her favorite quiet place to read her Sacred Script, while sipping her favorite mocha latte topped with a dollop of whipped cream. How safe he felt observing a simple routine that he usually would call boring. As much as Joe despises her God, he loves her patience and her peaceful countenance. Looking upon her again in this vision, after not seeing her for eighteen months, reminded him she really is beautiful, with long chestnut hair folding gently over her shoulders when she leans forward to read. Love welled up in his heart as he remembered when they first met...fireworks.

Suddenly Clarissa raised her hands to her invisible Lord and began to worship, startling Joe. He had never seen her do this, so he felt like he was invading her privacy. He had never seen anyone enjoying intimacy with someone invisible.

"My Lord and my God, I bring to Your throne my beloved Joe who still does not know You, nor does he even want You…yet. Please protect him from the enemy, all the demons whom he has allowed to rule his life in the land of barbarians, where he is serving his country. Open his eyes to his folly. I truly believe that you want none to perish in Gehinnom, but that all would come to repentance and live forever in the Land of Perpetuity. Thank you for restoring our marriage," concluded Clarissa.

"What does she mean 'thank you for restoring our marriage,' our marriage isn't restored!" sneered Joe out loud as if Clarissa could hear his criticism of her prayer.

"Besides she thinks that life, liberty, and the pursuit of happiness comes from the sovereignty of her country, which was established on the principles of the Infinite One. How archaic can you get?" he grumbled to himself.

"That old constitution is obsolete for a modern, sophisticated society, at least according to the Council of Foreign Servers to whom I have pledged my allegiance. We have become a global society which will be much better organized with one central government for the whole world: one military…one court…one religion…one monetary system…one global society. Aw…yes…everybody equal and fair to all…social justice," Joe murmured with much satisfaction for the truth he had embraced, while shaking his head up and down in agreement with the choice he had made for his life.

Joe continued to be plagued with contradicting tormenting thoughts, while he struggled to keep his mind focused on getting Gilly to the hospital.

"Please Gilly, don't die on me," he pleaded with the unresponsive battered body in his ambulance.

His last memory of his little Joey was sitting in his small rocking chair, absentmindedly rocking incessantly, not responding to Joe's hug and kiss goodbye. The doctors say he will improve some with their new medications and therapy. But Joe wants his son to be a "real" son, to play ball and go fishing and compete in sports. Or...maybe play a musical instrument if he desires, but this will never happen for seven year old Joey. Joe longed to hear his son call him "Dad."

"Why am I thinking these thoughts...I don't want to think these thoughts...go away," he cried out, thrusting his open right hand with fingers outstretched into the darkness, in a desperate attempt to push away this agony.

"I have to focus...focus...focus. I have to keep my mind on the things at hand. After all, I am well trained...calm, cool, and collected. I have been told that I have the perfect face for a spy...stone-cold expressionless face...as if ice water is running through my veins," he stammered. But... his mind simply refused to focus and kept wandering off to the past...the past he must keep hidden.

Joe had his perfect little world, well organized, predictable and in total control. When life threw him a curve like Joey's autism, he just went globetrotting. His wife could take care of it, he had convinced himself. That is her job anyway. So Joe could simply let her take full responsibility, leaving him scot-free to play in the world. Besides...Clarissa was trying to do something for Joey, or at least attempting to prevent other families from experiencing their heartache. Since he had no answers, it was easy to simply let her do her thing.

He did allow his mind to linger on what his wife was doing in her research for the cause of autism, and Joe was actually proud of her findings. Of course, he never told her. Government funds have poured into foundations that study this problem, but no answers so far. If they found a cause and cure they would lose tax-subsidized grant money. Once a foundation is set up and funded with taxpayer's hard-earned confiscated monies, it takes on a life of its own. So cause and cure will never be found by these Big Pharma promoted entities.

Clarissa told Joe that in her research of scientific tests completed by reputable research doctors (PHD's) who are privately funded, have proven without a shadow of a doubt that the excessive amount of vaccinations forced on little babies, is the cause of this pandemic malady. The aluminum, deadly ethyl mercury, and thimerasol adjuvant cause the tiny undeveloped brain of defenseless infants to inflame and swell, especially when several vaccinations are given at one time, harming the neurotransmitters irreversibly. Some babies are naturally protected because of their particular genetic makeup, but the increased stats are alarming: 1 in 100 births (more boys) now fall prey to this preventable suffering. The Amish sect does not vaccinate and they do not have autism.

The flu vaccine is now forced on pregnant mothers which is inflaming the brains of these little one's in-utero. Clarissa can hardly keep up with the data revealing the evil that is being perpetrated against an unsuspecting society.

Big Pharma lobbied congress to make it mandatory for children to be heavily vaccinated or they could not enroll in public school. This amounts to huge profits for these devious corporations...thanks to a bought and paid for Congress, who pass these egregious laws. With Big Pharma money in their campaign coffers, the clueless lawmakers continue to make laws that force a "free" society to subject their precious babies to this Frankenstein experiment...against their will.

No matter what are the facts now being revealed, the Medical Society must protect their flawed science, because the populous would bring lawsuits against them. Actually, there have been many lawsuits, quietly settled away from the eye of the public. So rather than support truth, they support a lie, no matter how great is the cost paid by the little ones and their families…forever.

"All they have to do is simply stop all vaccinations, repeal that stupid coercive law and quell the madness," thought Joe feeling anger rise within him, as he contemplated the simplicity of the solution in a convoluted society.

Charis, the magnificent angelic messenger, took advantage of Joe's moment of reflection and whispered in his ear, "Clarissa is a true reformer in a nation that has lost its way. The Infinite One has directed her to take a stand for truth and He will direct her path."

Joe perked up as he mulled over in his mind these cherished memories of his wife's valiant (crusader) efforts to ferret out the truth, amidst a bombardment of propaganda lies from the medical lobbyists to congress. He even remembered when she went to the Capitol armed with scientific facts and her own experience…very brave against the status quo.

A twinge of guilt washed over him like a wave from the ocean splashes involuntarily to shore. He seemed to be seeing truth for the first time. Joe realized, sadly not until now, that he had never encouraged his wife, nor did he help her in any way find the answer for their son's dilemma. Ignoring the problem was his line of least resistance. Of course, booze and pornography helped him maintain.

"Clarissa has the truth about autism and is truly a crusader for truth. Be sure and tell her you are proud of her when you see her," Charis spoke gently to Joe's weary mind.

Joe found himself agreeing with this new thought that suddenly appeared in his mind, and he didn't instantly cast it away, as he had in the past. Clarissa is a crusader, steadfast, and always patient and kind to everyone. He had never seen her act arrogantly. In fact, she always deferred to others.

"Hmm"...he thought, "Clarissa crusades for life...I crusade for death."

For the first time in all of his years with the IIA, he felt shame for how he had spent his life in the service of the CFS. He always wanted to be a Server with the approval of the Sinister Seven, even at the expense of his family... but now...he was seeing through different eyes. And...he didn't know why.

Again Charis, the powerful messenger angel whispered, "Could Clarissa be right when she assessed that the agenda of the Sinister Seven is to remove freedom from all citizens in the world, placing themselves in absolute power over all people?" Joe was always repulsed by this thought, when it previously came into his mind, because he had denied that possibility...until now. As suddenly as a bolt of lightning strikes, Joe was finding his conscience. His usual justification for defending the Plan was sloughing off like a snake slithering away in the grass.

"What is happening to me?" Joe mumbled under his breath, grabbing both sides of his head and shaking it back and forth, as if he could stop the bombarding thoughts that were softening his heart.

Soon he came upon a very sharp curve so he slowed down. Then suddenly he could see the illumination from the hospital against the blackness of night.

"Yea!" he yelled out into the darkness.

"We're here Gilly, we're finally here! You're gonna be okay now!" exclaimed Joe feeling the excitement of hope, as a jolt of adrenalin coursed through his veins stimulating alertness. Up the long driveway to the large door labeled EMERGENCY ENTRANCE, Joe maneuvered his long vehicle, backing into the opening to expedite the removal of Gilly by the staff. The back doors flew open, while two attendants grabbed Gilly's cot and swiftly removed him to their gurney, all before Joe could jump out and run to the back.

Much to his dismay, the attendants already had covered Gilly's face with a sheet. Joe was incredulous at their thoughtlessness, revealing this through bulging veins in his neck...but he couldn't say a word.

Dr. Hasad's soft dark eyes reflected perplexity, though his swarthy face was etched with creases of compassion, as he spoke gently, "Sir, your friend is stone-cold, eyes are set. He has been dead for quite awhile. Please come in, get warm and make your necessary calls. I am so very sorry."

Dropping to his knees, Joe's plaintive cry, "It's gonna be okay, it's gonna be okay Ahmir," could be heard inside the hospital, causing the staff to look out the window in dismay at the heartbreaking groans of a man in deep emotional pain. Then barely whispering he sobbed the last, "it's...gon...na...be...o...kay," while pounding his fist on the dirt.

Dr. Hasad and his attendants rolled Gilly's dead body into the hospital. Still outside, Joe finally arose from the ground. Then erupting like a volcano, he raised his leg and gave the ambulance door a swift kick, slamming it so hard the vehicle rocked. After he grabbed the second door and slammed it, he pounded his fists on the metal, screaming over and over, "Ahmir, you can't do this to me. You can't leave me on this assignment by myself. It is just too hard! What will I tell your beautiful wife Julie? Where did you go? Are you still alive?" Joe continued to babble like a raving madman, fists clenched, walking back and forth like a panther stalking his prey, tears flowing unabashedly, as he vented his helpless and hopeless condition.

Unseen by Joe during his outburst, someone walked up behind him and slipped a consoling arm around his shoulder. A soft voice said, "Do not sorrow. If your friend knows the Reconciler, he is in a wondrous place of peace and joy." Abhorred by these words, Joe turned abruptly on his heel to see the face behind the words that were not comforting to him.

"How dare you talk to me in this manner. Of course my friend Ahmir does not know your Reconciler. Why would he? This is not the religion of our land! That talk is a bunch of false garbage," growled Abrim through clenched teeth like a snarling guard dog.

He had to protect his IIA cover. Stepping back from Abrim's space, the soulful eyes of Dr. Hasad gazed upon the anguished eyes of Abrim, pouring, what felt like liquid love, into the depths of his hardened heart. It seemed that an eternity passed as the two of them were transfixed upon the peace exuding from Dr. Hasad. Calm washed over Abrim like a scarlet sunset upon a weary day.

Disarmed by the love flowing from Dr. Hasad toward him, Abrim pondered in his mind, "Who really is this man? I have never met anyone so full of peace in my whole life! He really has some of the attributes that Clarissa exhibits. Could this invisible Reconciler, to whom each gives homage, be for real?"

"I know you are an employee here. Would you like to contact Ahmir's family, or maybe your family? Do they live in Afgar?" inquired Dr. Hasad without explaining why in this foreign land, a man of his ethnicity would know about the Reconciler. Of course, Joe couldn't tell him he was with the IIA working a covert insurrection against Dr. Hasad's government.

Silently bearing their secrets they headed toward the hospital. Suddenly the door burst open by an attendant with a frantic countenance, breathlessly inquiring of Joe, "Are you Abrim Hahman?

When Joe said yes, his heart began to beat rapidly as he anxiously asked, "Is there good news about Ahmir…is he alive after all?"

"No, no, no sir. The Consular at the Embassy is on the telephone stating there is a life or death emergency. Someone in your family, I don't know who, but…please, please sir, just come to the telephone and the Consular will fill in the details," urged the attendant, grabbing Joe's coat almost dragging him to the telephone.

Chapter 4

Past Revealed

Hanging up the telephone, Abrim's countenance appeared as a dead man, whose color has all drained out, not unlike Gilly who lies dead in the hospital morgue. Scrambled thoughts raced through his mind seeking a game plan.

Once again quietly walking up behind Abrim, speaking in his mellow, reassuring voice Dr. Hasad said, "You appear as if you have seen a ghost. Is there anything that I can do for you?"

"No...no...there is nothing anyone can do now. It is hopeless," groused Abrim in his usual inimical fashion. Suddenly a pain struck Dr. Hasad deep within his spirit causing him to hastily grab Abrim's arm, hustling him into his private office and closed the door. Putting his hands on Abrim's shoulders, deep groans of grief uttered from his mouth, as he prayed an unsolicited prayer over Abrim, who stood in uncharacteristic silence, actually astonishment. There was a startling radiance emanating from Dr. Hasad, a strange, new and unexplainable experience for Abrim.

Neither of them saw the brilliant angelic messenger walking beside Dr. Hasad. Eleeo was very large. His head protruded through the ceiling and a gleaming sword was sheathed at his side. He pulled his sword against the demons of darkness crawling in and out of Abrim, when Dr. Hasad prayed, “Father grant to this grieving man a spirit of wisdom and revelation of insight, into the mysteries and secrets of the deep intimate knowledge of Yourself, by having the eyes of his heart flooded with Your truth. Cause him to trust in You for the deliverance of his daughter, so he will know that You live. I rejoice in You always.” Eleeo successfully held at bay Pheno and Kazab with his large golden sword.

Abruptly, without another word, Dr. Hasad disappeared leaving Abrim perplexed, but strangely encouraged, because of this unexplainable peace and the light that shone all around him. “How can this be?” he muttered.

“How did Dr. Hasad know so specifically about my dilemma,” pondered Joe. Then reality rushed in causing him to remember that he must get to the Embassy stat. A plane ticket is waiting for his 9,000 mile trek home to face the pain that he has caused his family.

Pensively he thought, “Will I be too late?” recoiling at the tangled web of unresolved issues that is now surfacing with this crisis.

“Where are you Gilly when I need you?” Joe probed his thoughts anxiously for some rhyme or reason for his compounding problems, as he rushed to his car to head for the Embassy.

“Don’t troubles come in three’s,” he pondered, “so I wonder what is next? How could I handle anymore? I am about at the end of my rope now!”

While he was inside the hospital a cloud cover had formed, shutting out the moon and the brilliant stars that had captivated him a few hours ago. In fact, a soft mist had accumulated on his windshield. Reaching for the knob to turn on the windshield wipers and the back window defroster, a sudden profusion of tears overwhelmed him while he backed out of his parking spot for the long trip to the Embassy.

"Too bad this car doesn't have wipers for my eyes," quipped Joe, smiling to himself at this lame attempt at humor during his desperate plight.

Stopping for a moment he decided that he better check his map since he is in unfamiliar territory. Pulling out his map, he carefully scrutinized the direction to his destination, though the tears would not stop. He wasn't hyperventilating, but hopelessness in the pit of his stomach encompassed him like a blanket of suffocating smoke. No answers were forthcoming. This was the work of Aporeo who slipped into the car along side of Joe, smiling smugly from ear to ear. Unseen by Joe, nonetheless, Aporeo had been very successful in his assignment, but his mission was not complete until Chloe was dead.

Aporeo was a disgusting looking character; putty-gray with vomit particles dripping from the edges of his wooly hair. He stunk to high-heaven and wrapped his iron fists around the heads of his victims until they succumbed to suicide.

There was no way that Aporeo would allow anything that Dr. Hasad had prayed over Joe to penetrate his spirit and cause him to seek out the Reconciler. Keep him in turmoil and confusion, heap troubles upon him, generating hopelessness and despair was the motto of Aporeo, while making sure the Infinite One is blamed. And...he was always successful. After all, he had practiced for centuries and had millions of notches in his belt, so he should be thoroughly skilled by now.

Joe could finally see the lights of the big city. He glanced once again at the map to zero in on the exact street of the Embassy. He had driven all night and was exhausted, but the sun was just peaking above a faraway mountain range, spreading golden hues of illumination throughout the rain-cleansed sky. Just viewing nature's wonder brought to his sagging spirit a twinge of confidence.This is because Aporeo had left him briefly to go help his compatriot in another part of the city who was having trouble subduing a believer in the Infinite One. But...he will be back.

Once on the long arduous flight Joe knew that he would finally be able to sleep. Finding his seat, he buckled in and the plane soon ascended, leveling off as it found its flight path. Joe nestled his head into a soft pillow and immediately conked out. But...Aporeo had accompanied Joe along with Chamas and Hega, joining the spirits of darkness who possessed Joe for so many years. They are very sure that the crisis they have created at Joe's home will drive him to suicide from guilt. Gleefully they high-fived all around. Then Aporeo sped off to Crystal Waters.

Then an omen appeared in the sky. Swirling aggressively around and around Joe's airplane appeared the blood-sucking vampire Thano, who had his next victim in his sights.

Joe's sleep was anything but peaceful. His invisible sleuths would enter his sleep with nightmarish horrors. Joe and his wife Clarissa have been married twenty-three years, but he has been on assignment with the IIA for most of those years. Basically, he had ditched his responsibilities, yet convinced himself that he had to make a living.

In his nightmare he saw his beautiful, but despondent, fifteen year old daughter Chloe dressed in black, while her countenance reflected a ghastly pallor, worshiping at the altar of Molech.

Joe knew she was attempting to fit in with the Goth sub-culture of acid rock music, but he thought it was a phase. Once, when he was home, he asked her why she liked the Goth life style? At that moment, the invisible demon Aporeo violently jumped into Chloe, causing her to transform into a creature-like being. Her eyes became fiery and her facial features contorted with her lips actually curling into a werewolf snarl shrieking, "Be…cause… they…love…me!"

Joe had only seen this type of morphing in sci-fi fantasy movies. At the time he was speechless, wondering in his mind (but did not say), "Who is this? She seems to have been taken over by some invisible force. This person certainly is not my little Chloe."

But as usual, Joe did nothing but turn-tail and run back to his safe covert/ops in a foreign county, leaving the solution to Clarissa…if indeed there was one.

In his nightmare Chloe's corpse-like face kept darting at him uttering an eerie mournful cry…help me…help me… pleee…eese…help me. Joe thrust both hands over his face in an attempt to crowd out this menacing specter.

On the telephone, when Joe was back at the hospital, Clarissa told him that Chloe was in the hospital near their home…in a coma. One of her ghoulish groupies actually attempted to offer her as a blood sacrifice on an altar to their god Molech, by plunging a dagger into her heart and slashing her throat. Thankfully he missed her heart, but she is barely hanging onto life.

Like a camera flash the next scene in his nightmare finds Joe running, running, running, down a narrow cobble path in dense fog. He has no idea where he is because he can't even see his own hand in front of his face, yet he is constrained to keep running into the forbidding fog, compelled by a frightful unseen force at his back. He knows innately that someone is chasing him, but he sees and hears no one. Terror has now gripped him, adrenalin is rushing, and his heart is pounding faster and louder, while Joe is running, running, running from the invisible energy force.

Snippets from his childhood were injected into this mishmash of buried unresolved memories, darting into his tormenting nightmare.

One day when he was walking home from school with his friends, he saw his mother hanging yellow-stained bed sheets on the clothes line yelling, "Now your friends can see how you wet the bed every night, because you really are a baby." This old buried memory emerged in his nightmare, and he could see himself, utterly ashamed, running, running, running as far away as he could get from his friends. The face of his mother was scowling. He was only ten years old and had no idea why he was targeted for this humiliation. No one guarded and protected his dignity.

At this moment, the seething hatred for his mother became murder. Joe watched horrified as a demonic being (Pheno) entered him, taking possession of his life from that day until now. Joe could see the fiendish grin on Pheno's face and he turned to run from his now revealed enemy. But…the enemy was inside of him and he couldn't get away.

Years later, a doctor found and repaired a urethra deformity, but the shame, and his unforgiveness toward his mother's unwarranted humiliation (and other embarrassments) was buried, molding him into who he was today. He emphatically denied that his childhood experiences had anything to do with forming his adult character…so Joe found himself running, running, running the rest of his life. Unforgiveness permitted the demon to posses his spirit, mind and body.

The nightmarish taunting continued with another flashback. Carol…displaying a menacing contemptible grin, overshadowed him like a dark ominous cloud…Ha Ha Ha. He remembered that she was that pretty little blonde in his tenth grade English class. How could he have forgotten! He had become very shy, especially after the hormones kicked in, but he mustered all of his nerve-reserve to ask her to the Homecoming Dance. She screwed up her face and said, "Ooh…aren't you…the one who wets the bed? Then she grabbed her books and ran off with her friends, laughing uproariously, confirming his worthlessness. Hatred and unforgiveness was reinforced in Joe's already stony heart.

Then Joe saw more apparitions leaving and entering his body at their will, and he was repulsed by this revelation in his nightmare.

It was a good thing that no one was sitting next to Joe on this flight, because his nightmares were causing him to flail and groan in pain. A concerned flight attendant walking by, gently tapped him on the shoulder asking if she could be of help. Startled, sweating, and heart still pounding fast, Joe jumped because he was disoriented. He was grateful, though, to be awakened from his horror. She said they had been flying for three hours and wanted to get him something to drink. Joe smiled, nodding his dazed head to affirm her kindness.

Shaken by these unfinished issues in his life, Joe was contemplative while he sipped his hot coffee, wondering what it was all about. A shiver ran through his body, mainly of disgust, because he could still see the contemptible grin on Pheno's face.

"Who is this creature living inside of me? Creepy! How do I get rid of him? Or…can I?" continued the demanding questions pressuring Joe's mind.

Gilly once again came to his mind. After all that Joe had experienced in the last 48 hours, he definitely was tuned into the fact there is an invisible world full of potential danger. Then his thoughts turned to Dr. Hasad and his loving, peaceful countenance…"hmm…who is he?"

His mind mulled over many tormenting questions, "Is Gilly alive in that invisible world? Is there really a good place and an evil place to live on the other side…the invisible world? If so, who decides which place you get to live? Oh…Gilly…I need you. Please…Lord…if you are real…please help me. I am so confused," whispered Joe under his breath.

Chapter 5

Gilly Faces Abbadon

Ker-thud! Gilly found himself rudely splattered spread-eagle upon volcanic debris, sliding until he abruptly and rudely halted, grinding his face into a pair of golden sandals. Instantly he thought, "What an incongruity! Who belongs to this splash of elegance in such a despicable environment?"

"Aw…ha…Mis…ter...Gillingham! I have been waiting for you, ohhh…soo…long," spoke a soothing mystical voice. "You think I am not dressed appropriately?"

Befuddled, Gilly scampered to his hands and knees to take a gander at the one who just read his mind. Sitting back on his haunches, his eyes slowly surveyed the one with the enchanting voice, beginning with the astonishing golden sandals and moving up. Instead of another menacing and gruesome creature, Gilly was transfixed by the beauty of this imposing figure who stood nonchalant, yet his arms were crossed in a 'gotcha' stance. While attempting to pull himself upon his feet, this gigantic being with the mesmerizing voice, reached his hand down to Gilly saying softly, "Let me help you up, Mr. Gillingham.

I am so glad to finally have this opportunity to meet you face to face."

Nonplussed, Gilly simply gazed...in a stupor... perplexed and questioning...still mute.

"Oh...I have forgotten my manners. Let me introduce myself. I am Abbadon. And you have arrived at my home in Gehinnom Land of Abandon; the person and place you do not believe exist. Remember? Ignorance of the truth is my most effective weapon. Do you not agree Mr. Gillingham?"

Gilly's head bobbed up and down in agreement, but he was still dumbfounded and unable to speak. Trembling, he watched in terror while Abdadon turned to walk up, what appeared to be Grecian-style tile steps, ascending to a throne covered with onyx and sardius stones. Actually, these stones appeared to be imitation rather than precious gems, because of their tarnished and garish appearance.

While Abbadon was ascending the stairway, Gilly perused the elaborate podium. There were several ornately scrolled shelves, each containing dozens of mammoth books exactly like the one sitting on top of the podium. After Abbadon reached the top of the stairway, he moved immediately to the open book on the podium.

By now, Gilly's attention had turned toward distant moaning sounds, someone crying out in unbearable pain, attempting to zero in on who was experiencing such agony. But it was difficult to see in this dusky environment, where a smoky haze hung so thick you could cut it with a knife. He could smell death and dying all around him, but he still couldn't comprehend what was the purpose of this deplorable place. Sadly, he really had little knowledge of spiritual things...but...apparently had just signed up for a crash course.

"Mis…ter...Gillingham" jolted Gilly from his intense surveillance of his new environment, "are you ready to have all of your questions answered?" goaded Abbadon, his voice lilting, yet laced with sarcasm.

Turning his head slightly to the left to better scrutinize the spine of the gigantic red gilded book, Abbadon erupted gleefully, "Aw…ha…yes…yes…this is the book of G's." Flipping through thousands of pages rather rapidly finally the page turning silenced, and Gilly could see Abbadon slowly running his finger down a column of names.

"There you are Mr. Gillingham. John Jeremiah Gillingham…father is Gerard and mother is Mary. Is this correct information so far Mr. Gillingham?" asked Abbadon shrewdly.

Something told Gilly that this was not going to be fun. He was so nervous about his impending doom, his knees were knocking together, and he could only stare at the filthy floor of this grave of the living dead. He was no longer the confident, keeper of secrets IIA Agent, but had been reduced to a cringing toady…the type of person he always despised.

"I almost forgot. Maybe before we get started Mr. Gillingham you would like a tour of your new abode?" invited Abbadon. "I noticed your attention was averted a few minutes ago as you attempted to find out the location of those voices of misery."

Quickly descending the stairway, Abbadon motioned Gilly by a wave of his left hand to follow him, "Come, come, I will give you a personal tour."

Reluctantly, Gilly obediently followed Abbadon down a narrow rocky trail in this tomb of gloom. Up ahead he could see a reddish-orange eerie glow, while the moans he heard previously, developed into distinct words as he drew closer, "Help me…help me…I will be good. Just let me out of here. I won't lie anymore….pleee…eese…I can't take anymore of this torment." Terror gripped Gilly's mind and heart like a vise, while his body wobbled like a drunk...but...he wasn't drunk.

Abbadon brought Gilly to a railing of barb-wire and stopped, motioning to him to look into the grotto. Gilly silently moved in beside Abbadon and fearfully peered over the barb-wire into the cavernous pit full of twisting and spiraling flames...intense...hot...fire, as far as his eyes could see. Gilly was repulsed as he viewed human beings only a few feet from each other, yet so deep in an individual cubicle of flame, they could not see one another. For miles unending, millions of flailing arms were attempting to climb out of these pits of torment, some were screaming curses, while others repented of their sins, provoked by their tormenting misery. A wave of nauseating horror swooped over Gilly causing his knees to buckle, falling to the rocky ground in pitiful convulsive sobs, as he contemplated his fate.

Out of one of those chambers Gilly heard a plaintive cry, eerily calling out his name. He craned his neck between the wires to get a closer look, at who was pleading with him to get him out of this fiery pit, but he could not see the man distinctly. As Gilly's sobs ebbed, he broke his long silence and squeamishly stuttered to Abbadon, "Wh... wh...who...is that man who knows me personally?"

Abbadon looked down at Gilly still groveling, and mockingly asked, "You don't recognize this political snob you so faithfully guarded when he presided over the second highest office in your country? Well...I...I guess he looks nothing like he did when he was dressed to the nines on Earth and flaunted his inherited wealth. You will remember him as the father of the global warming scheme. His propaganda was foisted upon all the little mush-heads in your government schools, inciting fear and hopelessness. He was the power-generator behind your EPA (Environment Prevention Agency). Did you not know this agency is my partner in removing all of your freedoms Gilly?"

"You are no longer on Earth, but this agency of social engineers will accomplish my goal by transferring the wealth of the working class citizens of your country, by sending all your manufacturing expertise to third-world nations. It is called redistribution of your wealth, and it is so easy to do. Just put the fox (corrupt leaders) in charge of the chicken coup," roared Abbadon with heinous laughter that shook the ground beneath Gilly's feet. Abbadon was unable to contain his rapture over his success at duping the naive citizens of the last free country on Earth.

Gilly had stood up by now, yet still wobbling, straining to recognize this persuasive person who seemed the consummate politician, able to lie his way into success.

"My," thought a perplexed Gilly, finally recognizing this woeful creature, "his global warming doctrine prevented us from extracting our vital resources for energy, oil, coal, and natural gas, with a big loss of jobs and heavily taxing the citizens for their carbon dioxide (breath) output. I think it is now called cap and trade, or cap and tax...oh…I can't remember."

Then, as if a light bulb turned on in his puny brain, a revelation probed Gilly's mind, "So that is why those electric shoe-skate cars have been forced upon us, and even those are scarce? I have believed an illusion manipulated by the Sinister Seven…organized evil. It is all about power and control! Why didn't I see this before now?" he mentally lamented.

Interrupting Gilly's intense self-examination, Abbadon answered his unspoken question saying, "Because you threw away your moral compass, allowing the entrance of my fearless champion Remira (deception) into your mind, who forced you to believe a lie, as if it was the truth.

And you were so easy to deceive, because you were filled with unforgiveness, pride and arrogance. This is the consequence of becoming your own god."

Abbadon continued, "I am especially proud of the work of this man. By lying and fear-mongering, he was able to amass radical changes in a very short time, subjecting the toadies of Earth to slavery. He was simply phenomenal. He was the best of the best, totally bereft of morality, and it was not my desire that he leave Earth. But since morality, based on the righteous Reconciler and His Sacred Script has been soundly rejected by your society, I have countless millions just like him, even the heads of all nations," declared Abbadon, leering at Gilly with contempt.

Abruptly and a bit gruffly, Abbadon grabbed Gilly's arm forcing him to walk deeper into the abyss. The deeper they descended into this bottomless gulf, Gilly could see a place, pointed out by Abbadon, reserved for greater punishment...the more detestable and despicable sinners, i. e., false religious bigots, witch doctors, witches, vampires, spiritualists, mediums, and fortunetellers (astrology)...those who revere Abbadon proudly and publicly. They believed that he had a special place in the afterlife set aside to honor their service to him...and... he does. The moans, groans and shrieks were nearly unbearable for Gilly.

Then Abbadon stopped their descent and pointed to a scientist, now languishing in eternal flames, whom Gilly did not know. Abbadon told him this scientist did wicked things against humanity during World War II. Then he was secretly emigrated to Gilly's "free" country during the IIA's Operation Paper Clip, along with other unethical scientists. They were placed in the research departments of elite universities to continue their experiments against humanity, those successfully carried out against the hapless prisoners, along with new, even more nefarious scientific experiments.

"This particular scientist, Mr. Vught, was an activist who lobbied your congress, convincing them that a poison he used in the water in his concentration camps to keep the population docile (mental stupor), should be placed in your drinking water," gloated Abbadon. "An additional benefit of this poison is infertility and chronic diseases with debilitation. I am astounded by his great success. And of course...you can see how I rewarded his allegiance to me, Gilly," chuckled Abbadon.

"Oh, Gilly, don't look at me with such consternation. Surely you know that fluoride is the waste product from manufacturing aluminum? Common sense tells you that toxic waste should be thrown away. But since you vote into office such money-grubbing corrupt representatives, groveling at the feet of Big Pharma, Big Agri, and the lofty medical/dental lobbyists, all you get when they confiscate your taxes is sickness, death and loss of freedom of choice," said Abbadon dismissively.

"Yea...what a great plan I have conceived. But...I could not have achieved victory without the corrupt, self-centered, agnostic intelligentsia of your degenerate society, who are possessed by my demonic minions who drive them to kill, steal from, and destroy your godless society."

"Keep in mind Gilly, what you will see on this tour are human beings who willfully refused the morality, purity and righteousness offered to them by the Reconciler. But it was totally their choice," stated Abbadon with condescending pity in his voice, yet his eyes revealed a glint of triumph.

All kinds of creepy creatures of various shapes and sizes were busy running back and forth often stopping to jab one of these woeful souls languishing in the fiery chambers, with a pole that had a razor-sharp spear on the end. Uproarious screams of agony could be heard, especially when the spears were twisted slowly upon removal. Gilly quivered, as Abbadon forced him to press on down, down, down, deeper into the chasm, where the heat intensified and fear wrapped around Gilly like a boa constrictor, tightening little by little, and wouldn't let go. He gasped for air.

Scared and shaking Gilly contemplated what soon would befall him, but Abbadon startled him back from his deep thoughts by joyfully proclaiming, "Oh, Gilly... this man will be your favorite...I'm sure," as he excitedly pointed to the skeleton of a human being with worms crawling in and out of every orifice, where once were his eyes, ears, mouth and nose. Gilly stared vacantly at this wretched human being wondering how he appeared to be dead, merely a skeleton, yet actually was alive.

"This man, Gilly," said Abbadon interrupting his bewildered thoughts, "fought through your corrupt court system to obtain your right to view pornography, anywhere at any time: porno movie stores, television, live stage acts, and, aw...yes...the Internet. Men now can legally corrupt their minds with images of perverse sexual acts 24/7, which will eventually incite them to look for an innocent victim to practice their new found techniques. And don't you just love it Gilly, the ravished victim is tormented for life because of constant remembrance of the abuse from this vile sexual deviate. And because many of your judges are corrupted by addiction to porn, the criminal is given counseling and put back on the streets to abuse again and again," roared Abbadon in uncontrollable laughter.

"My demons are so successful with lewd and lustful thoughts bombarding the minds of men, who pleasure themselves by viewing porn, it is my modern-day fly trap," bragged Abbadon with an ooh la-la, as he pranced around in a circle making sexual gestures.

"Shameful sexually deviant behavior has caused empires to fall, and simply disappear from the planet," declared Abbadon, disbelieving that humans could be so stupid. "In fact, it is so pervasive in your country Gilly, the empire will soon collapse...freedom...all gone. You can see why this depravity is one of my most successful weapons."

"Gilly...what do you think would be a just punishment in your society for these sexual deviates? Abbadon asked, as if to ensnare him.

To be honest...Gilly was always ashamed that he and Joe perused the porn sites on the Internet, but had thought there was no harm done. They never felt the urge to rape or sodomize anyone, so why would anyone else. After all, the learned psychiatrists professed that pornography had nothing to do with the escalation of sexual predators. As usual, Gilly bought the lie of the intelligentsia. This is probably because Gilly, long ago, discarded as foolish rather than wisdom, a proverb oft spoken by his mother, "One picture is worth a thousand words."

Gilly pondered the shocking revelations of these godless, self-absorbed human beings, floundering in the flames. He now could see how grievous were the actions of this man in the pit, who provided opportunity for Abbadon's demonic hordes to possess multiple millions of human beings, driving them into lurid and shockingly lewd crimes against humanity.

So Gilly answered Abbadon, "These sexual predators should be castrated immediately."

"That is the right answer! Yea! So glad you found your conscience, Gilly. It hasn't been seared after all. But the atheistic self-righteous (whom my demons possess) do-gooders in your society, lobbied your congress to produce laws that will protect the rights of these slime-balls, while the victims receive a life sentence...haunted by the horror, over and over in their minds...that is if they live," roared Abbadon with such delight, his laughter was contagious, inciting dozens of nearby demons to stop their work and join in the amusement. Depraved laughter rang out in this dark dungeon, echoing mockingly throughout the chambers of fire.

"Many of your pompous lawmakers are hooked on this junk themselves. What a grand scheme I have perpetrated upon you humans! Take another look at this worm infested soul and realize Gilly...there is justice after all," stressed Abbadon with a gleam in his eyes.

"Hurry along Gilly, there is one last place that I must take you," said Abbadon gleefully, "and this is my favorite sinner to possess and use against the innocent ones upon the earth. And I have ensnared millions of them through the likes of him...tee hee hee."

Gilly was getting tired, but knew he could not stop to rest, as they continued to descend deeper and deeper into the abyss. Out of this dank and musty darkness emerged creepy minions, who crawled all over him which he attempted, unsuccessfully, to push away. They clung to him like leaches, causing great pain. Vile sights and disturbing sounds were intensifying the deeper they descended.

Then from a distance he heard something contradictory to this environment. Screaming at the top of his lungs Gilly heard a man proclaiming from the Sacred Script.

"I know there is only one God. I will serve only You from now on...oh Infinite One. I will no longer lie, cheat, steal or indulge in sexual perversion. I will love the brethren. *Righteousness exalts a nation, but sin is a reproach to any people.*"

As Gilly and Abbadon approached the barbed barrier, the man stopped preaching and changed his tone to pleading with Abbadon, "Please, please give me a second chance. I have learned my lesson," begged the sorrowful, sobbing tormented Bishop who was attempting, unsuccessfully, to climb out of the flames. He would manage to curl his fingers over the ledge, pulling himself almost out, when a creepy vampire dressed in a black shroud came along and bopped him on the head. With a large rock embedded with spikes on the end of a pole, he continuously hit the poor slob until his bony fingers let go, plunging him back into the hungry fire. Heart-wrenching screams could be heard, until the flames muffled his regret.

Gilly glanced at Abbadon and saw a self-satisfied grin spread across his face, as he patronized the disgraced man by murmuring softly into the chamber, "Now…now… my son…you know you have already had hundreds of chances. Arriving here means you wasted every chance you were offered. You had a worldwide television ministry and wrote dozens of books, making millions of dollars. Thousands of people scrimped in order to send you money from their meager income. You lived sumptuously, even receiving accolades from heads of nations. The Illuminator spoke to you many times to repent and not pretend. You must exalt the Infinite One…not yourself. But you preferred the praise of the people…exalting yourself. The praise of the people is the only reward you will ever receive. At least now you are finally receiving justice for your schemes."

"Do you recognize this man, Gilly?" questioned Abbadon. Gilly shook his head no.

Perturbed…Abbadon grimaced, wrinkling his nose, "Is there anything in your society that you know anything about? No wonder evil people achieve the top of the pecking order. You paid no attention when your freedoms and rights were being pulled out from under you, one at a time. You even voted charlatans into office to rule over you. Actually Gilly, this man was the Bishop of the church where your wife once attended. You sat in two of his services before she had the good sense to leave this cult."

"Later this Bishop left this fast-growing cult and went to law school. Then he formed a venomous organization (Freedom from Believers) using his skills in the courts to eliminate any semblance of the Infinite One and the Sacred Script from the public square," boasted Abbadon.

"Of course, he fought for the rights of false religions in the same court that decimated the Infinite One. You can see why he was my most successful advocate in dehumanizing true believers on Earth. A man with a passionate mission, full of himself, loved being a guest on television programs, which was often, so I am surprised that you don't recognize him. Hmm...do you believe now that *eternal vigilance is the price of liberty*? Freedom is so fleeting," smiled Abbadon.

Turning away from the preacher, Abbadon pointed, silently indicating to Gilly he was to turn around and head back the same way they came. When they arrived back to the throne, Abbadon ascended the stairway again going directly to the open book on the podium. Gilly found himself in the lower level once again, staring up at this powerful ruler of the nether world.

"Do you have a preference as to where in your past that we might begin? asked Abbadon in a more sinister voice, yet with such delight he could hardly contain his excitement. But all Gilly could do was shake his head, indicating he had no preference.

Once Gilly's identification was confirmed in the red gilded book, Abbadon pressed a button beside Gilly's name in this book and *voila* a giant screen appeared with the name ASSASSIN printed in very large letters. Startled by this bold revealing of his well kept secret, a jolt of terror surged through him like a lightning bolt, causing him to tremble in fear.

"Personally, I like this time in your life because you were so…umm…I mean…you permitted such abominable acts against your fellow man. Do you remember this time in your career Mr. Gillingham?" inquired Abbadon wrinkling his nose mockingly.

Since Gilly did not respond Abbadon raised his left hand toward the screen, gesturing like an orchestra conductor, "Then let the saga begin."

Instantly in living color, Gilly could see himself at the Parthenogenesis Compound hidden deep in the forest, where the MK Ultra experiment was being conducted on unsuspecting IIA agents and lower level military personnel. This project would produce super-soldiers. Psychiatrists, who are also intelligence agents, experimented on these men to learn how to split the human core via electro-shock therapy, and mind-altering drugs. This process allowed them to remove the candidate's personality, and create a new sub-personality. By inserting certain key commands, this person will do as programmed the rest of his life. This is mind control at its best.

Once perfected, many undercover agents working as civilian psychiatrists were expected to program "troubled" private citizens to become puppets of mass destruction, especially rebellious teens. Keeping their civilian patients under mind control and dependent on psychotropic drugs assures success. Once the patients' personality is split a new personality is created. Each patient is programmed to take a gun, grenade or a time-bomb on command, then directed to go to a certain location and kill as many people as possible. He is programmed to take his own life…. automaton…nothing more. Because they have been labeled as misfit-psycho's, wing-nuts, or loners they can also be used to eliminate world leaders...a pretty clever scheme.

By cell phone call command, an "assassin switch" turns on his sleeper-personality, pre-programmed to assassinate and create chaos. If for some reason he does live after his barbaric deed, he will have no recollection that he did anything wrong, thus no remorse. "Chosen for Chaos" is their programmed moniker.

In this visit to his past, Gilly shuddered in horror as he watched his good buddies have their minds destroyed by the IIA, as he assisted, while protecting the barbaric psychiatrist from a crazed attack from his victim. He knew that eventually there would be massive anarchy in his country, when millions of these involuntary assassins will be unleashed upon society, at just the right time. Some already, one at a time, have been unleashed to see how society reacts to senseless mass murder. Some have been used as agents on foreign soil, but most are to be used by the Sinister Seven against a free people, provoking them to voluntarily surrender their personal guns in exchange for government protection. Tyranny always follows disarmament.

"Look at these ruined lives, Gilly. They have no soul. Someone stole it from them," declared Abbadon woefully, "and who did this unthinkable deed, Gilly?"

Teeth chattering due to his uncontrollable trembling, Gilly meekly said, "I... di...di...did."

"Really," said Abbadon condescendingly. "Do you really think you are that powerful? Actually Gilly...my power that controls your mind has done this injustice to your buddies and the world. You gave me permission to kill, steal, and destroy human beings through your allegiance to the Sinister Seven. And...how grateful I am for the millions on planet earth who are as cooperative as you have been. Don't you love the intelligentsia of your planet, who describe these poor souls as paranoid-schizophrenic, dissociative personalities, or multiple personalities? I cease to be amazed at such ignorance of my demon agents in my invisible world, who empower evil people," snorted Abbadon with a disdainful scowl.

Then Abbadon turned around and snarled loudly and gruffly at Gilly, "They…are possessed by my demons, at my direction, because I am the greatest power in the heavens and the earth!" Immediately Abbadon transformed into an ashen-gray grotesque creature, releasing a deep heinous cachinnation.

Gilly was stupefied, staring in disbelief. "Gilly…I'm so sorry to be so insensitive. Do you like me better in my 'angel of light' clothing?" he asked in a syrupy sweet ingenuous tone, instantly returning to his illusive magnificent form. No response from Gilly, but he was thinking that he now empathizes with the poor little mouse in the hands of a tormenting cat.

In a wink, the word on the movie screen changed to ENVIRONMENTALIST in gigantic letters, while revolving background scenes showed millions of human beings crammed into a few mammoth cities, no vehicles (except for the elite), where the populous was walking or using bicycles for transportation. Gilly was dismayed to see how his great and free country had, in many ways, regressed 200 years...almost returning to the Stone Age.

He could see government agents barging into citizens homes and forcibly changing all of their light bulbs from incandescent to mercury filled bulbs. Children were being dragged out of homes all over Gilly's country and placed in the youth corps…to be raised by the atheist-ruled State. No religious training allowed. Women were driven by gun point to abortuaries, because they dared to try and have a second child. Citizens were allowed one hour of energy to their homes per day, so people were scurrying to bathe, wash their hair, dishes and clothes in this allotted time. A camera was placed inside and outside of every home and business connected to the satellite, so the government could monitor every movement of every human being. They turned your lights on/off at their discretion...no privacy.

Gilly was horror-struck, and wailed loudly at his folly...his participation in the demise of his Constitutional Republic. He now could clearly see that these downtrodden 'global citizens' were sad and depressed, shoulders sagging from the weight of hopelessness, because they no longer owned private property and could no longer make choices for themselves, because they now served solely for the pleasure of the Sinister Seven... the Planetary Dictatorship...Globalism. They were over-taxed and over-regulated...no more Constitution...no more Bill of Rights. These hapless souls had surrendered freedom for government protection and provision. Tyranny was their reward. The Sinister Seven had finally been successful worldwide...bringing Order out of Chaos...the chaos they created.

Gilly was stunned to numbness watching the future of his country, because these sorrowful souls looked no different than the old films he had seen of the death marches in Viet Nam. But this was not war...it was the everyday life of every citizen of the world...Globalism. Gilly was abhorred by this site viewed now through eyes of reality, rather than the eyes of lies and deception from corrupt manipulative leaders. He had believed the rhetoric of the politicians, rather than looking at their record, or the books they had written.

"How could I have been so deceived by the rabid radicals?" the perplexing question pounded Gilly's mind like a jack-hammer. "I was so blind."

Vast portions of the earth, millions and millions of miles, Gilly could see were vacated by the 'evil' humans, inhabited only by animals, birds, bugs and snakes. Grand highways completely deteriorated from lack of use, bridges dysfunctional, hydro-power dams, which produced cheap energy were demolished. Worship of Mother Earth (created) had finally replaced worship of the Infinite One (creator).

But by now, the population of the earth had been violently reduced by 90% due to vicious viruses that had been invented by the mad scientists and released across the planet by the Sinister Seven. If the virus doesn't kill people, the cure will compromise their immune system making them vulnerable to terrible diseases, while also sterilizing them. Isn't that what depopulation is all about? This is a genocidal holocaust.

One aristocrat from the Sinister Seven crime family triumphantly announced in 2009...*the great culling begins*. Translated this means: eliminate the useless eaters.

"Man was created for worship, Gilly. Since you rejected the Infinite One, you had to find a substitute. Doesn't this single word, ENVIRONMENTALIST, define your worship of Mother Earth (Gaia)?" queried Abbadon.

"Save the trees you proclaimed with gusto, while sending your money to support abortuaries. My...my... Gilly, why did you condone the murder all of those little human beings? What did they do to harm you? You saved the bugs, whales, owls, and trees, but murdered your own offspring without a twinge of guilt," taunted Abbadon. "You are a perfect product of my propaganda."

"When you went on my tour of your new abode, did you see any of these 'murdered in the womb' human beings?" pressured Abbadon. "Did you Gilly...did you?" Gilly dropped his head overwhelmed with shame, silently shaking his head no.

"That is because they are not here! They are in the Land of Perpetuity, living eternally with the Infinite One," yelled Abbadon with indignant disdain, as he turned red in the face and the veins on his neck bulged.

Calming down some Abbadon continued. "Well…I may have lost them…but…I have their murderers here with me (those who did not repent). I will have to be content with these millions," snickered Abbadon flamboyantly waving his arm toward the grotto…miles of fiery pits of humiliated human beings.

"Your good wife Julie tried to tell you, or have you forgotten, the Environmental Movement was simply Big Brother confiscating land from a free people, causing energy prices to spike so high you can no longer afford to heat your home. Remember how you only voted into office the rabid community organizers who embraced this agenda? Now you can see the results of your choices. Are you happy with these results?" chided Abbadon.

Shame and condemnation shook Gilly to his toes. He remembered instantly the day that he accepted the Reconciler into his life when he felt pure and clean for the first…and…last time. Deep groans of sorrow agonized his soul, while tears of remorse flowed unchecked…because of regret.

"I always kept you deep in my heart…I never quit believing in you...oh my God...my redeemer. I was snared by my big bank account, and the glitz and glitter of the world. I am so sorry for my sins and for deserting You, the One who paid my ransom. If it is not too late, I will serve you the rest of my life," moaned Gilly to the invisible Reconciler he once served with joy, but had no idea if He…the merciful Savior…would hear his mournful cry.

Whoom! A sudden rushing wind exploded a shaft of brilliant light upon Gilly, just like a megawatt spotlight. Out of the light he heard a resonant voice proclaim,

"Abbadon...let him go! You have not succeeded in capturing his allegiance. You illegally dragged him to your abode. LOOSE HIM NOW!"

Whoosh! Suddenly...Gilly felt his spirit being sucked up, up, up, as if by a giant vacuum cleaner. Before long he could see stars and planets and all the glory of the heavens. He had never seen such a gorgeous sight in his life. He could clearly see the magnificence of the Infinite One. He wondered how he could have been blinded so long, when all of these universal wonders were in front of his eyes all the time. Unencumbered by a flesh-body, he was traveling at breakneck speed and enjoying the freedom...a titillating experience.

Then abruptly he began to descend at lightning speed. Without warning he re-entered his physical body, where it had been left on a gurney in cold storage in Afgar. His hands tangled in the sheet over his face, as he frantically struggled to remove it. Then he sat up and looked around the dark, cold, morbid room. Immediately excruciating pain gripped his body intensely, reminding him he again has a physical body. For a brief moment...nano-seconds... he grappled with the desire to go back to the Land of Abandon.

"Where am I?" he shrieked at the top of his lungs... then fainted.

Chapter 6

Chloe

Clarissa stayed day and night at Safe Harbor Hospital, known for utilizing the latest and greatest technology, right beside the bed of her precious Chloe who was barely clinging to life. Her breathing was shallow and very faint since she was still in a coma. Clarissa left little Joey with Gramma, who loves him very much.

The powerful and glorious messengers sent from the Infinite One, Charis and Harpazo, were with Chloe at the time of the stabbing and were able to intervene, preserving her life. The invisible angels cannot usurp the will of man, but they can come to their aid. Chloe had become a devoted disciple of the Goth sub-culture, finally allowing herself to be made a living sacrifice to Molech. Just as Aaron plunged the knife into her heart her thoughts silently screamed, "God...please...help me!" These two angels are now in Chloe's hospital room, but Clarissa could not see them. Yet...a powerful sense of peace pervaded the room, sustaining her faith.

Clarissa took hold of Chloe's limp hand, while gently laying her other hand on her brow, seeking the supernatural intervention of her beloved Reconciler.

Clarissa had already called her prayer partner, Sarah. The two of them had enjoyed a five year friendship full of fun, lattes, family and best of all, a passion for the Lord. When Clarissa and Sarah agree in prayer, good things always resulted.

It was now the third day since Chloe had been stabbed and throat slashed, but Clarissa was not discouraged by Chloe's lack of response. She had sought the Infinite One for so long to make her family whole, she wasn't about to give up now, especially since she believed with all of her heart this was an attack from the evil demonic realm. Besides…all of her life she heard "it is always darkest before the dawn."

Unbeknown to Clarissa or any hospital attendants, Chloe had an out-of-body experience, when she was taken to a virtual paradise of beauty and peace, by dazzling angelic beings who were sent to her from the Infinite One. While Charis stayed with Clarissa, many dazzling angels joined Harpazo who removed Chloe's spirit from her body during the third day of her coma, and she woke up on the other side of the visible world. Harpazo was so bright because of the glory of the Infinite One, she blinked her eyes several times in order to see clearly. When she finally could focus, his warm and gentle eyes and gracious smile put her at ease immediately, before he even said a word.

Looking around her new environment she noticed unique flowers of splendid colors, such as she had never seen on Earth. When she stepped on one it simply bounced back as soon as she removed her foot. She was speechless…totally awed. Harpazo noticed the wonder expressed on her face, so he waved his hand, spanning the whole area where she was gazing and explained, "These beauties never die, because there is no decay or death in this realm."

Chloe noticed another glorious angel standing by Harpazo, who introduced himself as Chrestos. Both were gigantic in size, emitting glimmering rays of golden light. She was nearly overcome by the majestic beauty of this pure and wholesome environment. Then she noticed a change in Harpazo's countenance, his eyes now stern and fixed on something behind her. When she saw him place his hand on his sword, terror nearly paralyzed her, yet she slowly turned to see who was behind her.

A whimpering grotesque, creepy ghoul, Aporeo, reached toward her, attempting to grab her and climb into her spirit body.

Harpazo intervened explaining, "This demon and his cohorts have ruled you since hatred and rebellion took up residence in your heart, seeking to ruin your life. Because of him you joined yourself to companions who worshipped Abbadon. Your mother warned you that evil companions corrupt good morals? But you screamed at her, 'You preach love, but all you do is judge my friends.' Do you remember any of this Chloe?" Chloe hung her head in shame saying nothing. She had no idea there was an invisible witness to her hate-filled words and actions.

With renewed boldness, Aporeo aggressively grabbed Chloe's arm causing panic to surge through her body. Chrestos wrenched Chloe away from the sneaky hairy monster, pulling her to safety, while Harpazo pulled his large golden sword. Though this ugly creature was the size of a hippo and stood on two feet rising high into the sky, several quick jabs into his massive body and the command to flee to Gehinnom, caused him to screech like a banshee.

Reluctantly backing away and cowering Aporeo sniveled, "Do I have to leave her? I was so successful in my possession forcing her to perform every kind of evil…I want to stay." He sounded like a crybaby.

"Yes!" commanded Harpazo. At his command, Aporeo simply evaporated like a breath in the wind...no longer visible.

"What happened?" exclaimed Chloe as her rapidly pounding heart began to calm down. Before anyone could answer she persisted, "Where am I and why am I here, and where is my mom? I heard her pray that I must live and not die...but...I couldn't open my eyes."

"Whoa Chloe, one question at a time," laughed Shalom who had just arrived and put his reassuring arm around Chloe's shoulder.

"Who are you?" she questioned nervously.

"We have come to your aid because of your mother's prayer of faith. She has beseeched the Reconciler to give you another chance to live, Chloe," Shalom whispered gently.

Extending his hand toward the giant gates of pearl, he continued, "The ruler of the universe who loves you so much...He dispatched us to you."

"Oh, my god," wailed Chloe, throwing her hands up to her mouth and falling to her knees, while regretful tears flowed into convulsive sobs.

"It really is true, everything my mother tried to tell me. We really do live after we die!" lamented a grieving Chloe.

Though still sobbing, her new revelations enabled her to finally analyze the situation. Standing up and wiping away her tears she announced, "Then...I...I...must have been sacrificed to Abbadon. He is real after all. I thought it was fun to rebel against my mother's religious beliefs, they were so stupid...not realizing this stuff is for real!"

Disgusted with herself, she placed her hands on her hips and looked directly into Shalom's compassionate eyes declaring honestly, "Well...I am the one who is totally...stupid! I had no knowledge, but acted like I knew everything...hmm...so much for being fifteen."

The soft voice of Shalom affirmed her confession. Then he said softly, almost apologetically, "Chloe...you must go back. The Infinite One responded to your mom's intercession. You have an assignment on Earth. Go in peace and remember to live for HIM alone...never for yourself. If you do, at the end of your life you will be able to return to this eternal City of Light. You could not enter today because you were not ready. You have the choice to eternally live here with us in the Land of Perpetuity, or you can chose to live eternally in Gehinnom Land of Abandon. Go back to Earth and find out how to make the best choice."

Joe's plane was delayed on the tarmac when he arrived, due to a terrorist threat. He knew he would be stuck awhile so pulled out his book and leaned back to read, while musing to himself, "It has already begun in my nation...freedoms disappearing...constant state of terrorism fomented by our own government. I will dedicate the rest of my life to stop them! Oh Gilly...I wish you were here to help expose the Sinister Seven. We were a good team," he reminisced.

Once the "all clear" sounded, Joe disembarked and hurried to find a taxi to go directly to Safe Harbor Hospital. Joe knew that Clarissa would never leave Chloe's side, where she would be praying continually. For the first time in his life the thought of her praying, brought an extraordinary tranquility to his heart.

He found three taxis waiting in front of the airport and jumped into the first unattended one, telling the driver to hurry to Safe Harbor Hospital. Joe had not told Clarissa his arrival time, because there is always a glitch along the way when he travels that far, even if it is a trumped up terrorist threat.

It took twenty minutes to get to Safe Harbor. Quickly he paid the cabbie and dashed into the hospital. After pressing the button to the fifth floor, his fingers absentmindedly and impatiently tapped on the elevator wall. His inner anxiety began an adrenalin rush to his heart, beating faster and faster, while he entertained desperate thoughts, "Please... please...please don't let Chloe die, before I get to tell her how sorry I am that I was never there for her. I so need her forgiveness and a second chance to be a real father."

Arriving to the fifth floor he passed many doors before he got to room 527. Before entering, he briefly paused for wisdom to know just the right words to begin repairing his fractured family. Bravely, he opened the door quietly, where he immediately saw Clarissa's head lying gently on the chest of his little Chloe, while warm tears fell softly onto her cheeks. A swelling compassion filled his heart as he observed this tender scene. He wanted to do what he had never done before, swoop them up in his arms and protect them from evil. He had never allowed such tender emotions to overcome him...and...strangely...he no longer desired to suppress them. In fact, it was a relief to have a moment of freedom from his stoic persona, and feel the emotions of a real man...the man his Creator intended him to be.

Clarissa felt the brush of air across her face from the opened door even though there was no sound. Just as she looked up, Joe pulled her into his arms wrapping them snuggly around her, so grateful to see that Chloe was still alive, even though still in a coma.

What Joe and Clarissa could not see was the entourage of ghoulish demons Chamas, Haga, Kazab and Pheno, fierce and intending harm, who barged into the room with him, planning to force Joe to take his own life. But these fiendish devils were met by an army of angelic warriors surrounding Chloe's bed with drawn fiery swords. These powerful angelic agents for good, charged the agents for evil with their fiery swords, forcing Chamas and his scary creepy ghouls to flee in terror.

Clarissa had not seen her husband for eighteen months and pondered in her mind, "What is so different about him?" as she fell into his arms like a wilted flower. It had been so many years since she had received such a strong, reassuring hug from Joe, so she was encouraged that he really would be a support to her this time, rather than deserting her once he paid his perfunctory visit.

Joe actually caught her as she fell limply into his arms. Holding her securely he whispered into her ear, "I'm here and it is going to be okay. The Reconciler is with us."

"Wow!" thought Clarissa as she peered into his dark blue eyes, soft, no longer steely, "did he say *the Reconciler is with us*?"

She couldn't explain yet what was happening, but that ember of hope residing deep in her heart had been instantly kindled by these five little words. Joe was different...a good different!

Gathering her composure, Clarissa gently took Joe's hand leading him to Chloe's side and backed away so he could get close to his only daughter, who looked so small and fragile. Uncharacteristically, Joe leaned down, picked up Chloe's small helpless hand squeezing it between his large strong hands, and tenderly kissed her forehead, while whispering in her ear, "I love you punkin. I'm going to make it up to you...I promise."

The moment Shalom told Chloe that she had to leave his heavenly realm and go back to Earth, instantly she was back in her lifeless body.

When her parents saw her eye lashes flutter, they were jazzed.

Joe and Clarissa were so excited they softly said in unison, "Chloe, you will live and not die." They held hands and stared hopefully as the fluttering stopped. Then slowly, her long curly lashes parted revealing her soft dark eyes. Turning toward the sound of her name Chloe saw her anxious parents...watching breathlessly.

Though her lips were parched and the tissues of her mouth thick because of all the meds, she managed to faintly say, "Oh, Daddy you did come for me," while her large soulful eyes filled with tears.

Together, Clarissa and Joe gently held Chloe's small hands, while Joe said humbly, "Yes Chloe, Daddy is here and will never leave you again." A peaceful stillness fell on the three of them...security...hope...a new and welcome experience for the Goldman family.

After Clarissa pressed the call button explaining what just happened, doctors and nurses rushed into Chloe's room to assess her awakening from the coma. They were astounded that her vital signs and reflexes were all within normal limits. Upon hearing this good report, Chloe sighed and smiled at her grateful parents.

Dr. Hope, Chloe's personal physician said to Joe and Clarissa, "Chloe is going to be fine now. We must do some more tests to confirm this, but you have reason to expect a complete recovery. Go home and get some rest, we will take good care of her. Come back after dinner and I will know more at that time," he reassured them with a big smile.

Once again Clarissa and Joe reassured Chloe of their love, telling her not to talk right now, but wait until she was stronger. They had no idea that Chloe was anxious to tell them about her out-of-body experience, meeting angelic beings and about the ugly demonic creep who had resided in her body...but..."There will be time for this," she mused, closing her eyes peacefully.

Joe grasped Clarissa's hand and led her silently out of room 527. He now wanted to see his son. Joe was so excited telling Clarissa, "I have been reading a book written by a medical doctor who uses natural means of healing, more than conventional. He has found that a chelating treatment, intravenously administered over a period of time, has brought new hope to the autistic child. Many are restored to nearly normal: to learn, do school work, to reason and even talk very well. This process gradually cleanses from the system the destructive adjuvant used in the vaccines that are stored in the body tissues."

As they drove to pick up Joey, Joe continued to share with Clarissa all that had happened to him since Gilly died. She was saddened to hear about Gilly, asking Joe if he had contacted Julie, since their families were so close.

Joe exclaimed, "I couldn't blow my cover, plus I went straight to the Embassy and immediately hopped a plane home. I'm sure the agency has informed her by now. We will call her as soon as we get home."

Clarissa was amazed, quietly listening to her "new" husband, who freely launched into a detailed description of his experiences of the last 48 hours: the bombing, Gilly dying, Dr. Hassad, and Joe's nightmare of unresolved issues. She could see his facial features change to pensive, when he described the demonic spirits who had entered and possessed his life, compelling him to do their bidding all of these years. His body even visibly shuddered as he detailed to her what he had seen in the dream, for he abhorred even the retelling of this horrifying experience. But he knew he had to share all of it, every last detail, especially his surrender to the Reconciler, so they could begin again. He didn't tell her, because there would be time for this, he planned to expose the Sinister Seven and thwart their efforts to rule the world.

"Where is that scum-bag who nearly killed my Chloe?" demanded Joe.

Clarissa patted him gently on the leg, while tears welled in her eyes as she hung her head. Sadness transformed her countenance as she spoke softly, "Those demons drove him to suicide. After the LSD wore off, he came to himself. After that, he couldn't accept the fact that he was capable of, let alone accomplishing, such a despicable act. Even though Chloe hadn't died yet, Aaron couldn't stand the guilt."

"I have been in touch with his alcoholic mom, trying to bring hope into her wasted and now grieving life. Oh Joe, it is so sad to watch people so willingly, though some unknowingly, serve Abbadon. All because they declare there is no God. But you and I know...*only fools say there is no God*," said Clarissa, wistfully looking out the car window into the fluffy white clouds skirting across the blue sky, pondering out loud, "Where did you go Aaron? The Sacred Script says that, *it is appointed unto man...once to die...after that the judgment*...hmm."

Compassion rose up in Joe's heart and he grasped Clarissa's soft hand. Looking into her sorrowful eyes he whispered, "I am so blest to have you, because you care more about others than yourself."

When they picked up Joey, Joe was no longer put-off by his lack of response, because hope had been revived that someday he really will hear his son call him Daddy, after he gets the new treatment.

As soon as they arrived home, Joe went out to the deck and sat down. The view of the mountains and valley from their mountainside home is breathtaking and serene. The deer came to feed on the chokecherries, two wild bunnies scampered around the giant evergreen and a resident squirrel stared at him from the limb of the old oak tree.

"Wow!" he mused, "I never appreciated all the blessings of my home...until now."

Clarissa quietly joined Joe, sitting next to him to drink in the tranquility, while not interrupting his soul-searching.

After about thirty minutes of peaceful silence, Joe said, "It is time we call Julie and see what we can do for her."

Chapter 7

Return From the Dead

Two male nurses rushed into the windowless, very cold, temporary morgue flipping on the light as they entered, so they could see what caused that horrifying shriek!

There were three dead bodies in their makeshift morgue waiting for family notification, before being sent to their final resting place. Surveying the three gurneys, the two scared men could find nothing out of order. It was eerily quiet. Scanning the gurneys one more time, one man's eyes focused on Gilly's gurney where he saw fresh blood dripping off the side and yelled, "A dead man doesn't bleed," and rushed to check his vitals.

"Dr. Hasad, Dr. Hasad, we have an alive dead man! Come quickly," shrieked the frightened nurse, while he frantically began to push Gilly's gurney toward the emergency room.

Dr. Hasad happened to be in his office, so was able to quickly arrive to the makeshift morgue to see what was causing all the commotion. None of the staff had ever seen a man come back from the dead, so there was a lot of excited conversation and speculation.

Seeing the fresh blood oozing from the dead man the doctor quickly checked Gilly's pulse and found that this man was alive, whom he had pronounced stone-cold dead yesterday.

"Get me this man's chart," he ordered the male nurse.

When the chart was handed to him Dr. Hasad mentally pondered, "Hmm...ah...yes...now I remember. That distraught ambulance driver Abrim seemed to know this man, but he left immediately on a family emergency before I could inquire further. I wonder what is their connection?"

Dr. Hasad spoke out loud the name on the chart, "Ahmir Abudaum."

At the sound of his name Gilly's eyes popped open directly into the assuring gaze of Dr. Hasad. While groaning in pain he weakly asked, "Am I alive on Earth?"

"Yes you are," said Dr. Hasad in a soft voice, "but we must get you into surgery immediately. You have survived a horrible van-bombing in Afgar and we must stop your bleeding. You are in Mount Hureeb Hospital just outside of Afgar, where you were brought by Abrim, the ambulance driver. Do you remember any of that?" Gilly shook his head no.

The next morning Dr. Hasad sat beside Gilly's bed explaining how pleased he was with the results of the surgery. But Gilly was anxious and compelled by dread when he abruptly grabbed Dr. Hasad's hand pleading, "I...I...must get home...right away...please!"

Wisdom, experience and his faith told Dr. Hasad that Ahmir went some place when he died. Softly he inquired of his apprehensive patient, "What happened to you, Ahmir, when you died?"

Gilly was perplexed and confused, but desperate to share with someone his experience in Gehinnom...but couldn't blow his cover. He just wanted to get a hold of

Joe who could help him get far away from Afgar. But... there was something about this man that captivated Gilly, something unexplainable engendered trust. Since he had been dramatically delivered from Gehinnom, he now was spiritually aware...able to discern good and evil.

Gilly was now determined to expose the whole globalism scheme. His mind kept mulling over and over the wicked schemes he and Joe had implemented for the Sinister Seven: 1) plundering natural resources from third-world nations, 2) protecting drug traffickers to support the habits of the banking cartel and corporate big-wigs, 3) supplying illegal weapons for the terrorists, 4) skewed intelligence reports in order to justify the inciting of war across the planet to fulfill the Plan. Once he found Joe and explained everything that he experienced in Gehinnom, he knew Joe would help him with this dangerous mission. After all, espionage was their expertise.

Ominous thoughts of retribution from Typhoo and Phobos kept pushing into Gilly's mind, warning him that the Sinister Seven would send the goon squad after him once they got wind of his plan to expose their corruption. But Gilly won the thought battle...because he must never forget...Gehinnom. He must warn the people...no matter the consequences.

Abruptly, and with difficulty, Gilly leaned on his elbow and demanded of Dr. Hasad, "Just who are you... really?"

Dr. Hasad stayed calm and waited a few moments before he answered. "Ahmir, who do you think I am?"

Gilly fumbled for words, something new for the man with nerves of steel, always in total control, but he finally blurted out, "There is just something about your countenance. Your whole being radiates peace, something I have longed for since my youth. Do you know the Reconciler?"

"Yes, Ahmir, I do. Are you ready to tell me where you went when you died?" questioned Dr. Hasad patiently.

"If you promise to get me out of here as soon as possible," bargained Gilly.

A smile wreathed Dr. Hasad's weary face as he said, "I have already set up a private line for you to make your arrangements...free of spyware."

Gilly was amazed at Dr. Hasad's wisdom to know in advance about his need. So it was time to bring Dr. Hasad into his confidence. Gilly was not used to "spilling his guts" to anyone at any time, but the great awakening he experienced in the last forty-eight hours, compelled him to trust this spiritual person sitting in front of him.

"First of all, my name is Gilly...uh...John Gillingham. I'm an IIA Agent from the West," he stated matter-of-factly. Then he embarked on a lengthy explanation of his and Joe's diabolical assignment from the Sinister Seven, to help set up world feudalism. He was surprised to hear that Dr. Hasad was privy to the Plan of the elitists, and was very knowledgeable about the shenanigans of the Council of Foreign Servers (CFS).

After all of this, Gilly began to impart to Dr. Hasad the gory details of his tour through Gehinnom Land of Abandon. Dr. Hasad sat transfixed as Gilly's story unfolded. He even visibly cringed when Gilly described his tunnel experience. While he was listening intently to Gilly's story, unseen by either Gilly or Dr. Hasad, several powerful warrior angels had entered the room with a message from the Infinite One.

Eleeo, a dazzling, mighty angelic messenger, moved close to Dr. Hasad and whispered, "You will write Gilly's experience in a book, publish it, then use it as a tool to reach the lost youth. You and Gilly will have a worldwide ministry which will usher in the end of the world." Dr.

Hasad could not explain the exhilaration that came upon him, but he suddenly knew the next step in his life.

Dr. Hasad only interrupted Gilly one time. He put his hand on Gilly's arm and said in a breathless whisper, "Minutiae, Gilly, is extremely important to me. Your experience will be effective in opening the eyes of our youth who have been lied to by godless government schemers. Since their parents have abandoned the Reconciler, they have no knowledge of spiritual things. I feel an urgency in my spirit, to write every last detail of your experience and get these truths into the hands of the kids, who believe the Infinite One is dead."

The passion of Dr. Hasad for those who do not yet know the Reconciler, brought tears to Gilly's eyes, along with a strong desire to serve something other than himself for the first time since his youth.

Doxes, an awesome winged messenger full of radiant supernatural strength, whispered to Gilly, "Do not be afraid. You are my 'voice in the wilderness.' Your story will help prepare my people for the end of the world and the return of the Reconciler."

Gilly suddenly knew he could spare no detail in the delineation of his experience in the invisible world. Dr. Hasad took copious notes, which later would help compile an exciting story for publication. With the help of the invisible messengers, he definitely was thinking ahead.

Over a period of eight hours, Gilly resting every hour in between, finally all of the sordid details of his Gehinnom experience was adequately recorded. Of course, Dr. Hasad was full of questions, but this interaction was important for it bonded these two men for life.

Dr. Hasad stood up without a word, but his countenance still reflected astonishment as he contemplated all he had heard about the invisible realm. Then he patted Gilly's hand, stating in a fatherly tone, "Gilly…we have a big job ahead of us, because the end is so near. Tomorrow, after you get some rest, I will bring in your protected line so you can make your arrangements. I will do all in my power to get you home, when you are well enough to travel."

Chapter 8

Reunion

"Joe...this is Gilly. You must find a safe line and call me back on my safe line," blurted Gilly into the phone, forgetting that the last image Joe had of him was in the morgue.

"Who are you and how did you get my private number," demanded Joe angrily, while dismissively throwing the phone into Clarissa's lap. Clarissa wrinkled her brow as she looked at Joe with concern over his outburst. All the color drained from Joe's face...chalk-white...so she knew this call had frightened him.

While staring straight ahead where they were still seated on the deck, Joe yelled, "No...this can't be true... Gilly is dead! This is a prank call...and ...it's not funny!"

Clarissa looked at the phone in her lap, then looked up at Joe's face...ghostly...expressionless. She really didn't know what to do, so she carefully picked up the phone and apprehensively said, "Hel...lo."

Immediately an anxious voice on the other end shouted, "Clarissa...this is Gilly. What happened to Joe?"

Without waiting for her answer Gilly continued, "I know this must be a shock Clarissa, but I have come back from the dead. I'm still at the hospital where Joe left me. Dr. Hasad got me a safe line so I could call and explain everything. So much has happened in the past three days, but I need Joe's help to get me home."

"Are you okay, Gilly?" asked Clarissa genuinely concerned.

"No, Clarissa, I'm not. I just got out of surgery because I have severe head injuries and a shattered leg. But Dr. Hasad has patched me up pretty good and I should be able to travel in a few days," answered Gilly excitedly.

"Gilly, did anyone ever inform Julie of your death, because we have not? inquired Clarissa.

"No, no, no Clarissa, she knows nothing according to Dr. Hasad. That is why I have not called her as yet. As soon as I have a date of departure I will call her and explain about my injuries and that I am heading home. I have to be there in person to adequately explain my horrifying ordeal. Take down my number," Gilly said hurriedly, "so that when Joe calls me back on a safe line I can update him.

Solemnly Clarissa clicked the off button on Joe's cell phone absent-mindedly holding it up against her chest, numb with disbelief, as she mulled over in her mind what she had heard. Joe was still staring ahead in silent skepticism, so Clarissa chose her next words carefully.

"Joe, this call is not a prank. I recognized Gilly's voice. As I allowed him to talk he explained how he had died, and was taken to Gehinnom Land of Abandon and was terrorized by Abbadon. Then a resonant voice in a shaft of brilliant light delivered him from the grave. Please call him!"

Without saying a word, Joe grabbed the note with Gilly's phone number and dashed out the door to the agency.

Ten days later Gilly arrived at the airport where Julie and their twenty-three year old son, Sean, were anxiously waiting. Sean had taken a leave of absence from his intelligence training, because of his dad's condition. Watching Gilly debark the plane on crutches with his head swathed in bandages, brought pain to their hearts. They had never seen him so vulnerable…so needy.

After eighteen months of separation this reunion was so sweet despite the circumstances. Hugs were plentiful while tears flowed. Sean drove with Gilly in the front seat next to him. Julie sat in the back seat content to observe her husband.

"I know he is badly injured," Julie mused in her mind, "but his voice is gentle, rather than caustic…indifferent. The antipathy once mirrored in his cold emerald eyes seems to have disappeared…hmm…I wonder."

The hum of the car engine produced a kind of rhythm that was soothing to Julie, as she contemplated her future with Gilly. She watched and listened intently as Gilly and Sean talked. Gilly, though he obviously was in pain, was not grouchy toward Sean or dismissive, as in the past. Actually, what Gilly was saying to Sean revealed introspection…something new for him.

"Hurry up Clarissa, we're going to be late to the Gillingham's," yelled Joe, hoping to be heard over the shower. Clarissa hurried to blow-dry her hair and get dressed.

What Clarissa and Joe did not know, the invisible entourage that followed him from Afgar did not give up on eliminating Joe. They may have been thwarted by the angels with fiery swords in Chloe's hospital room, but defeated…nonsense. Chamas, Haga, Kazab, and Pheno, who could no longer possess Joe because the Illuminator resided in his spirit, had been sent from Abbadon determined to attack his mind and body. Joe may not have committed suicide, but they can still make sure he dies.

In order to discombobulate Joe by igniting his old impatient personality, they surrounded him taunting in his ear, "Hurry, hurry, hurry. You are going to be late, late, late. You are never late. You hate to be late. And Clarissa is always late. Late, late, late, hurry, hurry, hurry. What will people think of you, if you are late. You are never late, late late."

Pretty soon Joe's anxiety caused him to talk rudely to Clarissa, who was doing her best to meet his demands. She had learned that when he was like this it was best to say nothing. When they jumped into their new red car the four demons gleefully jumped in too, and Chamas put Joe's head in an arm-lock exerting great pressure. Quickly, Joe headed for the freeway thinking that would be the fastest route to the Gillingham's.

They had been driving only about ten minutes when Chamas nudged Pheno and commanded him to take possession of the driver in a semi about ten miles away.

Chamas explained to Pheno, "Jack, the driver, has been drinking booze and hates red cars, because one killed his little girl about five years ago. When he sees a red car he becomes enraged, so all he needs is a little nudge from you…tee hee hee. Get the picture?"

"Yeah, got it," said Pheno already picturing the disastrous scene with delight.

In a wink Pheno entered the semi-truck taking possession of Jack. Many evil spirits already resided in this rebellious, revengeful man, but Pheno was higher in rank so quickly took control. After all, he had the distinguished assignment to murder a human being.

Pheno kept his eye on the road, peering through Jack's eyes. As soon as he had the Goldman's in his sight he shouted, "There's a red car…there's a red car. That's the car that killed little Katie! Make them pay, Jack, make them pay for taking your little Katie…kill…kill…kill."

Jack was resisting these tormenting thoughts that bombarded his mind relentlessly, as he gripped the steering wheel tighter. Beads of sweat popped out on his face. After all, he wasn't a man who took the law into his own hands he told himself. But the grief buried in his heart was rising to the surface, because of these relentless aggressive thoughts. With his moral resistance finally beaten down, he threw caution to the wind.

A hideous shriek of laughter rang out into the vast invisible realm from Pheno expressing his joy, as he relished in his mind the impending calamity.

When the Goldman's were about a mile down the road, coming in the opposite direction, Pheno screamed in Jack's ear, "There's the red car...now or never Jack. Make them pay now, now, now!" Spotting the car, involuntarily Jack began to maneuver his big rig over the double center line with the intent to crash into the tiny red car.

Joe was still being tormented by Chamas, "Hurry, hurry, hurry, you're gonna' be late," and he just couldn't shut off the relentless voice that pressured his mind. He became agitated and continued to fume, as he rehashed in his mind the incongruities of the past few days, distracting him from focusing on the road.

Chrestos shouted in Clarissa's ear, "Look up!" Just in time, she happened to look up to see the giant semi barreling into their lane. Pointing wildly she frantically screamed, "Joe, Joe, he is going to hit us!"

Then the invisible Chrestos shouted instructions to Joe, "Speed up...speed up...don't brake...don't swerve...step on it!" Joe's reflexes were always fast, but the adrenalin rush to his brain cleared his mind to be able to obey the thoughts injected into his mind by the angel. So he gripped the wheel with both hands and put the pedal to the metal. Clarissa clasped both hands to her mouth to muffle her terror, as the little car jolted into passing gear.

The little red car rocked from the wind created by the sheer force of speed from the powerful semi, as it barely missed hitting the rear of their car. The semi jack-knifed and tumbled over the cliff.

Joe and Clarissa were shaken but did not stop. Joe told Clarissa to call the highway patrol and report the accident. After all of this, they actually arrived at the Gillingham's early. When the Gillingham's arrived they all went inside to share the events of the past few days.

Getting Gilly comfortable was most important, especially elevating his damaged leg. Julie put on the coffee while the rest helped Gilly. Clarissa launched into a detailed description of the scary event that just happened to them. Actually her nerves had still not calmed, when she suddenly got a revelation blurting out, "Oh my God in glory…I believe we are under attack from the demonic realm! The Reconciler must have big plans for His people, and soon, for them to work so hard against us."

Gilly rolled his eyes and exclaimed heartily, "Boy Clarissa, you don't know the half of it. Wait until you hear about my experience in Gehinnom!"

"Gehinnom," yelled Julie from the kitchen incredulous over his claim. "Do you know what you are saying Gilly?" she asked, as she returned to the living room with the coffee and dessert.

"Yeah, I do," said Gilly cautiously. "I didn't tell you sooner because I was so far away. Telling you the unbelievable story that I was violently escorted to the invisible Land of Abandon to face Abbadon, could only be told with you right beside me," he said grasping her hand securely and lovingly gazed into her sky-blue eyes, "because it will frighten you too much."

Julie knew she had diligently prayed for a husband who would love the Infinite One, but she was stunned by this revelation, and troubled about the road he had to walk before her prayer was answered. She wasn't sure she was prepared to hear the details of his story.

As coffee was served, the five of them settled in to share their stories. As Joe's story unfolded, questions were numerous, as well as exclamations: amazing, thank God, and way-to-go Joe. But, when Gilly began to describe his experience of being dragged through the ominous creepy tunnel and his tour of the chambers of fire in Gehinnom, the response was more like muffled groans: oh no, oh my god, horrible, disgusting, sickening, and praise the Lord. As the story unfolded, Julie unconsciously held her hand over her mouth to muffle her panic and terror, tears silently flowed down her cheeks, while slowly shaking her head in disbelief.

Except for a comment or two, Sean essentially was quiet throughout the revelations of the spirit realm imparted by his dad and Joe. He had never heard his dad talk about spiritual things. In fact, his dad had showed little interest in him as he grew up. After college he went into IIA training because he thought maybe his dad would finally notice him. But, he really didn't like the tactics of the IIA, because of their lack of a moral compass. Their world view was in stark contrast to his world view. He hadn't said anything yet, because he feared condemnation from his dad.

Sean had left organized church. Rather than teaching how to be intimate with their Creator, through His Son, he felt they encouraged materialism and success in the natural world. He didn't want to disappoint his mom, but just couldn't stomach anymore of the legalism of sterile institutions, obeying man-made rules. He found no power to overcome his problems.

Sean listened intently to his dad, while he shared with Joe that Abbadon revealed to him about a scheme to destroy their freedom had been strategized long ago in a secret meeting on an island...Sorcery Sound...by the

Sinister Seven. The collapse of their great empire...the last vestige of freedom...was imminent. It was shocking to hear his dad and Joe confess how they had been pawns in the hands of the CFS to destroy freedom around the world, bringing all nations into serfdom under the rule of the Sinister Seven...criminal banking cartel...multi-billionaires.

Listening with excitement, Sean thought to himself, "Wow, now I am hearing about the real invisible world, not religious platitudes. I can't believe my dad actually died and visited the Land of Abandon! My church always said that supernatural experiences are a thing of the past. Visions, dreams, gifts of the Spirit, and the audible voice of God died with the apostles. The supernatural was only needed to establish the foundation of the church many centuries ago. But...I always felt we too needed all these things in our day, but I never saw it until now."

Then Sean, unable to contain himself any longer, suddenly spoke up, "You mean you two are going to leave the IIA?"

Both Gilly and Joe stopped talking and simultaneously turned to look at Sean with a stunned look on their faces.

"Sean" exclaimed Gilly, "how can I go back after all that was shown to me by Abbadon? I have invested every atom of my being to the destruction of my country, albeit out of ignorance. But now I must invest every bit of my new knowledge into rebuilding it."

"I know Dad, I just meant...well...maybe you won't be mad at me now, if I change careers," exclaimed Sean with enthusiasm. "I have recently been trained in the latest technology which will be the final nail in the coffin of the corpse of freedom."

"You got our ear, kid," said Joe as he winked at Gilly.

Sean began to tell how surveillance is being slipped, by stealth, into every facet of our lives. We are convinced by media propaganda it is for our safety from terrorism. People are manipulated into this trap voluntarily, when all the time, it is our own government who is our most terrifying enemy.

"Recently on television I saw an ad for a new car that has a GPS tracker installed by the manufacturer. The buyer pays a monthly fee to an agency. If he is in an accident, a voice talks to him in the car and sends help," said Sean distraught over the ignorance of a supposedly educated society.

"They don't realize they have volunteered to be tracked by their government 24/7. And…this agency can abruptly stop the engine of their car at any time…freedom to travel…gone," stated Sean, baffled by this unquestioning allegiance to tyranny.

"Really," said Gilly seriously, "Joe and I have been isolated in a backward country for three years. We came home only once briefly, so need you to update us. It is almost like we have dropped off the face of the earth, while progress rushed right by us."

"You probably already know about tracking us through our cell phones or computers," said Sean, remembering past discussions.

"Yeah" said Gilly, "we are aware of Project Echelon, a five-country collaboration to spy on their citizens through satellites with the ploy of protecting them from terrorists. But terrorists keep attacking and will continue to do so, until the Sinister Seven is finished using them. But that won't happen until all of us are global slaves…then terrorism will stop. The main computer…the Beast…is set up on nine acres, where an abundance of spying and recording of our techie correspondence is recorded and stored to be used against us."

Joe interrupted, "Can you imagine if you simply say the word 'bomb' in a conversation on phone, computer, or radio transmission, your conversation is immediately transferred to the main frame and held in a file on you? You may have said nothing more than a benign statement, i.e., 'I was bombed out last night,' meaning you were exceptionally tired. But no matter, that key word and sentence is recorded and may be used against you someday, especially if they think you are a threat to the Plan. And what is worse, one day you may find your bank account frozen, or your credit card cancelled, or phone and computer shut down. The Patriot Act gives them this power (no warrant needed) and no one will give you any information or explain why this happened to you."

Gilly couldn't contain his zeal interjecting, "What is really bad, the government goons can come into your home, when you are not at home, and take anything they want and you can do nothing about it. This is because they are protected by that damnable Act. Or, they can come into your home when you are there, dressed from head to boot in intimidating black uniforms, and terrorize you. If you tell anyone about it, even a lawyer, you could simply disappear to some gulag...or dead."

Clarissa cleaned up the coffee and dessert plates and told Joe they better call it quits for now, because they had to get back to the hospital to visit Chloe before it gets too late.

As they walked into Chloe's room she was just awakening and a big dreamy smile wreathed her sweet face, mirroring her delight in their arrival. After hugs and kisses Chloe asked if they would help her sit up. She had been in the hospital several days and now felt strong enough to share something very important.

Clarissa and Joe were nervous, expecting the worst, but sat down to listen to their precious daughter, whom they were so grateful to still have with them. Slowly and very seriously Chloe said, "Mom…Dad…I know that I have not listened to your advice…especially you Mom. Those kids I hung out with you told me were trouble… well…you have nooo…idea."

The day all this came down, we were all sitting around a blazing fire passing around reefers, getting high, and chanting mantras over and over. This ritual is supposed to conjure evil spirits. Of course, I didn't believe in that demon stuff, but wanted to be part of the crowd…you know…accepted," as she shrugged her shoulders and looked down…embarrassed.

"For incantations we always wore our black hooded capes and chalked our faces. It kinda reminded me of Halloween every time we did this," she said with an innocent child-like grin.

Then Chloe's voice dropped and her eyes shut briefly as if to collect her thoughts, then she said, "But…this night was different." A visible shudder went through her body and she gritted her teeth as the memory of that night came into her mind.

"Aaron…you know…my boyfriend was sitting across from me on the other side of that blaze. There were about forty of us. Earlier he had been smiling at me as we chanted 'oh great god Abbadon' over and over. I think he dropped some acid, because suddenly and without warning, he…he…transformed right before my eyes into some gruesome creature…a monster right out of a sci-fi movie. Yuk…I can't even bear to recall it," she lamented, throwing her hands up to her eyes as if she could erase the horrific memory.

Clarissa and Joe were sitting on the edge of their chairs by now horror-stricken, but did not interrupt Chloe. Chloe gathered her composure and proceeded. "First… Aaron's eyes became black with fire behind them. I couldn't believe what I was seeing. But…then…his face began to twist into something…something ugly…like… like with knots and lumps instead of a face…oooh. Hot fire shot out of his mouth and fangs…oh my god…fangs instead of teeth. You know…like…like in those movies about vampires and werewolves!

Then she lowered her voice, speaking nearly monotone, "But…this wasn't a movie…it was for real!"

"We always have an altar for sacrifices with a ready dagger. Usually cats, dogs, goats or sheep are sacrificed. But the invitation is always open for a virgin to offer herself as a sacrifice to Molech the idol, but she must be a virgin. But those people have all been around…you know what I mean?" said Chloe, expecting her parents to understand her insinuation.

All Clarissa and Joe could do was swallow hard and nod their heads, because they were frightened, hearing this type of confession from their little girl. They had no clue how serious was her devotion to this cult.

Before she got to the scariest part of her story, Chloe calmed herself by taking a deep breath followed by a sigh. Then she continued, "In an instant Aaron jumped up, ran through the fire, grabbed that dagger off the altar, pushed me onto that altar flat on by back, and plunged it into my heart and slashed my throat. And it was so strange…I had no ability to scream out loud or even resist his power."

By now tears were flowing down her cheeks and Chloe looked straight into Clarissa's terrified face and said emphatically, "Mom…it's your prayers that saved me that night…nothing else. It was a miracle that a forest ranger came by to check on that blaze, because he saw me laying on that altar bleeding to death and called 911."

By now everyone was crying and praising the Infinite One for this momentous occasion. Then there was just silence between the three of them…contemplation of the events. No one could deny this was supernatural intervention.

Then a big smile could be seen on Chloe's face which prompted Clarissa to ask what had caused her joy. Chloe became a teenager again with wondrous bubbling excitement, only expressed by the young, as she embarked on what transpired when she was removed from her body.

None of them were aware that Chloe's room became filled with powerful angelic messengers, but their presence could be felt…peace.

Chloe's countenance seemed to glow as she shared with her mom and dad about Chrestos and Harpazo, their dazzling, other-world brilliance, and the extraordinary City of Light. She told them she was not allowed to go into the city through the mammoth gates of translucent pearl, but she saw the surroundings which were, "Sooo… awesome!"

Then Chloe's eyes opened wide in wonder as she shared, "Harpazo is my guardian angel! Can you believe that…a guardian angel?"

"And he even protected me when I was up there," she exclaimed excitedly while pointing upward, "when a gross demon grabbed me and Harpazo took after him with his sword. Oh…mom, my life has changed…forever. Now I know that I am loved," she proclaimed with a sigh of relief.

While Chloe finished her story Joe reached over and gently took Clarissa's hand giving it a reassuring squeeze, which she returned. Both knew that they were in the presence of a holy happening, which had not lost its luster in the retelling.

Chapter 9

Hidden In Plain Sight

Going home from the hospital Joe and Clarissa recapped the startling yet, very exciting events of the day. They hadn't recovered from Gilly's dreadful supernatural experience, when they were plunged into Chloe's perilous journey. Everything was happening so fast, their heads were spinning with new revelations. As the scarlet sun set behind the snow-covered mountains, they still pondered the meaning of these phenomena. Sleep was very welcome.

The shrill ring on the telephone startled them awake. When Joe answered he heard, "Get up you lazy dog." The enthusiastic voice of Gilly stated he wanted to take them out for breakfast. He had been talking to Sean last evening, while Joe and Clarissa were at the hospital, and felt the five of them must get together to strategize. They also must hold some meetings to awaken their sleepy seaside community of Crystal Waters.

Down at Dixie's Diner their favorite breakfast place, with plenty of room for Gilly's injured leg, they got their coffee and made their order. They were not aware they had been joined by a troop of invisible angelic messengers, who surrounded their table to impart ideas from the Infinite One.

With a concerned look on his face Joe said, "Sean shared things last night that just boggled my mind, so I have asked him to update all of us so we can brain storm an offensive plan."

It was hard for Sean to know just where to begin because he had learned so much in his year of training, besides what he researched on his own. But Karmel, his powerful and intelligent guardian angel who had protected him all of his life for such a time as this, was sitting next to him to help him prepare for the end-time battle. This brilliant angel imparted ideas to Sean's mind to help him implement the plan of the Infinite One.

"The most insidious, yet seemingly innocuous stealth surveillance is the Internet," Sean said seriously.

"The military who developed it, first called it the Arpanet. Then the devious government saw its value to invade the privacy of every human being around the world. So they linked up with a brilliant techie nerd to promote their evil scheme, which made him filthy rich, so he could promote Globalism for the Sinister Seven. Every move we make can be legally tracked...thanks to the Patriot Act. Once Globalism merges every country into ONE, the Sinister Seven will become a Planetary Dictatorship."

"How can we stop this?" asked Julie, revolted by what she was hearing.

"Mom, we can't stop them. It's too late," said Sean shaking his head in frustration and helplessness. "It was already too late before I was even born."

"But why has none of this been ferreted out by the press?" questioned Julie in her naïveté.

"Oh Mom...are you for real? We no longer have freedom of the press in any country. The press is owned by the Sinister Seven global banking cartels and oil rich Dawaism?" said a bewildered Sean.

"Why do you think the news is always filled with the immorality of celebrities or some horrible gun crime? This keeps your mind off the fact that our treasonous Congress is passing heinous bills in the dark of night. Their skulduggery is no longer constrained by our Constitution... so...bye bye freedoms. Eventually Congress will say, *time to wake up dunderhead your freedoms evaporated while you slept."*

Karmel imparted more thoughts to Sean's mind influencing him to say, "I'm really concerned for the kids who are falling hook, line and sinker into their lying trap. You see, when you follow the money and the path of investors, you find that the IIA set up the latest Internet phenomenon, targeting kids...Casebook. By this means they can examine carefully the likes and dislikes, sexual preferences, religious habits and daily routine of each user. They also connect families worldwide with their networking process, something not possible before," Sean continued, "and all recorded by Casebook voluntarily provided by us."

"Well, it's not just the kids," said Joe, showing signs of anger on his face, "most adults refuse to believe that a free country could be manipulated like this, so they pay no attention to the 'signs' hidden in plain sight. Did you hear the interview with the president of the search engine 'Goober' the other night, where he claims his giant data base will be called the 'Mind of God?' He bragged that he has the largest information gathering corporation in the world. All searches using his search engine are stored forever and given to any government authority to be used against us. They are watching us. We must be more vigilant and less trusting."

"Sean," asked his dad, "not to change the subject, but have you heard about that book titled…1984?"

"Yeah," said Sean, "I found it on the Internet. We better appreciate the freedom of the Internet while we have it. That freedom will be gone soon. That book was published in 1935, written by George Orwell, predicting a government takeover by 1984. I also found a book 'Between Two Ages' by Z. Brzezinski, published in 1970, which outlines in detail the…Plan...of the Sinister Seven. In it he states that in order to have one central government rule the whole global family, one obstacle must be eradicated."

"What is the one obstacle?" asked Julie innocently.

"I know," chimed in Gilly. "It is the same one that Abbadon fears the most…the Reconciler and his Sacred Script. For centuries tyrannical regimes have burned millions of Scared Scripts in an attempt to wipe out the Infinite One and his son the Reconciler. But…they cannot. But…will keep trying."

"No one bothers to pay attention to what is hidden in plain sight, because Brzezinski's book with its radical agenda, has been on the market all of this time for anyone to read," said Sean.

Sean explained, "Brzezinski predicted that governments will have total control of the weather. Now it is 2010, and sure enough they completely control most, if not all, storms. Nature still intrudes on their best efforts. China has 35,000 weather control scientists…why? Did you ever hear that info on your nightly news? No…they lull you to sleep with disinformation. Scientists can create snow and rain in one nation, producing drought and famine for their neighbor. Pretty nifty weapon! Tornados and hurricanes are easy, and earthquakes can now be generated by oscillating electro-magnetic fields. Then they scream 'global warming' is caused by CO2…man caused. If any unnatural climate change is taking place, it is because of the weather control scientists. It is simply unimaginable what corrupt man, driven by demons of darkness will scheme against humanity. This is because modern society has discarded the moral pinning of the Sacred Script," exclaimed Sean with a discouraged look his face.

"But why do they want to do this," questioned Clarissa with a perplexed look on her face.

Joe, with all of his years of undercover work, intuitively knew why, "Because of hubris. Total control of people, places, and things is the name of the game. And depopulation by any means must first be accomplished...disease, wars, destructive storms, devastating earthquakes, tsunamis, mind-controlled mass murders, and abortion, all of which are promoted by the Sinister Seven...global banking crime families."

"Another of Brzezinski's devious and sinister schemes is to create new diseases intended to eliminate millions, if not billions of human beings. That means their Frankenstein scientists have been hard at work. Everything he outlined in his book forty years ago are the schemes of Abbadon," concluded Gilly, since Abbadon personally confirmed this information.

"Wow," exclaimed Julie, "I was just reading the other day in the Sacred Script that because of disobedience against the Infinite One, diseases would come upon us that were yet unnamed. There will be madness and confusion of heart. There will be no humans to save us, because the tyrannical rulers will be the head and God's people will be the tail...all because of our disobedience to Him. And it is happening now!"

Remembering something important about weather schemes Sean said, "The Sinister Seven have top secret scientific organizations that have been altering the jet stream in the ionosphere, which in turn modifies the weather. They must inject chemicals into the atmosphere in order to accomplish their macabre deeds. Along with deadly radioactive materials, another deadly component is aluminum...deadly to any living thing. These chemicals blasted into the ionosphere have to come down. When they do, our water, soil and food supply is poisoned resulting in degenerative diseases. It has been going on for fifty years, but has escalated exponentially since the 80's."

"Hmm...all since Brzezinski's book was published," concluded Gilly as Phileo whispered the thought in his ear.

Then Chrestos whispered remembrance to Julie's mind of an article she read about a year ago by a neurosurgeon, turned preventative medicine scientist. She was so excited about remembering something so important she interrupted Sean saying, "This...this...neurosurgeon I read about, found that in the brain tissue of the cadavers of Alzheimer's patients, aluminum and mercury had been embedded, interrupting sensitive neurotransmitters. He went on to explain that aluminum and mercury create inflammation of the brain with interruption of its function, creating a myriad chronic diseases. Wow, now it makes sense," she exclaimed, "like that Brzezinski guy said, they would create chronic diseases. And here they are big time...oh my...what can we do?"

Then Clarissa piped up, "That is exactly what the honest scientists are trying to explain about autism. In my research to help our little Joey, I found that the aluminum, along with ethyl-mercury and thimerosal in the vaccinations, cause immediate inflammation to the brain of the wee one's (in the womb or outside), and many endure lifelong neurodegenerative chronic diseases. Because there is a cumulative effect from these poisons, especially in brain tissue, many immune-degenerative diseases are directly linked to inflammation of the brain, stimulated by aluminum, ethyl-mercury and thimerosal."

Joe was so proud of Clarissa's efforts to reveal the truth about autism so he asked, "If someone works in an aluminum processing plant are they warned about toxicity from this dangerous chemical?"

"Oh yeah," declared Clarissa with assurance. "They are supplied a warning pamphlet. The symptoms they may suffer if toxicity occurs are: attention deficit disorder (ADD), sleep disorders, personality disorders, convulsions, stuttering/stammering, motor disturbances, fatigue, dementia, tremors, or memory loss. Most of these symptoms can be found in the autistic child or an Alzheimer's patient."

"Have any real laboratory tests been applied just to aluminum toxicity?" asked Julie.

"Oh, my...thousands," answered Clarissa with a sigh.

"My research took me back to 1928 to an amazing book written by a dentist called 'Aluminum Poisoning,' which clearly describes aluminum toxicity and his warnings to manufacturers to eliminate it from all foods and implements used for cooking. Because of corrupt political power brokers his warnings were not heeded, the same as today. Depopulation through poisoning is one of their weapons," declared Clarissa.

"But to answer your question regarding laboratory tests," she continued, "A study in adults and children receiving dialysis, aluminum is one component, regression of speech was pronounced in some kids. A fully developed small child regressed not only in speech, but also motor control (tremors), development was delayed with much smaller heads, memory loss and ADD. Some adults developed Alzheimer's. Most of the symptoms of Alzheimer's and autism parallel. But get this...the tests done on lab rats revealed dying motor neurons and brain cell death. And all of this is kept from the public. But all you have to do is an Internet search. A lot of it may get scrubbed by the government...soon...to continue the cover-up."

"With all of the information available is aluminum in any products at this time," asked Sean, as his brow furrowed with concern.

"Oh, I wish I knew all of them, but it is allowed in everything you can imagine. It is still in baking powder, sunscreen, antiperspirants, antacids, public drinking water, soy products, buffered products, makeup, pouch drinks, cans, and pans...the list goes on and on. Remember, a small amount in any one of these things would probably do no harm...but it is the cumulative effect, since it is stored forever in brain tissue."

"Well...that is certainly a sinister plan Clarissa," declared Gilly, "Your researchers must be ruffling the feathers of the Sinister Seven, because I heard just yesterday on the news that a ten-year research study proving everything you just said tonight, has now been disputed, and labeled a false study. The grant study program will now censor the scientists severely for bogus reporting. All I can say... someone has threatened their lives and/or cut off funding. After all, the populous must stay asleep and suffer from the barbarians."

"The Sinister Seven have been plotting and implementing their evil schemes against us from our founding, and we are the last free nation to fall. And what have God's people done about it? Nothing! Most have folded up like a flower at midnight, submitting to the chains of politically correct propaganda. Their salt (witness) has lost its flavor...their light no longer shines for the Reconciler. Although, a few of us are still twinkling. I learned this from Abbadon while I was in the Land of Abandon," lamented Gilly..."of course...he was gloating over his victory."

"Since it is now 2010, well past the 1984 prediction of total global governance, they will have to create a crisis of monumental proportions, something that will terrorize the people so much, they will grovel and plead for the government to save them and protect them," interjected Joe with his accurate and practical, yet always cynical conclusion.

"Do you think with all this talk about the swine flu pandemic, which many credible scientists believe is laboratory contrived, that this will be the crisis that will bring them the control they require to push us under the bus?" questioned Joe.

"Maybe, but probably bio or chemical missiles will be launched into our country. They need a really big plan to scare the people into submission. But they do plan to use the military to force the populous into Civilian Inmate Labor Camps for mandatory inoculations, if we don't volunteer. If the virus doesn't kill us, what they secretly put into the vaccination will kill us...bio-weapon. Why else is healthcare the biggest industry in our country and is now under government control? The esoteric Georgia Guidestones boldly proclaim that world population must be maintained at 500,000,000 to balance with nature. So how will the Sinister Seven reduce the population to their predicted perfect number?"

"Well...there is so much these wicked tyrants could use to create the most debilitating crisis we have ever experienced. They have to be careful not to create a crisis that will affect them negatively. Oh yes...we must protect the pampered Sinister Seven," mocked Sean in a sissy voice with puckered lips. Everyone roared with laughter watching him prance around mimicking a girlie-man.

"They already are helping rogue countries develop a nuclear missile that will reach our shores. The warhead could also carry an EMP (electro-magnetic pulse) that would explode above cities and immediately disable the power grid. Even our cars would cease to function, phones interrupted, along with the internet and all electricity. I noticed that the purchase of power generators has gone up 500% by those in the know...corrupt insiders. Think they know something we toadies are not privy to? But... you won't hear that bit of info on the propaganda media," explained Sean, "because truth might wake up the sleeping giant."

"We must not forget the motto of the Sinister Seven... Order out of Chaos. They will create the chaos, then come swooping in like the knight in shining armor to save the day. Ooh...I just cringe when I think of their malevolent plot," decried Gilly, as his body visibly shuddered.

Sean went on to describe the most recently developed technology. "The satellite has given corrupt leaders a close-up look at our everyday life. They can even see you taking out your garbage. Microphones are hidden in roof tops and utility poles. We are being monitored 24/7 by the masters of illusion. They even have radar guns that can peer through concrete. Soon it will be mandatory for all citizens to have finger prints, iris scans and DNA samples stored by Big Brother, biometric ID cards, transponder tracking on vehicles (gas tax) and the most abominable of all...microchip implants.

"Right now," Sean continued, "microchip manufacturers are pushing only medical chip implants which store your whole medical history. But tracking, financial, and purchasing implants are on the back burner waiting for enforceable laws from our treasonous congress. Propaganda is already in the media lauding the benefits of being chipped, especially to protect children from kidnappers. Their advertising really tugs on your emotions and fears...Snow White's poisoned apple."

"Just think...all of this wickedness has been revealed in the publications of these evil globalists...hidden in plain sight. We are so stupid to believe political rhetoric," snarled Sean like an animal caught in trap.

"Yeah," confirmed Gilly, "and these elitists include movie moguls who produce movies in the guise of sci-fi... fantasy. All the time it has been truth by stealth...clearly prophetical. The Plan has been hidden in plain sight. It was all made so clear to me when I was in Gehinnom...a diabolical world takeover plan of mammoth proportions, by a small cabal of money changers (bankers).

"Do you remember a Communist leader who said, 'If I have control of the money I care less who makes the laws' asked Joe? "Our country surrendered the control of our money in 1913 to the money changers. Soon they will control the populous by the implanted chip. This is no conspiracy...it is Abbadon's carefully constructed Plan. His demons possess these people who will fulfill his Plan to enslave mankind."

"Oh, I almost forgot," added Gilly. "Smart Dust...does anyone have any idea what is this stuff?" All of them shook their heads except Sean who did know. "Well... Abaddon showed me while laughing uproariously, that Smart Dust is RFID's in micro form."

"What in the world are RFID's?" asked Clarissa.

Sean answered, "They are radio frequency identification tracking devices. They are already embedded in many products, passports and drivers licenses. At strategic areas, i.e., airports, government buildings, etc, they simply throw the micro RFID's in the air or sprinkle on the floor, where they cling to your feet and clothes, which in turn trigger a video or listening device to monitor your movement or conversation. They even have antennas that can be aimed at your computer monitor from outside of a building, and reconstruct that information on their screen. These people are simply treacherous and dehumanizing."

"Also," added Sean, "in airports and any government property these snoopy snakes have placed Smart Carpet or Smart Cushions. They have embedded biometric censors, which send signals to government agents who are monitoring your voice and body pulses. The arrival/departure windows at the airport have been implanted biometrically. While you are reading this window a single word might suddenly pop up, like jihad or terrorist, while a hidden camera monitors your reaction. Any suspicious response could get you arrested."

"Is it true Sean that airports will soon install behavioral screening scans, which will read your mind or reveal your hidden intentions...or so they say? Joe asked.

"Absolutely," answered Sean, "And think about it...who has the power to challenge their interpretation of the scan in a totalitarian government?"

"We have to get all this information laid out, analyze it, plan our strategy, and then present it to the church community to get their input," concluded Gilly.

"Oh, boy," grimaced Sean, "good luck with that idea. The church is so afraid of the government, you know, losing their tax exemption and such, there is simply no spiritual boldness to confront wickedness head on. I think there motto is 'don't make any waves and the devil won't get you.' Sadly...they don't even know he already has them under his feet."

With the help of Karmel sitting invisibly next to Clarissa influencing her thoughts she suddenly said with strong conviction in her voice, "Well...we better teach them that the weapons of our warfare are not carnal (guns & bombs), but are mighty through the Infinite One to pulling down all of Abbadon's strongholds that he places against us. This is a spiritual battle with only a spiritual solution."

Chapter 10

Strategy

IN THE CENTER OF EARTH

Shrieks and screams of horror-stricken human beings could be heard throughout the realm of Gehinnom Land of Abandon. All entrances to this dark dungeon of nightmarish horror were jammed packed with rejecters of the Reconciler, waiting their turn to be tossed into their permanent abode of fire and torment by the ghoulish servants of Abbadon. Millions of fiendish monstrous demons are running helter-skelter, due to the volume of new denizens of the damned waiting to be assigned to a particular den of dread.

The determined malevolent vampire spirits of death had been extra busy on Earth, so the 'keepers of the deep' in the center of Earth, cavern of the living dead, simply were not prepared for this influx of new residents. Chaos reigned because of this population explosion.

Pyra, the fire-breathing spirit of the flame, was in charge of all the 'keepers of the gates' who manned the entrances into Gehinnom, so with a booming voice that could be heard for miles he screamed, "Enough already! Stop the madness."

All the clamor of the robotic minions stopped instantly. The only sound that could be heard was the moaning of a multitude of sorrowful human beings backed up in the tunnel…contemplating their fate…waiting to be processed and assigned their final punishment. It must have been horrible for them to realize that this place is for real… knowing now…they had bought the lie while they lived on Earth. And now they are squished together like sardines in a can, where the stench is unbearable and the dusky darkness exudes hopelessness. Hundreds of demons, all sorts and sizes, crawled all over them pawing, pulling and pounding various parts of their bodies…non-stop… as if they were play things.

Pyra simply didn't have enough trained foot soldiers for a smooth transition for this unexpected number entering the eternal fires of the Land of Abandon…all at one time. So he needed to send his captains to every entrance of Gehinnom to make a clear plan of distribution for these eternal captives, to their specifically designed punishment.

Strategically placed underwater volcanoes on Earth are referred to as the Ring of Fire, because of their mysterious and violent activity surrounding many oceans. Actually they are entrances to Gehinnom. Because of the extensive use of these entrances Pyra assigned Katara, Rasa, Krino and Seol, to receive and process the damned. These characters are the most wicked of the wicked with vile curses and condemnation pouring from their mouths, humiliating the human victims in their fiery hell-hole.

Pyra explained they will do alternate shifts at the North and South Poles, the two major entrances to this subterranean city in the center of Earth. He showed them the master guide they must follow, which should help them bring order out of chaos. With a wave of his hand gesturing them to follow him, Pyra grabbed his clipboard and headed toward the East entrance.

"Seol, you are in charge of this entrance." Pointing to a life-size screen embedded in the wall of this woeful cavern Pyra continued, "Now look at this monitor. You can see the numbered markers along the tunnel, and right now there are at least five-thousand sorrowful souls waiting. It won't get backed up like this if you keep the process systematic and orderly. You have hundreds of ushers at your disposal, so put them to work," said Pyra with a crisp authoritative tone to his voice.

Pyra turned toward the East entrance to demonstrate to his nefarious captains. He paused to observe the next victim waiting to enter the Land of Abandon. The poor soul was being perversely fondled by a lust spirit, which amused Pyra immensely, noted by the smirk on his face.

Running his finger down the list of names, passing those already processed, Pyra stopped when he reached the name of the man standing at the entrance, "Ah…here we go. This next one is…ah…yes…another false religious bigot…my favorite," as he winked and wryly smiled at Seol.

Gazing contemptuously into the eyes of his trembling captive, who was gasping in horror, attempting to catch his breath as he surveyed his new surroundings, Pyra said, "Oh…umm…you must be very disappointed sir. Are you looking for the umm...umm…seventy-two virgins?" raising his eyebrows in a look of triumph. "We have millions of your type who are residents here in the Land of Abandon."

The captive, contemplating his fate said nothing, but was still gasping from the horror of it all. The intense heat in this tomb of gloom had apprehended his sensibilities.

With the exuberance of sudden revelation Pyra exclaimed, "Ah…now I understand why our lust spirit was appointed to greet you today! It says here in your record that you humiliated many females by rape and harsh torture because of your religion."

"Hmm...my friend...now it is your turn. But your humiliation is for eternity." Shrill laughter erupted from Pyra and his captains, because they were thoroughly amused by their torment of this captive.

It was pitiful seeing the despair in the man's eyes, but Pyra couldn't help turning the screws a bit tighter when he said mockingly, "If it makes you feel any better, the Prophet who taught you how to hate and murder, and his cruel leaders who lied to you, are here with me now experiencing a much harsher eternal punishment than you will my friend."

Then Pyra turned back to Seol continuing his instructions, "See how I have checked off his name on your master sheet. Everything is updated hourly from headquarters for every entrance."

Pointing to a column on the right side of the page Pyra said, "Across from his name you can see the cubicle number and section of our great city where this damned denizen is assigned, along with the name of his eternal tormentor. Simply look around for that minion, or several may be assigned, hand him a sheet of instructions, and he will escort him to the chamber of horrors...fun, fun, fun," grinned Pyra.

"Any questions?" All four shook their heads no.

"Be sure you understand, because I must leave now and go to the other side of our principality to cover our UFO unit. So I won't be available for a couple of days," cautioned Pyra.

Abbadon had confided in Pyra that the UFO unit had been one of his most effective weapons on Earth. The intelligentsia has rejected the Reconciler because He requires them to repent of their sins. Since they would have none of this Abbadon has their total allegiance. All humans hunger for supernatural knowledge, especially since they innately know they cannot explain life and creation without it. So they easily fall for the lie about some superior race visiting them from the great beyond, imparting ancient wisdom. Because of the UFO phenomenon, Abbadon assured Pyra that the humans easily accept them as their 'spirit guides' on Earth to the great hereafter. He was able to perpetrate this fantastic hoax, because the humans have rejected the Sacred Script as a book of lies.

"Of course...we are their spirit guides whom they conjure through channeling, but they describe us as Ascended Masters. Don't you just love the rationale of the demon possessed intelligentsia?" laughed Abbadon.

"And we don't guide them into eternal bliss...either," snickered Pyra, then exploded into raucous laughter.

Smugly, Abbadon bragged to Pyra, "Have you seen how those scientific idiots explain how Earth hangs in the midst of the universe with no obvious support?" All Pyra and Abbadon could do was laugh uproariously, because of the lies they have been able impose upon the minds of the intelligentsia...those who have become their own god...inventors of evil.

"These godless government leaders have kept secret, all of the supernatural scientific knowledge we have imparted to them through our visits in what they call... UFO's. They have even duplicated my UFO's fooling the people on Earth. No matter...at least I have their total allegiance," gloated Abbadon. "I'm winning."

"But...I am not getting credit for providing these secrets that make these scientists gods in the sight of the people, who mindlessly laud them as miracle workers, because they can grow body parts in Petri dishes. This must end!" roared Abbadon. "I will share my glory and honor with them no longer."

Abbadon headed to the Colosseum, while Pyra went to the UFO unit to ratchet up their appearances upon Earth. He told him to direct his pilots to make more appearances to ordinary humans, so the selfish scrutinizing eyes of government can no longer steal and reproduce his crafts. They must direct ordinary human beings to organize and proclaim these wonders to all. They are to continue to invite humans on board their crafts so they can testify about the "superior race" they meet. Allegiance to Abbadon is demanded. He will no longer tolerate allegiance to scientists or government gurus.

The Colosseum was filled with worried demon generals. "You cannot enslave a people who absolutely believe in the Sacred Script," bellowed Abbadon to his conclave of generals, whom he had commanded to return from Earth for new marching orders. "The Reconciler has set them free!"

Pacing like a panther while holding a copy of the Sacred Script in his hand above his head, he continued to bellow, "Why is this book still in print? How many centuries have I given you to get rid of this thing? Let me demonstrate to you imbeciles."

Then he walked to a receptacle of crackling flames, ripped out one page at a time from the Sacred Script, and tossed them into the hungry fire…relishing with delight the disappearance of every last page.

"B…b…but," whined a cowering Chamas, "we have influenced most of the global population to disdain what is written in it…sir."

Abbadon stopped and stood erectly, an imposing and intimidating figure, crossed his arms and glared at the hordes of demonic imps cringing under his critical eye.

"And you…you are my elite forces…fierce and full of power…and all you cowards can do is cringe and tremble? Is it because you know that you have not yet accomplished my Plan on Earth?" shrieked Abbadon turning red in the face as his temper exploded.

"My Plan was supposed to be fulfilled in to...tal...ity by 1984...and what year is it now you morons, or do you even know?" demanded Abbadon.

"Umm...uh...it is 2010 your majesty," offered Apisteo meekly, while staring at the ground.

Since there was no rebuttal from Abbadon, no humiliating remark, Apisteo mustered the courage to look up and declare, "The majority of the global population no longer believes in the Infinite One and His Sacred Script, and it is being burned at the rate of one thousand a day across the globe. B...b...it is those believers in that 'free' country who keep printing and mailing them back to those countries enslaved by Dawaism."

While Apisteo was talking, Abbadon walked up to a giant map of Earth on the wall behind the platform. When Apisteo had finished with his nauseating arsenal of excuses, Abbadon turned abruptly and with black fiery eyes blazing, he glared so long at Apisteo he could feel holes boring through him, causing him to squirm uncomfortably.

Finally Abbadon spoke, though condescendingly through clenched teeth and steaming with rage, "And you...you who are endowed with all of my power...can't stop them?"

Then Abbadon turned back to the map and placed his long pointer to a very large continent asking, "Is it this country in the West that you call a free country? He was laughing so hard that eventually the whole stadium of generals joined him, creating quite an uproar.

"That empire is no longer free. It is an empty shell, devoid of virtue. But, it is cracked and soon will collapse like a house of cards," promised Abbadon.

"B…b…but remember how in 1963 we got the Sacred Script outlawed in the government schools…a country founded on the laws of the Sacred Script? That was a feat in itself! I know it took awhile to corrupt enough people, and place them in powerful positions of the judiciary, but you have to remember who is the real power that we are up against. The Illuminator (Spirit of the Infinite One) covers the whole earth at the same time, persuading humans to follow the Reconciler, while we are limited to one human at a time," complained Anomos, the most powerful general in Abbadon's army.

"Excuses, excuses, excuses are all I ever get from you," sneered Abbadon as he waved his arm back and forth gesturing that all of them are at fault.

"I am the greatest power in the heavens and the earth… and you give credence to the Illuminator! No wonder your growl is worse than your bite…wimps," screamed Abbadon.

They wanted respect for their accomplishments, not humiliation. They had snared most of the citizens of Terra Firma in a net of elitist lies and were very proud of their victory.

"Despite our losses Master," declared Aporeo bowing low before Abbadon, "we have not been unsuccessful. Hopelessness and despair, produced by fear and terror, reigns on Earth revealed by global hatred…war…murder… suicide…sexual depravity…corruption…anarchy. Those who work in my expertise roam the halls of governments in every nation, federal, state and city, possessing and corrupting these lawmakers to make self-serving laws that will enslave their citizens. And…it is working," he gloated.

"We are especially proud of our pernicious scientists who have engineered a terminator seed for major crops. These seeds (GMO's) are genetically manipulated to grow bigger crops with greater yields. The seeds will die at the end of each season and will not regenerate. Big Agri and their malevolent invention will cause those who ingest these poisonous crops, to succumb to chronic diseases," laughed Nega. "And...we added a surprise twist."

Nega stood up straight, proudly thrust back his shoulders and began to pound his chest, while looking around with a grin mimicking the proverbial Cheshire cat he revealed, "Surprise, surprise...those who eat GMO food will become infertile...humans and animals alike."

A most ingenious scheme for depopulation...don't you think Abbadon...my master?" offered Aporeo bowing mockingly.

Before Abbadon would address their arrogant declarations, he walked back to the giant map and placed his pointer on the union of twenty-seven nations across the Atlantic Ocean. Tapping wildly and loudly with the pointer at this group of nations he declared vehemently, "And what about these nations...you fools?"

"My GMO scheme was first embraced by these nitwits. B...b...but you sniveling slackers let the People of the Book rise up and demand the removal of our delicious poison... and their voices were heard. Now they have made a law against my terminator seeds. And...and...what are you going to do about it?" demanded Abbadon, flashing a disgusted fiery glare at his haughty generals.

They hung their heads...shamed again...and silently returned to their seats. None of them answered Abbadon's question. But Abbadon said smugly, "Ah...ha...just as I thought."

"Quick...back to Earth. The monitor flashed that a very bad scene is transpiring and you must dismantle that meeting in Crystal Waters. Hurry," commanded Abbadon with urgency in his voice.

BACK ON EARTH

The meeting was called to order in the Community Center of the beautiful seaside town of Crystal Waters. B. A. (Bob) Warrior, pastor of the local Church of the Redeemer had invited Gilly and Joe to give their testimony. Pastor Warrior was very excited about this opportunity to rally followers of the Reconciler to roll up their sleeves and turn the world upside down, as did the early apostles. He just needed someone from inside the government to expose the corruption from first-hand experience…not just from books.

"Shall we pray?" asked Pastor Warrior, as the very large gathering of citizens arose from their seats.

"Lord we beseech You to send forth Your angels to protect us as we embark on this dangerous mission to expose the wickedness of the Sinister Seven, who have destroyed freedom around the world. Our freedom is hanging by one slim thread. Thank you for the Illuminator who lives in our hearts to guide and direct our path to glorify You."

At the command of Abbadon, hordes of demonic spirits arrived in the beautiful city of Crystal Waters, heading directly to the headquarters of the local community organizers who are funded by the federal government. Abbadon's demonic minions already have possession of these rabble rousers, who inflict strife upon this city. They are very involved in fraudulent voter registration, at tax-payers expense, along with many other vices.

Chamas and Pheno rallied these community organizers quickly, since their minions already possessed them, barking orders to prepare for agitation and harassment at the Community Center. Within fifteen minutes about forty demon-possessed organizers darted out the door of their headquarters with intimidating signs in their hands, marching toward the Community Center in peaceful downtown Crystal Waters.

Before long an explosion shook the Community Center causing all who were inside to come dashing out into the street to see who was attacking them. As soon as the attendees of the meeting appeared outside, they were pelted with rocks and other debris from the hate-filled chanting and screaming radical protesters. Pastor Warrior could see that their dumpster was in flames, so quickly called 911, while the rest of his group doused the fire with an outside hose.

The police did nothing because the community organizers have free speech rights, and no one was hurt. Since no one witnessed the bombing destruction of the dumpster, their hands were tied. Or...so they said.

Energized by the Illuminator, Pastor Warrior led the peaceful citizens to pray for their enemies, as they are instructed in the Sacred Script. He told the people that the Sacred Script empowers them with spiritual weapons. When he began to pray the rest of the people agreed, because there is power in the prayer of agreement. "In the name of our blessed Reconciler, we bind the power of Abbadon, and command all of his demon spirits possessing these community organizers to desist from their evil maneuvers and leave our meeting NOW!"

After they had prayed, everyone in the Community Center sensed a presence of peace. They suddenly felt energized to go forth with the task at hand.

They were unable to see that their room was filled with gigantic angelic warriors sent from the Land of Perpetuity. They were bright and shining wearing golden breastplates and flawless snow-white linen tunics. They moved effortlessly amidst the people, whispering hope into the ears of the faithful who were seeking the will of the Infinite One.

Several of these angelic warriors went outside to encompass the Community Center. Simultaneously they turned toward the onslaught of Abbadon's evil forces. With their flaming swords drawn, Eleeo yelled to Dunamis and Phileo, "Advance!"

These three radiant angelic warriors with streams of shimmering light emanating from their bodies, brandished gleaming razor-edged swords, advancing on the thousands of malevolent demons, who had converged on the Community Center, while one angelic warrior, Doxes, continued his vigilance around the building.

As Eleeo, Dunamis, and Phileo led the charge against Chamas and his demons of darkness, cries, shrieks and howls could be heard throughout the invisible realm, as the angelic warriors thrust forth their fiery swords, commanding the terrorized demons to flee. Instead…they fell to their knees groveling like beggars, complaining and whining, "Oh please…please…don't make us leave. We mean no harm. Can't we please stay?"

Eleeo pulled back his shoulders revealing his magnificent and powerful stature then shouted, "You must flee…NOW." Millions of retreating demons sounded like a roaring tornado, as they high-tailed it out of there shrieking in terror.

Unaware of the invisible spiritual warfare, Gilly was introduced to testify to the faithful people gathered at the Community Center, who wanted to know what they could do to save their country. His testimony was so gripping he captivated his audience. Then Joe spoke, explaining everything the Illuminator had revealed to him about his past, and the demons who possessed him, causing him to betray his country.

Although Pastor Warrior had done his homework regarding the world takeover by the Sinister Seven, probably two-thirds of the curious people who gathered there this night were vaguely informed, but were seeking valid facts.

"The church at large has been defanged by political correctness," explained Pastor Warrior. "Our salt has lost its savor, our light has ceased to shine, because of our tolerance of every sin known to man. We now tolerate sexual perversion, idolatry, paganism, and we heartlessly murder our own offspring. This tolerance is an abomination to our Creator. If we don't lift the banner of truth, deception shall continue to reign holding us in bondage to sin. We must crush the chains of tyranny."

Joe jumped up to inject a warning. "Gilly and I have participated in an evil plot to enslave third-world nations through monetary debt...the wicked Plan of the Sinister Seven. The Sinister Seven covet the natural resources of all poor nations of the world. They already have ours tied up by environmental laws. So the Plan is to send 'economic executioners,' evil economic advisers, to the leaders of poor nations to help them obtain loans from the World Bank. With this money they could modernize their nation by digging wells, building power plants, roads, schools and airports for their citizens. Of course, only major corporations from the West would be allowed to contract for this development. We do hire the locals, but as laborers at slave wages. We drill their oil, mine their diamonds and other precious metals, but the nationals receive only a small portion of the profit, while the Sinister Seven receives the lion's share."

By this time, Gilly had rejoined Joe at the podium saying, "These poor nations are required to pay back the loan with interest, while the corporations become disgustingly wealthy. Of course, in time, since they receive such a small return from the development of their own natural resources, their billion dollar debt soon falls in arrears. The Sinister Seven gets richer and the poor nations get poorer. Their debt default gives the West authority to rule that nation. We set up the rich people to rule the new 'democracy' allowing the people to vote...but...the vote is rigged. Our elitist puppet government stays in power. Then we set up a military base and *voila* another nation is added to, and under the control of, the global empire of the Sinister Seven....the Planetary Dictatorship. So far we have military bases in 130 nations. This madness must stop."

Then Joe finished up their testimony. "If the 'economic executioners' are unable to convince the leadership of a nation to borrow these vast sums, the IIA sends Gilly and I to stir up hatred and rebellion against the ignorant leadership. Once destabilized, we plot a coup d'etat and topple that government by force. Our puppet ruler is put in place and we still call it democracy...under the thumb of the Sinister Seven."

With a furrowed brow of concern Gilly added, "The sad thing is...the Plan is nearly completed. We are the last empire to be toppled...and the water is up to our necks... blub...blub...blub."

"For aeons these elitists have planned the eventual slavery of all the toadies of the world," declared Pastor Warrior, "while the People of the Book were lulled to sleep by their prosperity and pursuit of equality with the world.

"But...it is time...it is past time...for the sleeping giant to awaken, repent of her idolatry, and rise up in the strength of the Lord to do exploits...or...we will be ruled by Dawaism," loudly proclaimed a very animated Pastor Warrior. He was getting excited to take back his country and was hoping to ignite passion in this crowd of seekers.

Chapter 11

Empire Falls

Sirens were blaring non-stop, flashing red and blue lights splashed the darkness with eerie shadows...at the midnight hour. Citizens were hiding in their homes, because they heard on the grapevine that the President had suspended the Constitution, and ordered the military to invoke the help of local police to remove all firearms from every residence in the country. Now they are pounding down the doors of law abiding citizens. The Patriot Act provided ample provisions to harass and suppress citizens of their freedom, overturning the protection of Posse Comitatus. Posse Comitatus was a law enacted by Congress in 1868 to protect citizens from the military taking up residence in private homes and cities, or collaborating with local law enforcement to bear arms against citizens. Now...we are no longer protected from our domestic enemies.

After all privately owned firearms are confiscated, all citizens who refuse to be inoculated against any pandemic they contrive will be herded into Civilian Inmate Labor Camps. Long ago the government began closing military bases to refurbish many of them, so they would be ready to imprison citizens who resist the Plan, whom they call terrorists. They describe a terrorist as...People of the Book, veterans, anti-government, anti-war, anti-abortion, as well as those who are social/fiscal conservatives or constitutionalists. So it is easy to herd them into labor camps on the pretense...they refused the vaccination intended to prevent spreading the viruses, the government unleashed upon its own citizens.

"Bam, bam, bam...open up," was heard at the door of an elderly couple in their eighties. The noise did awaken them but they were unable to rise quickly due to their age. By the time they arrived in their living room to see what was causing all the commotion, they came face-to-face with five AK 47's pointed at them, because evil personified had already beaten down their front door. These five men were obviously military, but the words they were shouting were a language Bud and Molly did not understand, nonetheless menacing and terrorizing.

Hordes of invisible demons accompanied these wicked intruders. Chamas was barking orders to Haga and Pheno to rein in their minions. These creepy slimy monsters were running all over, climbing in and out of the five gunmen, spitting and defecating on them, and forcing wicked thoughts into their minds commanding them to shoot...shoot...shoot. But Chamas wanted them to stop, for now, because he wanted this couple to suffer torment before they die. Chamas thrives on torment and torture.

This sweet old couple had experienced many changes in their great country over the years, which they did not like, because the freedoms they had enjoyed in their youth were being systematically removed. As followers of the Reconciler they held fast to the Constitution and the Bill of Rights provided by their founders. They had given contributions to certain organizations who desperately lobbied congress to retain their godly foundation. Because of their allegiance to freedom, the couple was well aware that they were on the Homeland Security terrorist watch list.

Molly and Bud Dunbar had faithfully served their country. Bud was in the Air Force during the Korean War, then he came home to serve his community as a building contractor. Molly was a homemaker, raising four children, while volunteering in her children's school and the PTA. During this time they were unaware that evil plotters, who actually hated their Republic, had gained congressional and judicial positions where, by stealth, they could blackmail representatives of the Republic into passing corrupt laws and sign corrupt foreign treaties, which would transform their great Republic into a tyrannical third-world nation. Bud and Molly could not believe their beautiful freedom-loving Constitutional Republic protecting individualism, had been transformed by these treasonous charlatans into a Collectivist government, where taxes are confiscated from hard working citizens, and transferred to those who do not want to work. They call it Utopia.

Rising taxes and the inflated dollar caused questions to come to their minds, but they were busy with the responsibility of raising their children to be honest citizens of integrity. They could never have imagined that corrupt, compromising betrayers, could ever get into a position of authority. They were trusting and naïve...and wrong.

Then one day Bob Collier, a sub-contractor who worked with Bud handed him a book...*None Dare Call It Conspiracy*. Once Bud and Molly read this book the missing pieces to their puzzling questions began to fit together, forming a clearer understanding to the clandestine and dubious activities of their government. They began to research and found many books written by the elitists who serve the Plan, which is to destroy the Republic (sovereignty). They were amazed at the audacity of these elitists to boldly declare in writing, their step by step Plan for the demise of the Dunbar's country. They were horrified at their own ignorance to this devious, well constructed...Plan. They dared to look beneath the veil of government secrecy, by becoming involved in a patriot network...Sound the Alarm.

Now their greatest fear had suddenly and brutally been shoved in their faces. Bud suffered from bladder incontinence. While he was being terrorized by these thugs, trembling from panic and revulsion, he could not stop the warm urine from pooling around his feet.

Shiman, a mighty and brightly shining warrior angel, though invisible, wrapped his arms around this patriotic saint of the Reconciler. Then Shiman whispered in Bud's ear, "Stand your ground, my friend, be courageous for I am with you."

This honorable man, though embarrassed, sensed new strength surging through his veins, so he could resist his fear and shame. Bud pulled back his shoulders and stood tall, proud of his God and his country...boldly staring down his oppressors. Molly grasped his hand with a gentle squeeze, conveying to Bud her faithful love of sixty years, assuring him they will go down together...martyrs for their Reconciler.

From behind the shouting commandos appeared a local cop, strutting like a peacock because of his important orders to takedown the terrorists...two helpless citizens of the Republic.

Molly and Bud clung to each other, shaking now from the cold because they were scantily clad in nightwear, as the terrorizing threats continued by these foreign thugs. Once Officer Outlaw appeared the thugs stopped their incessant shouting. Whew!

The invisible arrogant demon Typhoo, escorted Officer Outlaw into the living room shouting commands into his mind to be ruthless and merciless. Like a panther salivating over his prey, he circled Molly and Bud, looking them up and down with the intimidating swagger of a slave-master.

"Bring out all of your firearms Bud, and lay them right here," commanded the officer gruffly, tapping his index finger loudly on their dining room table indicating the exact spot to place them.

"B...b...but...I don't have any firearms," stuttered a very nervous Bud. And this was true, because his guns were hidden in a secret place known only to his adult sons.

Slamming his fist hard on the table, Officer Outlaw screamed, "You lie! I have it on record that you own two rifles and a .45 Colt. Where are they?" Bud and Molly simply stared at him, but uttered nothing. Kletos and Shiman, the faithful angelic warriors stood fearlessly beside them, whispering encouraging words, enabling them to confront the enemy victoriously.

With a snap of his fingers and a wave of his hand, the ruthless military brutes, with cold steely demonic eyes, instantly obeyed the command of Officer Outlaw to begin a search of the Dunbar's home.

While their home sweet home was being trashed by these goons, Molly and Bud finally sat down on the sofa. Hands still clasped together Molly looked into Bud's always twinkling, blue eyes and lovingly said, "We have faithfully followed our dear Reconciler all of these years together and He has never abandoned us. No matter what happens to us tonight, my beloved Bud, if it is our time, I will meet you on the other side of the veil in the Land of Perpetuity."

Officer Outlaw was infuriated that he could find no firearms and verbally berated a silent Bud and Molly.

"I will burn down your house," screamed the officer as the veins on his neck swelled and the carotid pulsated wildly, as his face turned red with rage. Molly and Bud had prepared themselves for this moment…that it could actually happen. So they were not persuaded by his threats, because all of their material things they counted as nothing when compared with the glories of the Infinite One in the next life.

Then harshly, and with indifference in his voice Officer Outlaw demanded, "Produce your inoculation certificate."

Molly answered politely, "We do not have one."

Typhoo barked orders to his creepy ghoulish imps who were running around wildly, spitting, clawing and defecating on all of the military and Officer Outlaw, shouting obscenities and forcing wicked thoughts into their minds to destroy the enemy…Bud and Molly.

Enraged at Molly and Bud's disobedience, Officer Outlaw rallied the five thugs to handcuff these terrorists and put them on the prison bus waiting in the street.

Spotlights were charging through the night sky, nearly as bright as the sun, so Bud and Molly could easily see the contemptuous "I told you so" on the faces of some of the on-lookers. Nevertheless, Bud and Molly proudly, with heads held high, joined the other resisters of Big Brother who were chained on the bus. The whole time, they were rejoicing in their hearts that they had been obedient to their Lord to the end.

Five days after they were incarcerated in the Civilian Inmate Labor Camp one hundred miles from their beloved little home, Bud Dunbar died from a severe reaction to the forced vaccination…government bio-weapon. Shiman, Bud's guardian angel, took him by the hand as he departed his old worn-out body, and escorted his spirit safely through the maze of Abbadon's slimy, grungy, demonic minions cluttering the invisible realm, creating anarchy. Bud was awed seeing his, no longer invisible angel, after all of these years, brilliant, powerful and glorious, ascending together hand-in-hand to the longed for, and dreamed about, Land of Perpetuity.

A few days later, Molly heard on the grapevine that her beloved Bud had departed this life. Molly was already ill, so within a few hours of hearing the bad news, her heart simply stopped beating while she slept. Kletos, her invisible guardian angel, who had continually been with her during the unimaginable indignities she experienced at the Civilian Inmate Labor Camp, took her spirit from her worn-out body. As soon as she opened her eyes on the other side of the veil, she gasped in wonderment when she gazed upon the radiant brilliance of Kletos, who emanated rays of shimmering light.

"Oh, my," she exclaimed with breath-taking joy, "your purity and beauty is beyond my wildest imagination!"

Kletos smiled and said, "Hold my hand tightly because we must press through this conclave of wickedness surrounding the upper atmosphere of Earth."

Molly curiously looked around this formerly invisible realm and saw slimy creatures with beady eyes, snarling and grabbing at her. Creepy hairy one-eyed monsters crawled over smaller fiendish ghouls, jutting out their hands attempting to seize her. Strangely...Molly had no fear... just repulsion at finally seeing clearly those from whom she had to endure harassment on Earth. No...Molly was not afraid, she was ascending out of all the wickedness of the world, evil men clamoring for recognition, jealousy, competition, hatred and wars, all soon would be removed from her psyche forever.

Kletos soared smoothly with no hesitation, through the chanting, cursing and impious gestures of these condemned demoniacs. Once past the clamor Molly looked back. All she could see was a black misty fog surrounding the whole planet. Kletos explained that the black mist actually was billions of demons on assignment from Abbadon, all crammed together to form, what appears to be sludge encircling the planet. This is not visible to the natural eye. Kletos explained that the sins of the people have empowered (permitted) the demons to govern on Earth. Since they were so far away now, it simply looked like a black misty fog.

Molly was never able to visibly see these scary creatures while she lived on Earth, but she felt their oppression and harassment everyday. She and Bud had been relentlessly attacked by these foul children of the Prince of Darkness, because they took a firm public stand for freedom and their faith.

Molly noticed how light she felt, like a feather, since she had discarded her body. This was real freedom! It was just too marvelous and incomprehensible to describe. As she and Kletos continued to ascend, surveying the scintillating cosmos brought overwhelming joy to her heart. Before long Molly spotted at a distance, a spectacular brilliance illuminating the royal blue firmament like a sparkling diamond, radiating colorful streams of light.

"Wow...what is that most glorious site?" she pondered in her heart.

Kletos smiled, having read her thoughts and said, "We are almost there."

In a twinkling of an eye Molly was standing with Kletos in front of two massive gates, delicately crafted from translucent pearl. Upon their arrival, the gates slowly opened automatically. With anticipation and excitement she could hardly contain, Molly waited impatiently for her first glimpse of the City of Light. Joy unspeakable flooded her spirit, when behind those beautiful iridescent gates was her beloved Bud...arms outstretched to welcome her. She almost didn't recognize him, so youthful, wrapped in the glory of the Infinite One.

After they embraced and rejoiced, Bud whispered softly to Molly, "Let me take you to meet our blessed Reconciler, whose blood paid your entrance fee through these gates of splendor into the Land of Perpetuity."

Whistleblowers, like Bud and Molly, have tried to awaken the populous about what is going on behind the walls of some deserted military bases, but they were marginalized by the mainstream press, as kooks and conspiracy theorists. The mainstream press was very successful with their bombardment of disinformation through their Sinister Seven-owned newspapers and television/radio networks. But Bud had firsthand knowledge. While he was in the Reserves, the government closed a nearby base. Insiders told him why.

The day of Paul Revere has returned, but the warning was not heeded. Only citizens who previously established a means to communicate with fellow patriots, could be alerted during the crackdown...many communications have been interrupted.

Screams and shrieks of fear and horror, expressing disbelief, could be heard throughout the beautiful peaceful city of Crystal Waters. Shots rang out in the darkness of this ominous night, as many citizens refused to surrender their firearms. These quiet tranquil neighborhoods only yesterday were filled with happy children playing ball, hide and seek and riding bicycles, but now have become combat zones, as working class citizens, the disabled and the elderly of this great "free" country were being hauled out of their homes, kicking and screaming, and placed in huge military prison buses.

The blood of the citizens was splattering all over the beautiful shrubs and flowers, those who unsuccessfully attempted to protect their "castle" from these tyrants. Men, women and children lay dead or dying on their porches, lawns, and driveways, because they pulled their guns against this mighty military assault of Big Brother. There was more freedom in dying than submitting to a life sentence in a Civilian Inmate Labor Camp, or a painful death by a bio-weapon. All the personal belongings, as well as the home of every dead citizen was confiscated, becoming the property of the State. Power corrupts, and absolute power corrupts absolutely.

Most of the military hauling honest, hard-working citizens of this once great free country, off to the Civilian Inmate Labor Camps, were from foreign countries speaking limited or no English at all. Since they have no allegiance to this country or to its people, if they kill someone obeying a command there is no guilty conscience. They have been secretly trained in the closed military bases, by our own military, preparing for years the perfect strategy to conquer a free people. The element of surprise was essential to assure the success of this monumental kidnapping of a free citizenry…the whole country at the same time. Of course, it was done in the darkness of midnight, because most of the freedom loving, hard working, taxpaying citizens were asleep, making them vulnerable to the dirty deeds of those who are transforming their country…from freedom…to fascism.

TWO YEARS EARLIER

One crystal clear day with the sun shining brightly, spreading its warm rays through the fluffy burgundy shears hanging at the bedroom window, the shrill ring of the phone startled Gilly, awakening him from a cozy slumber.

'"Hel…lo," whispered a groggy Gilly.

"Hello, hello, my dear friend Mr. Gilly," the voice boomed with excitement, but Gilly did not recognize his voice.

By now Gilly was sitting on the edge of the bed trying to get his bearings, while glancing at the clock. It was 7:00 o'clock. Before Gilly could say anything, the voice on the other end of the line said, "Gilly, this is Dr. Hasad. I know I should have contacted you before this, but I wasn't sure how long it would take me to get out of my country. Then suddenly…I am here in this great country of yours!"

Gilly couldn't believe what he was hearing, but was so glad to be reconnected with Dr. Hasad. He asked, "What do you mean you are here…where?"

"I am at Hotel Crystal Waters room 102, Gilly. Could you come and get me so we can get started on your book?" asked Dr. Hasad enthusiastically.

"Oh Dr. Hasad," exclaimed Gilly, "you are just in time. We have an organization now called, Sound the Alarm, which has helped us distribute our message all over the world in real time. Now you will be able to help us."

By the time Dr. Hazad arrived, Pastor Warrior, the Gillingham's, and the Goldman's had educated hundreds of the citizens of Crystal Waters through their Sound the Alarm organization. So many materials are available, because in order to concoct such a gargantuan world takeover plot, there has to be a paper trail. Dr. Hasad did an exceptional job writing Gilly's experience in Gehinnom. His finished and published book was easy to read for all ages…exciting…compelling. It was added to their arsenal of distribution materials. Many kids have contacted them for more information, because they were totally clueless about who lives in the invisible realm.

Through contributions to Sound the Alarm they have been able to alert friends and relatives in many states of this great nation, supplying DVDs, CDs, books and literature that delineate the Plan of the Sinister Seven in detail. Each person receiving information from Sound the Alarm was instructed to share the materials with others.

By networking, all citizens interested in the truth could be supplied materials in every state, as well as around the world.

Pastor Warrior was well aware that his colleagues of various denominations were very afraid, refusing to see the truth of the Plan, preferring to live in denial. Reflecting the opinion of the mainstream media, they told him that he was a conspiracy nut, because they insisted that People of the Book (believers) already have the Constitution to protect their religious freedom. In other words, don't confuse them with the facts. Since they desperately want to protect their 501(C)3 tax exempt status, allegiance to the pagan government is the result. The Sacred Script says that man cannot serve two masters. The modern-day progressive church has chosen allegiance to mammon (money).

Nevertheless, the intrepid Pastor Warrior, motivated by the Sound the Alarm team was undaunted by the naysayers, because he was a man on a mission to awaken as many people as possible. He is well aware that his task is an uphill battle. This is because the corrupt Congress has enacted laws to protect the tyrants, and eliminate the freedoms of the citizens with the ease of discarding a used tissue in the trash. They sit in their ivory towers of privilege totally disconnected from the needs of those whom they are supposed to represent.

There really is no place to hide from what is coming down the pike, unless you have a hidden underground bunker. Of course, there is an underground city with seventeen levels built underneath the People's House (at the Capitol) to hide the president and the congressional turncoats from an enemy. Many countries have such hideouts for their elites. There is some evidence and many rumors pointing to a subterranean submarine chamber and underground bases...not on any map, because it is all hush-hush to those who pay the bills...taxpayers.

Pastor Warrior put a notice in the newspaper that he was having another meeting at the Community Center. When the day arrived there were many more people in attendance than at their last meeting, and he was encouraged.

"We have only one way to prepare for this unthinkable onslaught of wickedness against us," declared Pastor Warrior, as he paced back and forth in front of the patriot believers.

"As we draw close to our Lord and Savior, He will draw close to us. From the beginning of civilization, our Creator has desired our dependence upon Him for all of our needs. But we are so intelligent we meet our own needs, devoid of Him who created us. It seems that only during a crisis, an impossible situation, do we even call on His Name. Shame on us," shared Pastor Warrior with a grimace on his face. "This ought not be so."

Julie raised her hand to share a warning and an encouragement. "That which is coming to Earth will be the greatest hour for the church since the martyrdom of the early church. If we don't learn to depend on the Infinite One now for all of our needs, we will simply be mowed down. It was prophesied in 1909, by a humble saint of the Lord during a mighty revival, that in one hundred years the greatest revival known to mankind, trumping even the outset of the church, would come upon the whole world. That hundred years has passed...it is now," she proclaimed enthusiastically.

The crowd jumped to their feet in uproarious joy, clapping, and whistling with vociferous shouts of praise to the Infinite One. This thunderous exultation lasted a full fifteen minutes.

As their praise ebbed, Julie continued, "We may face the loss of food and water, electricity, and other forms of energy. Deprivation could invade our whole country."

"Are you really ready for empty kitchen cupboards like was experienced by George Muller when he fed hundreds of orphans in the 1800's? Are you ready to pray in every morsel of food you eat as did Rev. Muller, waiting faithfully on the Infinite One to supernaturally supply your need?" Julie questioned seriously.

Looking around, trying to read the enthusiastic faces in the crowd, she asked again, "Are you REALLY ready? Because that is the way it is going to be for survival. Oh, I know...some of you will say that you are not afraid of dying, and neither am I. We know where we are going," she agreed with a big, knowing smile and a nod. "But... someone else may need to see the supernatural provision of the Infinite One through your example."

Jumping up to stand beside Julie, Gilly reminded the crowd, "We can't forget who is the strongman attacking us. We wrestle not against flesh and blood, but against the Prince of Darkness in the invisible world. So our real warfare is not with carnal weapons...guns...bombs... tanks. In the spiritual portion of the battle, only spiritual weapons...helmet of salvation...shield of faith...sword of the Spirit (Sacred Script)...breastplate of righteousness... will provide victory. Even though in the natural world we still use protective tanks, guns and grenades, we need the guidance and power of the Reconciler and His mighty invisible angelic army, to be able to pull down all demonic spiritual strongholds placed against us."

"Since I met Abbadon personally...I know you believe me," proclaimed Gilly with a victory shout... "Hallelujah!"

"The Sacred Script in our generation has been demeaned and devalued, by the smug seminary scholars, as not divinely inspired but simply a fragmented document of the early church infiltrated with myths and men's ideas," explained Pastor Warrior.

Holding up the Sacred Script in his hand, the pastor proclaimed, "Our faith will be sorely compromised, promises not fulfilled, if we do not believe this is the divinely inspired word of the Infinite One. The angels act on the word of the Infinite One spoken in faith...not in doubt... to supernaturally help us," warned the pastor. "In other words...when you speak His word (Sacred Script) the angels hear, and are energized to manifest that promise in your life."

The door of the Community Center squeaked rather loudly, causing everyone to turn to see who was arriving in the middle of the meeting. They marveled when they saw Chloe with her mother Clarissa come to the front, where Pastor Warrior was speaking. He gave her a big hug and told her how happy everyone was to see her recovering so nicely, since her ordeal three months ago.

Her soft brown eyes began to fill with tears which caused the pastor to ask, "Honey, what is wrong?"

Clarissa answered, "Chloe wants to testify to the youth gathered here, what led her down the wrong road to death, her out-of-body experience, as well as what delivered her. She knows the dirty work of Abbadon first hand, and believes the kids may wake up to the evil that has, and will continue to come against us."

Pastor Warrior ushered Chloe behind the podium and adjusted the microphone to her height. Chloe was very nervous, not just because she was so young, but she had never before addressed a large audience. Sensing her apprehension, everyone in the room simultaneously jumped out of their seats and began to clap and whistle their approval of her courage.

Timidly she began to speak. "I walked into the temptation of the Prince of Darkness boldly and with my eyes wide open. I have a praying mother whom I rejected... her God...not for me. I rebelled against every good thing she tried to teach me. I told myself...all she cares about is my brother. So I was jealous and angry. My dad was never home. He was always in some other country doing great things for someone else. So I convinced myself, with the help of the unseen demons, that no one loved me, so I could do whatever I wanted...when I wanted... who cared."

"My mother never accused me of my sins and would never throw me out of her home, even though I challenged her to do so. I was always in her face. She didn't come after me or force me to come home, when I disappeared a few days at a time. Of course, I told myself this was because she didn't love me. I could die, for all she cared. At that time, I had no clue that she had covenanted with the Infinite One that she would live her life according to His example. She would trust Him for all of her cares and needs, including my rebellion and hatred of her...even to her loss. I didn't understand that kind of sacrificial love," lamented Chloe with sadness in her voice and on her face..."until now."

Clarissa perceived that Chloe was experiencing cotton mouth, not just from talking, but from her pain medication she still needed, so brought her a cold glass of water and quietly sat it beside her.

"I look at all the young people in this audience and plead with you to resist temptation, do not fall into the Abbadon's trap of sensual love. He is a liar! There are severe eternal consequences for continued rebellious sinful pleasure. Right now I feel like fifteen going on fifty because of my horrible experience. Rebellion against what is right does not bring freedom...trust me! It brings bondage to sin, pain, sorrow...and maybe even early death. But for the grace of the Infinite One, and my mother's prayers, I would be dead right now," implored Chloe, as her voice became stronger with a tone of urgency…"living eternally in Gehinnom."

"Most of us get into sex, drugs, and rock'n roll. After all, isn't sex shoved down our throats in the government schools? To them we are no better than animals…no morals...no commitment…no respect...just raw sex. At least that is what I got out of sex-ed and my friends, too. If the temptation of sex is shoved in your face, day in and day out with no restraint, you are going to indulge. This is Abbadon's dirty little secret. I personally resisted sex, but threw myself into drugs, alcohol and magical arts, séances and the worship of demons. This got me jazzed."

"Because of your government school teachers," Chloe continued, "many of you have already fallen for 'you're going to do it anyway,' so study our sex manuals and get the most pleasure possible. Actually, the pornography shown in your Sex-Education class compels you to experiment, because you are curious, self-centered, hormonal and foolish. But no matter, if you get pregnant a teacher or counselor will take you to an abortionist without the knowledge of your parents. They have a special slush fund to pay for the murder of your baby…and some of you have used this fund. All the time they convince you it is a lifeless blob of tissue…but…you really know in your heart that is a lie. But…it is a slick, quick exit from sin…but not from the consequences…trust me."

The silence was deafening in the Community Center for Chloe had their rapt attention. She could tell she was touching a sensitive cord, but was compelled by her heavenly experience to press on with her testimony. Her large brown compassionate eyes were now clear, no more tears, as a sense of mission surged through her whole body, strengthening her resolve. She knew her magnificent guardian angel, Harpazo, stood right beside her. She could never forget his dazzling brightness and his powerful physique.

Chloe took a deep breath and paused briefly before she continued her difficult confession. "Because of the hatred and unforgiveness I nurtured in my mind and heart, I permitted (without realizing) the invisible demonic spirits to take charge of my life and they led me into the Goth sub-culture: demon possession, witchcraft, mediums, psychics, Ouija Board, vampires…the whole nine yards. Becoming a vampire was an obsession with me…power… respect. So after a few months of worshiping Abbadon around the great fire of sacrifice, I thought that I might want to offer myself as a sacrifice…but not to the Infinite One like my loser mother…but…to Abbadon. I was awed by the power of the Prince of Darkness, who was mystical… exciting…defiant. All of this led to Aaron reading my mind and attempting to sacrifice me to Molech."

Taking a drink of water and gathering her composure Chloe continued. "When I died and left my body, a dazzling angel bright as the noonday sun, took me by the hand and led me to the beautiful Land of Perpetuity. It was awesome. I will never be able to truly describe the glories I saw in that brief moment of time, but I do know that I want to go back and live there forever," avowed Chloe, as she turned toward the rays of sunlight streaming through the window, with a dreamy faraway smile on her face.

"While I was enjoying the beauty of this enchanting haven of peace, I felt so clean…a purity I wanted to capture and hold onto forever. Then suddenly a creepy, slimy, monster, with drool oozing out of his mouth matting his hair into smelly clumps (vomit), who had possessed my body and mind on Earth, tried to climb back inside of me."

Grimacing and cringing she said, "Ooh…it was scary and disgusting. But…my guardian angel stopped him.

Then...sadly...I was commissioned to go back to Earth to testify about what I had seen, and to compel you to surrender your life to the One who gave it to you in the first place...our Creator."

A seventeen year old boy stood up to ask Chloe a question. His name was Jason, the son of the President of Crystal Waters Bank, who was sitting beside him. Jason, trembling a bit, was so moved by Chloe's testimony that he was compelled to ask, "Chloe, why did you have to come back? Why couldn't you stay in that wondrous place?"

With a smile Chloe answered, "I am so glad you asked that question. I was kidnapped by sin and did not understand that the Reconciler had already paid my ransom. After I returned to Earth, I gladly repented of my sins and accepted the Reconciler into my heart. Now I will be able to return to that wondrous place at the end of my earthly life. But first, I must finish the work He has called me to do here on Earth...like sharing with you. We are not born to serve our earthly father, but we are born to serve our heavenly Father," she admonished.

"So if you have what you consider a mean father or mother, or a lonely and unhappy home life, or rejected by your peers...what does that matter?" questioned Chloe. "Each of us must experience some adversity and pain in this life."

Tears began to well in Chloe's eyes once again, as she drifted off in her memory to recall her majestic experience, causing her to pause briefly. Then she slowly scanned the audience as her tears dried, and her eyes widened with wonder. Her voice was soft, almost a whisper, "If you could only see what I saw, you would be convinced beyond a shadow of a doubt that you have an eternal Father that loves you unconditionally, and He has a very special plan for your life. Please trust what He says about you...and...about the City of Light in the Sacred Script, so you will not have to face the consequences that I have endured from my unbelief and rebellion."

"The end of the world is drawing near and we must be about our Father's business," entreated Chloe. "And...I want to help you be ready."

Chapter 12

Traditions Outlawed

"Mom...Mom...Mom," screamed a terrified Chloe running through the back door in a hurry to tell Clarissa what happened at her school today.

"I'm in the laundry room, Honey...what's wrong?" yelled Clarissa as she darted out of the room to see what was causing the panic in her daughter's voice. "What... what...what is going on?"

"Oh...mom...sit down," invited a breathless Chloe slipping into the blue leather-covered booth of their cozy breakfast nook.

"You're never going to believe what happened in our school today," said Chloe launching right into her story.

"Do you remember when Dad and Gillly told us about the jihad movement in our country...well...it has arrived in our school," she said with terror in her eyes.

"We had an assembly today and they passed out a pamphlet titled 'Dawaism School Guide.' It's right here," said Chloe as she reached into her notebook and pulled out the pamphlet to hand to her bewildered mother.

Clarissa slipped into the other end of the half-moon styled booth, where the late afternoon sun filtered through the blue paisley, ruffled curtains, and began to thumb through the pamphlet without saying a word... but the terrified look on her face revealed what she was thinking.

Then she asked Chloe, “What does Dawaism mean? I know it has taken over dozens of countries already, and has been flying below the radar in our country, but do they translate the meaning in this pamphlet?”

“No mom, they wouldn’t dare reveal the truth, because I remember that Dad said ‘duty to conquer’ is what it means,” explained Chloe. “But after this pamphlet was passed out, a Dawa girl sitting across from me, just glared with dark angry eyes saying under her breath, “Umma is greatest.”

“Have you ever had a problem with her before now?” asked Clarissa.

“No...mom...never. We have actually worked on classroom projects together and I never experienced any animosity, just school friends...at least I thought so. She can’t have friends to her home because of her religion, except those of her religion, but that never bothered me. But since we are now going to have this program to study her religion, suddenly she became hostile. Really...I don’t understand. But...I do know...Umma is not greatest. That ticks me off.”

“We all know how that Communist Legal Union (CLU) was successful in removing any semblance of our country’s traditional religious beliefs from all schools in this country, even labeling our Sacred Script contraband. Now this cruel and vicious religion, who kills anyone who doesn’t believe their way...is legal in our schools!” screamed Chloe as she got up from her seat and began to walk back and forth crying frustrating tears, grabbing a tissue as she walked past the box on the counter.

Then she threw her hands in the air exclaiming, "What are we going to do Mom? This is the worst day of my life!"

"First of all we are going to call Pastor Warrior and have him come to dinner, so he can read this pamphlet and see if he knows about any of this," stated Clarissa calmly for she tended to internalize shocking information before she reacted.

"We knew this was coming, but we didn't know that laws were already in place to propagate Dawaism in our schools. From what it says here this program to embrace this dangerous religion is mandated by our state. This is treason! But...evil laws are made in the dark of night then thrust upon the populous against their will," said Clarissa shaking her head in disbelief, while putting a reassuring arm around Chloe giving her a big hug.

Clarissa picked up the telephone and called Pastor Warrior, briefing him on the contents of the pamphlet. He had no idea this kind of clandestine activity was going on in their state. He yelled, "What!" so loudly that Chloe could hear him across the room. "Our kids are commanded to celebrate their holy month and our school district has outlawed Christmas! What time is dinner Clarissa...I'll be there." Clarissa dialed the Gillingham's and invited them to dinner.

Then Chloe got a bright idea. "You need to invite Dr. Hasad, too. Didn't he leave the jihad movement and is now a believer in the Reconciler?"

"Oh...great idea Honey, I forgot about his past. He is such a beautiful believer in the Lord, it is hard to imagine him a killer of infidels. He can give us great advice," Clarissa agreed. "I'll call him...then let's get busy on dinner. It's going to be a long night."

When Joe walked through the door Chloe ran up to him and gave him a big hug, which he returned. Without saying a word she simply handed him the pamphlet, but he noted anger in her eyes. He looked at the title and without saying a word glanced at Clarissa, who rolled her eyes and shrugged her shoulders conveying through body language, "We have a big problem and I don't have a solution." So without question, Joe sat down and began to read the pamphlet.

About 5:00 the back door suddenly burst open and in walked a happy Gilly, as he thrust his hand toward Joe for a shake saying, "Hey...bud...how the heck are ya?"

Before Joe could answer, Gilly patted him on the back continuing to talk without taking a breath, "Haven't seen ya for a few days. What's up with the dinner in the middle of the week?"

Joe had just finished reading the pamphlet and simply looked up at Gilly, handing him the pamphlet. "Whoa... if looks could kill I'm a dead guy. What caused the black cloud to rain all over you?" asked Gilly as he received the pamphlet from Joe, reading the title at the same time.

Astonishment flashed across Gilly's face, but he said nothing and sat down to read the pamphlet. Sean sat next to him, peering over his shoulder so he could read it at the same time. Julie went to the kitchen to help Clarissa, asking her what was in the pamphlet.

Just as the ladies put the roast beef dinner on the table, Dr. Hasad arrived with Pastor Warrior right behind him. As they sat down Joe asked Pastor Warrior to pray.

"Our most merciful Father, we thank you for bringing the patriot believers together once again. We are united in Your love, desiring to do Your will only. Grant to us Your wisdom and guidance as to how we are to proceed in this new mission. We are grateful for Your provision and ask You to bless this food for health...that we may better serve You. Amen!" said Pastor Warrior with gusto. Everyone at the table said, "Amen."

As they passed the dishes of delicious food, Chloe launched into the events that transpired at her school that day. Dr. Hasad had not read the pamphlet, but he didn't have to because he knows the lies this religion tells in order to manipulate their beliefs onto unsuspecting people to accomplish their Plan to rule the world. He knows that adherents of Dawaism always claim they serve a religion of love, yet, their religious book states that they can lie in order to persuade someone to become a serf to Umma.

That which Dr. Hasad greatly feared has come full force upon his new country, creating deep pain in his heart, although he knows that Dawaism has a hundred-year Plan to takeover western civilization. Dawaism is a religion, behind which they hide their true agenda... political ideological goals...so they actually are more dangerous than Communism or Marxism. It seems that any "ism" means bondage.

Dr. Hasad told them, "Stalin stated that the West would fall without firing a shot, because he knew that even during his reign, Communists had been covertly planted in our government. Now in 2010, they are openly invited to positions of authority in our government. But what is worse, Dawa adherents are also serving in our government, having proclaimed that one of them would be our president by 2008...compliments of the Sinister Seven. I often wonder if there will be a standoff between these two power brokers...Communism and Dawaism... for ruler-ship...or...will they join forces during the time of the final takedown of our country?" he questioned, wrinkling his brow as he contemplated the horror of his reasoning.

After Chloe finished her story Dr. Hasad asked, "Is it true that it is illegal for you to have a copy of the Sacred Script at your school?"

"Yeah," said Chloe with a twinkle in her eye and a mischievous smile, "but I have one hidden in my desk covered by one of our schoolbook covers, and I read it during our allotted reading time. Ever since I visited the Land of Perpetuity, the most glorious place I have ever seen in my life, I must read the truth in our holy book, and I am not going to let that false cult come into my country and steal my traditions and my religious beliefs. We know before we die, that we are guaranteed a place in the Land of Perpetuity, if we accept the sacrifice of the Reconciler who paid the price for our sins. My Dawa friend said she must try hard to do good deeds to her people, as required by the Prophet, but she still won't know until she dies if her good deeds are acceptable to Umma…how sad."

"Chloe, I am impressed with your passion," said Dr. Hasad in his richly accented, deep soothing voice, exhibiting a warm smile. "It is the youth, full of passion for their Lord, who will bring revival to this nation. We elders are the advisors and intercessors. I do believe that just before the return of the Reconciler, He will allow one more great revival of supernatural healings, creative miracles and many raised from the dead. One last demonstration of the love and mercy of the Infinite One toward wayward man…calling him…wooing him."

"You are absolutely right Dr. Hasad," said an excited Julie. "I have been reading about many cities across the globe where all of these things are already taking place. Even a few college campuses in our country are experiencing the sin-convicting power of the Illuminator, kids weeping their way to repentance. Classes have even been canceled because students are prostrate before the Lord for hours. And…it is only going to accelerate."

"*Where sin abounds, grace much more abounds*," shouted Julie and Clarissa at the same time. Excitement was beginning to stir around the table.

"*Greater is He that is in me, than he that is in the world,*" said Dr. Hasad with enthusiasm.

While everyone was talking and eating Pastor Warrior had been thumbing through the pamphlet. Then he soberly interjected in the middle of their conversation, "I believe our first step is to go see our lovely Congressman...you know...what's his name? Oh yeah...Chance...umm...Slim Chance. That's it! He apparently is a participant in this legislation. Well...I guess I don't know yet, if he voted for it, so I must withhold judgment...but we will soon find out."

"I have to go, too," chimed in Chloe with enthusiasm.

"Oh, you bet Chloe," confirmed Pastor Warrior, "this is your baby."

"Your mom and I will go along for moral support. Your mom knows her way around the halls of congress since she has done so much for the cause of autism," he said as he patted little Joey gently on the head, who was eating quietly beside him.

"Tomorrow I will call his office for the first after-school appointment he has available," confirmed Clarissa.

Dr. Hasad warned, "Now...expect that he will give you some mumbo-jumbo about multicultural diversity. That is...if he voted for this intrusion in our public school system. So be sure and see where he stands on the issue before you vent," he said with a devilish grin, "but I hope he will be your ally. It will make it so much easier to get the ball rolling to oust this false god."

"How did you get involved in this religion?" asked Chloe.

"I was born into it," explained Dr. Hasad. "I was raised with our religious book in one hand and a machete in the other. If someone refuses to be persuaded by our religious book to follow our Prophet, then with the machete I was commanded to whack off his head. I was taught from infancy to hate the People of the Book…and I had never even known one…so sad."

"Ooh…how horrible," expressed Chloe with a grimace on her face, as her body noticeably shuddered at just the thought of such violence…especially violence in the name of religion.

"D…d…did you ever whack off anyone's head Dr. Hasad?" she asked cautiously, hoping he will say no.

"No child…no," he answered with a sigh of relief. "Even though I was a rabid follower of Umma, a first class bully in order to please him alone, the first time I was commanded to kill an infidel, I quietly laid down my machete and walked away from my religion and my family. How could a 'supreme being' ask me to kill any human being? If he wants him dead…he must do it himself. So I left my country to go to a university in Israel. It was there that my roommate, who was a believer, gave me a copy of the Sacred Script. Oh my…what a difference from the religious book I had studied all of my life!" he sighed raising his hands high, then clasping them together reverently in a prayer symbol.

"Reading it was like pouring water upon parched ground. It truly was living water to my thirsty, truth-seeking, spirit," he said crossing his hands on his heart, indicating the fullness of joy he has experienced.

"The Infinite One means…I AM or THE BEING…who is, was, and always will be…self-existent…eternal. Does Umma have a meaning?" asked Sean.

"Domination," answered Dr. Hasad without hesitation. "Umma certainly is not a god of love, nor does his name indicate that he is self-existent or eternal."

Everyone at the table darted glances at each other expressing on their faces, without saying, they had a better understanding of who they were up against. Since they all knew that Dawaism meant "duty to conquer" everything began to make more sense with this new information from Dr. Hasad. Domination...conquer...murder are not commands from their Reconciler. The Infinite One sent the Reconciler (His Son) to Earth to save lives...not destroy them. The only one that was overwhelmed by the Reconciler was Abbadon...not humans.

"I learned from reading the Sacred Script that I had been a tool in the hand of Abbadon, who came to kill, steal, and destroy," said Dr. Hasad with sadness on his aging, yet kindly, face.

"But why were you in Afgar," asked Gilly somewhat perplexed.

"I believe I was...what you call...a missionary," he said as his eyes danced with enthusiasm.

"And boy, you sure ministered to me," Joe chimed in.

"At first you made me mad, but the Lord was dealing with me...as I learned a bit later. But I just couldn't get you out of my mind. You just didn't fit in that violent country. You were...so...so kind and your countenance glowed with peace," said Joe fondly remembering.

"And then you had knowledge about my daughter, and I hadn't told you what was said during my phone call. All of that was just...well...just supernatural. Can't explain it any other way...definitely a new experience for me," added Joe as a big smile wreathed his face.

"And I'm so glad, Dad," said Chloe as she placed her hand on her dad's hand giving it a gentle squeeze.

"Does your pamphlet outline what you will be required to do in these classes?" asked Dr. Hasad.

"Pretty much," answered Chloe. "We have to learn the five pillars of their faith, memorizing portions of their religious book. It says that our founding fathers believed in Dawaism, which of course is a lie. We will have to chant prayers and profess Umma is the only true god."

"That is blasphemy," declared Pastor Warrior slapping his hand down on the table, which shook it slightly. "I am incensed that our lawmakers would make such an egregious law behind our backs, especially after they did nothing to retain our country's religious foundation. Let me have that pamphlet back so I can study it and know what I'm talking about at our meeting. I will get it back to you in a couple of days. After you make the appointment, let me know the date and time, Clarissa."

"There is a lot of audacity in this program they are planning to foist upon our trusting kids," offered Gilly. "The kids will even be required to dress in their religious garb."

"That's just great!" erupted Chloe. "Can't you just see me in a burqa."

"No," said her mother softly, as she caressed Chloe's long hair. "I wouldn't be able to see your pretty face and gorgeous hair"...everyone laughed.

"They will have to take a new name," Gilly said as he finished describing what he read, "one that is condoned by this religion. And eventually they will learn a jihad prayer of war. Wow...that is blatant!"

"I think I read in the pamphlet that every school must designate a specific room for prayer for the followers of Umma. But the People of the Book are denied any rights, their religion is illegal and even the Sacred Script is considered contraband. How did we degenerate to this degree without noticing?" lamented Joe.

"If Congressman Chance won't help us, I know a good patriot attorney...and we will sue...just like has been done against us by that Communist Legal Union. The fight is on," declared Pastor Warrior vociferously.

"Boy," declared Sean, "we have millions of illegal aliens crossing our borders demanding that our hardworking citizens pay for their schooling, medical treatment and food stamps...the Sinister Seven has taken over our government driving us to bankruptcy after de-industrializing our nation...all good jobs gone overseas...and now this false god replacing the true God. Our forefathers would turn over in their graves, if they knew what has become of the nation they fought tooth and nail to give to us. Woe is me!"

"Well," said Gilly, "we did start our Sound the Alarm organization to inform the public. We'll just add this cause to our agenda," he laughed. "We knew we would have to eventually."

The following Monday Clarissa called Congressman Chance's office and made an appointment for Friday. Chloe had to get out of school early because there was only a 2:00 appointment left at the congressman's office. Clarissa picked her up at school then swung by to pick up Pastor Warrior. Once they arrived at the congressman's office they only had to wait about five minutes.

"Please follow me," said the secretary.

The three of them got up and followed her to Congressman Chance's office. Slim Chance, a tall slender man, offered a hand shake greeting to each of them, before they sat down around his gigantic polished oak desk. Awards and pictures of him with politicians and celebrities, as well as family, adorned his walls and shelves. The walls were a rich dark blue, while burgundy and blue vertical striped draperies adorned the glass French doors, which opened onto a Victorian style balcony with a breath-taking view of the ocean. The glass doors were open allowing a faint whiff of the sweet seaweed to permeate the room, while the peaceful sounds of the waves gently splashing onto the shore provided serene ambience.

"What can I do for you?" asked Congressman Chance in a firm, yet welcoming voice.

Both Pastor Warrior and Clarissa silently looked at Chloe who was sitting in the middle. Chloe looked pleadingly at each of them, but they just smiled. So Chloe, very slowly and softly said, "Congressman Chance, we came here today to see why our school district is required to teach a religious program called Dawaism," handing him the pamphlet while she finished answering his question. "Do you know anything about this?"

As he took the pamphlet he wrinkled his brow and shook his head gently, worry appearing on his face, while he leaned back in his burgundy overstuffed chair framed in warm polished oak. Silently and soberly he thumbed through the pamphlet, stopping to read a paragraph here and there.

Then he looked up at the three of them. "I knew this day was coming…and I was dreading it. But here you are and we will face it together. Yes…legislation has been passed by a narrow margin…and not with my approval. It wouldn't take much to reverse this legislation, but would take a lot of work and a lot of time. I believe the best route for permanent results is a lawsuit. Are you willing to give of your time?"

"How much time?" asked Pastor Warrior.

"Well…one or two years…maybe more," answered Congressman Chance.

"This will be proven unconstitutional. After all, the Communist Legal Union has been successful in removing from our schools across this country any semblance of my beliefs," he said with a sad countenance, as he hung his head in shame at the shenanigans of his fellow congressmen.

"And what are your beliefs," asked Chloe.

"The same as yours…I think. You see…I was paralyzed after a car hit me one day when I was riding my bike. I was ten years old. About a year later Mom took me to a revival meeting where the people seemed so happy praising and worshiping the Lord. I felt warm and secure in that environment, yet, I couldn't explain why at that time. Suddenly I heard someone yell excitedly that she could see...her sight had been restored. There was a lot of excitement. Then the evangelist came to the mike and said, 'There is someone here who is paralyzed from an accident. If you stand up by faith, you will see that you are healed.'

"Were you the one healed," asked Chloe softly, sensing she was on holy ground hearing his remarkable testimony.

"Yes," he whispered, mentally recapturing that moment of so long ago, "and I am grieved that laws against my faith...your faith...have been passed. I have fought hard against it...to no avail. But if you are willing to file suit there is a non-profit organization that will be more than happy to take your case. We need someone who is brave enough to do so," he stated wondering if they knew what they were getting themselves into.

"What do you mean...brave enough?" Clarissa inquired.

Buying some time, Congressman Chance cleared his throat, and hesitated. Then slowly, haltingly he said, "Well...umm...umm...it is dangerous to come against this religion."

"How so?" asked Pastor Warrior, now revved up for a good fight.

"First...they own all or portions of, all major television networks, radio stations, newspapers, and even the film industry. The power of persuasion is through the media...a propaganda tool. Through intimidation and threats, because of their financial investment, they can prevent anything truthful from being revealed about their religion. Without media scrutiny, they can quietly transform our country. So you will experience telephone threats against your life. Always record them. You could be stalked by ominous looking men. Gossip and disinformation about you could be spread around your school to ridicule and humiliate you, with possible bigotry from your teachers, whose union lobbied us for this law. Because they are bullies, it could get really ugly," explained Slim, hoping that he hadn't discouraged her. But he knew he had to lay it all out clearly, so she would be able to make an informed decision.

"Wow," said Chloe with a serious look on her face, "I had no idea so much would come against me for only asking for equality."

"When the followers of Dawa moved to our country, we gave them freedom to worship whomever they desired. Now…they have the audacity to make a law to exalt Umma. I'm mad and I am willing to suffer anything to bring back reverence for the Reconciler who provided the freedoms of our country, as well as respect for our traditions," she said emphatically.

"This organization you talked about," asked Clarissa, "does it have a good track record?"

"You bet," answered Slim. "In fact, you will find that once this gets out, others will come out to support you. There has already been success in quashing this movement in another state. We can get a copy of the court records and see their approach to victory."

"When you said there would be a lot of support once the lawsuit became known, do you mean from the churches?" asked Pastor Warrior. "Because my experience with the churches standing up for anything that might bring a little persecution, causes them to run like cockroaches from bright light."

"Have you met Pastor Brawn from Believer's Patriotic Chapel asked the Congressman?"

"No," answered Pastor Warrior. "You mean there is a bold witness in this town?"

"He just moved here about six months ago, and he already has about 200 in attendance. I attend there. A farmer sold some of his land way out on Allegiance Hwy so maybe he is too far away for you to have heard about him as yet," said Slim.

Congressman Chance picked up his phone and dialed. He had a conversation with someone, then cupped his hand around the receiver and asked Chloe, "Can you meet with Freedom Force next Tuesday at 4:00 P.M.?"

Chloe looked at her mom then Pastor Warrior, both nodding, so she said, "Yes, we can be there."

Tuesday rolled around pretty fast. The three of them drove up to an historic brownstone, parking right in front.

"Wow...they have done a beautiful job of restoration on this hundred-year old building," exclaimed Clarissa. "I love that...that solid...dignified... eastern look." Pastor Warrior and Chloe agreed.

"It appears that all three stories belong to Freedom Force," assessed Pastor Warrior as he read the calligraphic words on the window. The three of them went inside, checked in, and took a seat in the stately waiting room.

Chloe pointed to the handcrafted mahogany spiral staircase saying, "Mom, that is so cool."

The wall paper had an ecru background with an outline of forest green and mauve human figures dressed in clothing reflecting the 1800's. Also there were buggies with horses reminiscent of those times, outlined in dark brown. The plush forest green carpeting completed the motif. Soon the secretary ushered them down the hall to a very large conference-style office. The double mahogany doors slide open and disappeared into the wall.

Chloe glanced at her mom with a look that said, "That's cool...please explain this most interesting architecture."

Clarissa whispered, "Craftsmanship that is lost to history."

A well-dressed dark-haired man with a splash of silver at the temples, walked up to them with his hand extended to welcome them. "My name is Sam Champion...please call me Spunky...a childhood nickname."

With a little shrug of his shoulders indicating resignation, yet with a devilish twinkle in his eyes he added, "I think it still fits my personality, although, not especially professional. I kinda like it...Spunky Champion...fitting for what we do here. Please sit down and let me know what I can do for you."

"Slim Chance said that he was sending me a very brave 15 year-old girl...so that must be you," he stated pointing to Chloe with a big smile on his face.

Chloe smiled, dropping her eyes slightly to gather her thoughts. Then she looked straight into his friendly hazel-green eyes and began to tell her story. She handed him the pamphlet and asked him if he knew anything about it. Spunky took the pamphlet, settling back comfortably in his mahogany chair padded with plush cushions upholstered with mauve brocade, woven into a feather-swirl design. The three of them waited politely and quietly while Spunky thumbed through the pamphlet.

Pretty soon Spunky looked up and asked Chloe, "Is this going to begin in your school soon?"

"Yes," she answered, "in two weeks and I will leave school before I will be forced to say that Umma is greatest," she declared, as her brown eyes widened, flashing determination.

"I am aware of what is happening in our schools, but we need a complaint of 'harm done' that will allow us to go to court. No one has been willing so far, because they are terrified of retribution from this threatening and intimidating power-broker. They have powerful organizations that lobby congress for laws sympathetic to their cause. They are funded by the oil cartels in the East. They teach jihad in the schools they have established in our country and no one stops them...because they are afraid. So you have to be sure you are willing to see this thing through to the end, because we may have to go clear to the Supreme Court...I mean to the federal Supreme Court. Are you committed to the end?" he asked Chloe seriously.

"My dad has been an IIA Agent all of my life and I have learned so much from him. Although I can't be sure of everything they will try to do against me...I do know...I am committed to the victory. The Reconciler and His angels will help us," she said flashing him a confident smile.

"Wow...you are sure of victory...and so am I. You have the courageous spirit we need to accomplish just that, Chloe. Now I can slap an injunction on this program preventing it from proceeding in the schools of our state until the court settles the religious issue," said Spunky with a confident smile. "You don't realize how excited I am to get this case."

"Will your modus operandi be the same as the Communist Legal Union, who has successfully removed our traditions and religious beliefs from our schools?" asked Pastor Warrior.

"Absolutely the same MO," said Spunky emphatically.

"In the past the churches would not take an offensive approach, even though our rights slipped away as fast a snowball in the sun. All of this happened before my time, but I have read many of the cases and am appalled at the apathy of the churches. Adherents of Dawaism have already proclaimed victory in our country, even though they represent less than 1% of our population, so we have desperately needed this case to plug up the hole in our sinking boat," he informed them.

"What if I get threats or abuse from the school teachers, school kids, or maybe my name smeared in the newspaper?" asked Chloe.

"Count on it kiddo...count on it. But the newspaper and even the school is prevented from naming you as the plaintiff, because of your age. But in school the antagonist can release your identify through a student, and that will probably happen...especially from this sect," explained Spunky.

"But...just let me know the name, if there is a death or bodily harm threat, and I will take care of it. It looks like you have a great support team, with your pastor and all, so prayer will be your best strength," he added.

"So what do we do next?" asked Clarissa.

"First I have to file the injunction. Then the state will be served, who in turn will notify the schools to stop this program dead in its tracks. When I have the paperwork ready in a day or so, you will come back and sign the complaint Chloe. This religion will turn to the media in an attempt to demean and ridicule this lawsuit, but eventually we will go to court. Chloe will be needed during most of the court hearings, but you will be coached by me regarding your testimony, as well as how to answer questions from the defense. Eventually you will meet my colleagues for their help will be needed in this landmark case," explained Spunky.

Then Spunky leaned forward placing his elbows on his large desk calendar on top of his shiny polished desk. After carefully intertwining the fingers of his hands and placing his chin on top, he sighed, gazed intently into Chloe's eyes and asked tenderly, "Chloe...do you realize the impact your case will have on our religious liberties?

Chloe, a little embarrassed, looked wide-eyed and a bit teary, but could only shake her head no.

"Well my dear," said Spunky, flashing a big warm smile, "this case will be as monumental as Roe v. Wade...but in the positive.

Then he stood up and walked over to them giving each one a big hug saying softly, "I'll be in touch in a few days."

As they descended the steep brick stairway of the elegant brownstone, Chloe said, "I feel all tingly. I know that Harpazo my guardian angel was sitting right next to me, helping me speak the words of the Lord and giving me courage."

"And he is not going to leave you, Honey, or us, as we face the giant," encouraged Pastor Warrior.

"I can hardly wait to tell Joe how well this all went down," declared Clarissa. "This sure has been a God-moment. Wow...to actually be a part of a landmark case... how exciting."

Clarissa and Chloe dropped Pastor Warrior at his home then proceeded home to prepare dinner. During dinner they explained everything that happened at Spunky Champion's office to Joe. Then Joe explained some of the intimidating techniques used by Dawa propagandists in major cities, where their religious temples are established. There isn't one in Crystal Waters, which is to their advantage. In fact, there is only one in the whole state. He also encouraged Chloe by telling her that he and Gilly are only on leave of absence from the IIA, so they will go down to the school at the first show of intimidation expressed toward her and show a little muscle. They plan on resigning soon, but will wait until this case is on a sure footing.

After listening to her dad's pep talk Chloe looked into his strong loving eyes, while clasping his large hands between her small manicured hands, she said in a positive assuring tone, "Dad...you're the best. What would I do without you? But...a strange thing has happened to me.

I...I...can't really explain it...but I believe I have been called by the Reconciler for such a time as this. Do you understand?"

Removing his hands from between hers, Joe clasped her small soft hands securely between his brawny ones. Holding them firmly he said, "My dear Chloe...I couldn't be prouder of you. You certainly have been called for such a time as this...led by the Creator of the universe to make a difference for freedom," he declared, as his eyes became misty.

For a moment dad and daughter gazed lovingly into each other's eyes, knowing they will work together for this great cause, achieving victory for their wonderful country...and for the Reconciler.

The telephone was ringing when Chloe entered her home after school. She wondered...*where is mom*...but dropped her books on the table and quickly answered.

"Goldman residence," she said with a cheery voice.

"Hey...is this Chloe?" the unfamiliar voice asked.

"Yes it is. Who's this?" she questioned.

"Chloe this is Spunky. I'm calling you with our first court date," he exclaimed with excitement in his voice.

"I know it has taken awhile, but that is the nature of the beast. Of course, there was also much opposition using legal shenanigans to prevent this case from ever seeing the light of day. But we finally made it. Now I will need you and your team in my office this Friday at 2:00 to go over what to expect and how to answer questions. Will that work out for you?" asked Spunky.

"Oh yes Spunky," answered Chloe.

"I am sooo excited," she squealed.

When Friday rolled around Pastor Warrior, Clarissa and Chloe appeared at Spunky's office at 2:00 o'clock sharp.

Spunky was cheerful and welcomed them into his elegant office. After he shook hands with each of them and they sat down, he pulled out a stack of papers for the court.

"Now Chloe, you are going to be asked to declare how you have been offended by the State for requiring you to learn and participate in this religion, other than a passing reference in the history of comparative religions. Since participation in your religion has been outlawed from your school, you demand that participation in all religion be outlawed from your school. Just stay focused on this simple statement no matter where the defense lawyer tries to take the questioning. He will attempt to get you into a defensive argument to persuade the jury that you are a bigot.

"But I'm not," protested Chloe. "I respect their right to choose their religion…I just don't want to be forced to embrace it."

"That Chloe…that is what is so good about this case. Your protest is not contrived…it is genuine…from a pure heart," encouraged Spunky.

"But they will think they can break you down and reveal some clandestine motive…and they will try. So don't get rattled, just give brief answers. If he gets antagonistic I can step in and stop him," he advised.

"Are we allowed to be there," asked Pastor Warrior.

"Absolutely," answered Spunky, "and bring any of your friends that may be interested. But get there early, because this case is already in the news. But…I don't have to remind you of that. How has it been at school?"

"Well…Dad and Gilly did have to go down there and set them straight, but most of the kids are behind me because they didn't want to learn about that religion either," she answered. "I can't believe how terrified they are that they may be killed, or their home blown up, if they openly support me. It's spooky!"

"The people are very informed about the tactics of this religion, but it's our government that gives them the freedom to bully their way into power," offered Spunky.

'Yeah," said Chloe excited to share her knowledge. "Dad told me just the other night that their Prophet has outlined in their religious instructions how to accomplish global conquest, and they have faithfully followed his instructions to subdue many countries so far."

"That's very interesting Chloe," said Spunky. "What are the instructions of global conquest?"

"Well...Dad said there are just three rules: 1) immigrate, 2) increase, 3) eliminate. While the West is aborting their offspring there is great loss to their godly heritage. But this religion is multiplying exponentially because they average eight kids per family...but of course...each man has three or four wives," explained Chloe.

"So your dad is saying that they are required to immigrate to every nation on Earth. They must continue to have a lot of babies per family, who will be indoctrinated from birth to hate all who do not believe as they do. Then they must eliminate...kill...those who refuse to follow their Prophet?" asked Spunky, whose face appeared ashen, as he contemplated this diabolical plan for tyranny in his country.

"Yes!" answered Chloe with gusto, sitting on the edge of her chair ready to explain to Spunky all that her dad has revealed about this dangerous religious ideology, who have been emboldened by our government to rip apart our freedom-loving Constitution and replace it with their tyrannical religious laws of bondage.

Then the four of them sat quietly for a few moments to digest all that had been shared. Spunky glanced at his watch. Sensitive that he may have another appointment waiting, Pastor Warrior stood up to leave saying one last thing, "I went to visit Pastor Brawn, and his group is going to come to one of our Sound the Alarm meetings, and will support us in court. Thanks so much for telling me about him. Sure hope you will be able to come to a meeting sometime."

"You are more than welcome," smiled Spunky. "I do plan to attend when my schedule allows. Now...I will see you next month on the 5th at the court house...9:00 A.M."

"You bet...if the Lord hasn't returned by then," quipped Pastor Warrior with a hopeful grin.

None of them could know the drastic changes that were just ahead.

Chapter 13

Terrorism

The grapevine whispered that Marshall Law was soon to drop its hammer on the citizens of this free nation of the West. Too many citizens were rising up and demanding that their leaders restore the Constitution established by their founding fathers and adhere to the freedoms outlined in the Bill of Rights. Yet, Congress, in the past one hundred years had been systematically making new laws and regulations contrary to these great documents that were established on the natural law revealed in the Sacred Script. The Supreme Court has enforced their schemes.

It has taken a long time, but finally many citizens were awakening to the shenanigans of their Communist infiltrated government and judiciary, and they were madder than a wet hen…so must be silenced.

B.A. Warrior and Sean jumped into the pastors' little blue sport car and sped north to a little hamlet nestled in the cove of Sea Shell Bay. During the breath-taking coastal drive, surging breakers rose high then crashed, rolling gracefully to shore with melodious rhythm.

As they were basking in the beauty of the Pacific Ocean, Pastor Warrior broke the peaceful silence saying, "Sean...thanks for coming with me to visit Pastor Coward. I thought we would sit in on his morning service to see what he is telling his people. Except for Pastor Brawn, Pastor Coward is the only colleague of mine who is at least reading some of our materials, and he agreed to our meeting today after his service. I would love for him to have an informational meeting in his county. I have encouraged him to just look around at all the check-point roadblocks, with dog sniffers, that have been strategically placed all over our great state on a daily basis, demanding our ID card, while insisting that we declare our destination...bye bye 4th Amendment to the Constitution!"

"Yes sir...it is only a matter of time before our freedom is completely gone...puff," opined Pastor Warrior.

"Does Pastor Coward teach his congregation they will be raptured off to la-la-land and won't have to experience the removal of our religious freedom and the fall of our empire?" asked a concerned Sean.

"Yep," answered Pastor Warrior shaking his head in disbelief. "I only hope by now, after reading our materials, that the truth has overcome his deception. But when you have believed a doctrinal lie for so long, another concept seems like heresy."

"I do know," said Pastor Warrior looking Sean straight in the eyes with angst, "that propaganda letters have been received by all church pastors in every state, constraining them to admonish their congregations to follow all the mandatory requirements of their government, to protect them from terrorists, which of course is a lie. Whether it is vaccines, fingerprints, iris scans, imbedded chips, or unwarranted searches of their homes and vehicles, the clergy is responsible for the unquestioning submission of our flock to the pagan government. And we are supposed to report to them anyone who appears suspicious."

"But…I will have none of it," he said slapping his knee, "no sir, I will not be a partner in their clandestine anti-Constitutional schemes."

"In your ministerial meetings, can you tell if the other pastors are going along with this high-jacking of our freedoms?" questioned Sean.

There was a long silence while Pastor Warrior maneuvered a hair-pin curve. Sean could see that Pastor Warrior's jaw was set as he pondered his question.

"Sean, my boy," said the gentle saint of the Reconciler, "I'm so proud that you have done your research. My colleagues, twice and others three times your age, have been bamboozled by false church doctrine and government propaganda for decades, so it will probably take the total collapse of the economy, the dollar, and the loss of their cherished material things (idols) via bombs or sent to Civilian Inmate Labor Camps, before they will awaken to the truth of the matter."

"The non-believers are awakening faster than those pew-warmers. None of them have a clue that they have become tools in the hands of the Prince of Darkness," he said with alarm in his voice, "and I seem powerless to change their minds."

Sea Shell Bay is a delightful little hamlet…always clean streets and the mom & pop shops freshly painted. The variety of bright colors used by the shop owners always reminded Pastor Warrior of a field of the Creator's beautiful fresh-faced flowers, vibrantly alive after a soft misty rain. It worried him that these small business entrepreneurs, the heart of freedom, will be crushed by the heavy foot of Big Brother…heavy taxation…over-regulation. Pastor Warrior and Sean found the church easily and were in time for the

10:30 service. It was already packed so they slipped into the next to last, center pew.

Unseen by anyone, the persistent purveyors of evil showed up on assignment from Gehinnom...Abbadon's demonic hordes. The angelic warriors present were not allowed to prevent them from fulfilling their orders from Abbadon. During the singing and praise, these gross and slimy demons from the abyss, Typhoo, Kazab and Apostasia tormented the congregation by crawling in and out of their bodies, squatting and defecating all over the people, continuing their disgusting contempt by spitting, while Chamas tackled Pastor Coward. Despite the fact the people in attendance were well dressed and dignified, real spiritual power was minimal. When there is spiritual deadness, demons are permitted to oppress or possess all who are yielded to them.

After a time of song and worship, Pastor Coward came to the pulpit. The invisible dark and foreboding Chamas was laughing hysterically, as he grabbed the pastor's head under one arm, while hitting him with his fist. At the same time he was forcefully spewing into his mind, "You are mine and you will do my will. You will be embarrassed... you will look like a fool if you don't walk the safe road. Keep your mind on the doctrine you were taught in seminary... you are no crusader. Tell the people what they want to hear," yelled Chamas, relentlessly pounding his thoughts and false ideas into the mind of Pastor Coward.

Due to his inner torment, Pastor Coward became visibly weak as a flash of nausea surged through his body. He grabbed hold of the pulpit to steady himself. The terror Chamas was forcing into his mind formed a tight band around his brain, pressuring him to doubt the new truths he learned from Sound the Alarm. Chamas was succeeding in breaking down his resistance.

Then he heard a soft, alluring, audible voice ask, "Are you rea...lly sure you want to be labeled an extremist? How about heretic? Do you rea...ly want to lose your respected position in the community...do you...do you?" questioned Remira, the demon who mimics the voice of the Illuminator.

After wrestling with his conflicting thoughts, mulling over the idea of humiliation from peers, Pastor Coward capitulated to the invisible, influential Remira. After he gathered his composure, he discarded his new ideas and proceeded to exhort his congregation to look for the soon coming rapture, which would prevent them from experiencing the devastation that will soon come upon the world.

"Yes! Fear of shame and humiliation always works. It shows how much pride rules his life," Remira chuckled to himself with satisfaction

Chamas, Remira and the rest of their entourage in that room laughed and laughed and laughed so hard, that tears flowed down their ghoulish cheeks, because victory was...oh...so sweet. They high-fived all around then went right back to work their deception on the congregation.

Pastor Coward explained, "In prophecy, years ago we the clergy believed the ten horns on the beast symbolized the revived Roman Empire, creating a ten-nation European Union. That was false. The European Union now includes twenty-seven nations...but no revived Roman Empire. When Mussolini transformed Italy into a Fascist state (1925) the West sent pastors to Italy to confront him as the anti-god-man, telling him that his rise to power would trigger the seven-year great tribulation. That was false. We told you for years that the 200 million-strong army in prophecy was China. That was false. We now understand that this army represents Dawaism, because their Prophet exalts himself as the Savior of the world, challenging the true Savior…the Reconciler.

Typhoo, Kazab, and Apostasia were busy directing all the demons who arrived with some of the attendees, putting them to work menacing the minds of the humans, making sure they will continue to embrace the false doctrine. It was amazing how much sleepiness and yawning they were able to stimulate in a majority of the attendees.

Pastor Warrior and Sean were protected by their giant shining guardian angels, Pestos and Karmel, who had drawn their fiery swords creating a shield of protection around these two believers of truth.

Then Pastor Coward told them that the clergy now has a new interpretation for the beast with the ten horns. "The ten horns represent dividing the planet into ten bioregions ruled by the anti-god-man. But we don't have to worry about the identity of this depraved leader, because we will be swooped away before he comes into power and commands every person to take his mark…the RFID chip…mark of the beast. Nope…we will be gone!" Everyone in that place jumped up and began to clap loudly and praise the Lord for His expected deliverance.

Sean's eyes were drawn to two ladies, two pews forward and to his right, who were dressed very classy. What caught his attention was the strange transformation of their facial features when the noisy praise began. Their demure lady-like countenance subtly turned slightly witch-like. Out of their mouths they whispered guttural sounding words, perplexing him.

He leaned close to Pastor Warrior whispering, "What is happening to those two ladies?" whom he pointed to discreetly, keeping his hand below the pew.

Pastor Warrior watched the ladies for about thirty seconds then whispered to Sean, "They are High

Priestesses from a local coven. The facial transformation and strange sounds means they are conjuring demons."

Sean looked at Pastor Warrior in wordless astonishment, then turned back to watch the ladies, not understanding at all.

During the tumultuous praise, Pastor Warrior nudged Sean with his elbow and pointed to the isle, indicating that he wanted to leave while all the hoopla was going on. They were escorted safely from that building by their angels.

After they got into the car Pastor Warrior said, "Son, let's go get a good breakfast. I know a place downtown called Gramma's Goodies that has the best homemade food you've ever tasted. Her biscuits simply melt in your mouth, and she always has pecan cinnamon rolls, hot and buttery...yum."

Then Pastor Warrior's brow furrowed as he contemplated how he would explain to Sean what they observed in church, although it is imperative that the subject is addressed.

"Sean…about ten years ago those two well-dressed socialites became board members of Pastor Coward's church. Through my counseling ministry, I have counseled people desiring to escape covens, so I have first-hand knowledge that these two ladies are part of the occult hierarchy of a powerful world-wide coven. They are practicing witches. Doctors, lawyers, businessmen and women, teachers, therapists, and blue-collar workers belong to secret societies of various names, but come together in their local covens to strategize how to infiltrate every church that believes in the Reconciler, in order to compromise their effectiveness in the community. And… they have been very successful. They also infiltrate all secular governments and scientific communities worldwide. I think you already know what has happened in our schools...thanks to them."

"Bingo...now I understand what has happened in our schools. And...this explains to me why I was turned-off on church for so long. All they pushed was self-improvement programs, modern music only, and just plain activity to keep kids (and adults) busy, busy, busy. I wanted to know more about the Sacred Script and its author. Now I know this would have provided true self-improvement," reasoned a now enlightened Sean.

"There is no better place for these witches than on church boards," explained Pastor Warrior.

"Because of their money and prestige, their leadership in the church body is coveted, so with this power they are able to covertly plant their destructive occult ideas with the veneer of modern spirituality...angels of light. They have been able to remove the old hymns, declaring them too antiquated for a sophisticated youthful generation, which demands modernization. Their undercover wickedness became outwardly evident about twenty years ago... revealed by the numbers game," he explained

"What in the world is the numbers game?" asked a confused Sean.

"Well...rather than teach the Sacred Script like the church has done for centuries, drawing people to the Reconciler by His sin-convicting salvation, a new program has been outlined by these witches. These covert witches make pastors feel guilty if a congregation is small, even if it is spiritually thriving. They designed a plan to ratchet up their numbers so the world will see them as successful. Programs to lure in the youth, by modern rock music, basketball courts and any other worldly enticement would be required, to make the numbers go up," explained Pastor Warrior.

"But even if the numbers go up, does that mean all those kids are believers...spiritually changed?" asked Sean.

"Of course not, that's the point. Although some kids are believers, but lukewarm in intimacy with their Lord... they also like all the hoopla. The busier they keep the kids, and adults, doing 'things,' the more certain they are to abstain from seriously studying the Sacred Script, or seeking intimacy and direction from their Savior," explained Pastor Warrior.

"The Sacred Script will renew one's thinking producing honesty, integrity and humility...not some religious program," he concluded accurately.

After they were seated in Gramma's Goodies they ordered. While enjoying a mug of fresh brewed coffee, a perplexed Sean could finally ask, "Why did we sneak out like that, before we had our meeting with Pastor Coward?"

"After hearing what he said today, do you really have to ask?" a disillusioned Pastor Warrior asked, with his eyes cast down staring vacantly into his steaming cup of coffee.

After looking up, he glumly added, "Of course, how could I have expected more of him with witches planted on his own board? I was hoping if he read the truth in our literature, it would finally sink in and he would remove their evil influence. I have tried to help him see that our churches have been sabotaged, but he won't talk to any of the former witches I have counseled."

"I totally understand," said Sean with sadness and compassion in his voice, especially now that I know about the covert operations of Abbadon's witches. I am still so stunned by this information that I can't wrap my mind around it yet."

"Did I hear Pastor Coward call the RFID surveillance chip, the mark of the beast?" asked a perplexed Sean.

"Well...yes you did...I'll try to summarize his ideas," offered Pastor Warrior. "In the Sacred Script there is a passage that explains about the image of a beast, who will rule men and place his mark (666) on them," he explained. "And...anyone who takes his mark, which the modern-day church has interpreted as the RFID chip, will face the wrath of God, ending up in Gehinnom Land of Abandon."

"Since I am a church history buff I have proven that this mark is not a physical mark. Picture this Sean," explained Pastor Warrior, "two thugs grab you and forcibly insert a microchip (RFID) into your body against your will. You gonna tell me that the Infinite One has condemned you to Gehinnom, because you have that chip? I don't think so."

"But Sean I would be remiss if I didn't explain that the Plan of the Sinister Seven is to insert a chip into all humans. After we become a cashless society needing the chip for all transactions, they will control us electronically. If they don't like what we are doing they will simply inactivate our chip. Since the beginning of time tyrants have cut off their citizens from food, water and shelter...this is nothing new...just another mechanism.

"You're right...history reveals this. Even at this very moment people are fleeing their country, because their despotic leader has burned their homes, taken their land, killed them or chased them to another country, denying them jobs, food, water and shelter. This has been done at the point of a gun or a machete now...but later by a chip. There really is no difference," confirmed Sean. "But if it isn't a physical mark or a microchip, what is the mark of the beast (666)?" asked Sean.

"Oh that is simple…but our learned theologians in our seminaries have concocted strange ideas about the end of time," answered Pastor Warrior.

"This is a perfect example of the infiltration of witches in our churches and seminaries. It has been going on for over a hundred years. The witches have planted the doctrine of an anti-god-man rising who, after the church is raptured away, will force his mark in the forehead or arm of his followers. The old translations of the Sacred Script disprove this idea, but the new translations have inserted certain words so as to prove this doctrine. Abbadon has always been the anti-god power that is coming to rule, prophesied by his covert representatives in the church."

"You see Sean," he continued, "the Sacred Script clearly tells us that we are not to interpret prophecy of scripture, but these pompous theologians proclaim they have uncovered the mind of God…no wonder we have so much error regarding the return of the Reconciler. In the Sacred Script, numbers have symbolic meanings. The number six symbolizes the sum total of man's achievements."

Chuckling, Pastor Warrior said, "I add something to this definition, but it really doesn't change the meaning. The number six means the sum total of man's achievements… incomplete without the Infinite One."

"I see," said Sean. "Man cannot serve two masters. Man's allegiance must be totally surrendered to the Infinite One…not half in the world and half in the kingdom of the Infinite One. The sum total of man's achievements (666) doesn't amount to a hill of beans…without the infinite One," Sean summarized finally understanding the concept.

"Right on Sean, my boy," said Pastor Warrior as he took another sip of his coffee, "you have captured the essence of the subject…and so quickly. Everything is spiritual. Always remember that the mark of Abbadon is allegiance, and the mark of the Infinite One is allegiance. To whom will you give your allegiance?"

"Ya know Sean," said Pastor Warrior with a serious tone, "not to change the subject...but...since they passed that 'hate crimes' bill it sealed my fate as a pastor. This is a sinister conspiracy to prevent clergy from preaching the truth in the Sacred Script...or we could be jailed. In one state, People of the Book have been arrested for simply passing out pamphlets at an alternative-sex rally that only expressed forgiveness and salvation from their Creator. Pastors in the North have been arrested during services, because they were sharing out of the Sacred Script, where it says that sex between people of the same sex is an abomination to their Creator. I cannot suppress this truth from them. To call evil, good, invokes the wrath of our Creator. Their rebellion against the truth of the Sacred Script already provoked the Creator to give them over to vile affections, perverting the natural into that which is against nature."

The powerful angelic messenger Pestos, spoke into Pastor Warrior's thoughts, "Always walk in love and forgiveness toward those who are driven to unscrupulous acts, because if they receive the Reconciler as their Savior they will not do these vile things. Pray first for your enemy."

Concern brought a frown on Pastor Warrior's face as he lamented, "If I am constrained by law to let them die in their sin, I am a most miserable servant of the Infinite One, because I want no man to end up in Gehinnom."

"Yet...the love of the Infinite One constrains me to set men free from the grip of demons, which means that I must disobey man's law," he reasoned.

"Boy...this is serious stuff," declared Sean, as he tried to absorb these revelations shared by Pastor Warrior.

"I have been so involved in the surveillance encroachment of our freedoms, I was not aware that this really is a spiritual battle...until now."

Then his powerful guardian angel Karmel spoke a thought into Sean's mind, so he asked Pastor Warrior, "Did you consider the possibility that the Sinister Seven is pushing this alternative sex style, because it supports their depopulation agenda? Same-gender sex produces no offspring. *Voila!*"

"Wow Sean, I think you're onto something. I like your wise reasoning," agreed Pastor Warrior, patting him on the back affectionately.

"But," said Sean soberly, "they are twisting and confusing the minds of our precious little ones to accomplish their wicked, self-serving agenda...and we have to stop them. They have the freedom to do what they chose for themselves, but they cannot choose for our kids!"

Pastor Warrior agreed saying, "We must take up this issue with the Sound the Alarm team."

After they began to eat their breakfast Sean noticed that Pastor Warrior was just staring at his chicken-fried steak, after taking only a couple of bites, so he asked, "Is there something wrong with your breakfast?"

Pastor Warrior seemed lost in his thoughts so Sean's question startled him. "What, what...oh...I...I'm sorry Sean. I was just thinking into the future. If these radical tyrants running our government have their way, we will no longer be able to buy beef, or any meat for that matter. Some of them believe a strange religious doctrine where animals are sacred and should be worshiped...not eaten. They plan to foist upon us their vegan ways, which flies in the face of the Sacred Script, where the Creator tells us... kill and eat the fatted calf. Of course...they have thrown our book in the trash-heap of mythical nonsense."

"I am still amazed and puzzled why a free people would so willingly surrender their freedom, to subjugate themselves to the whims of godless tyrants," said Sean shaking his head in disbelief.

"Besides...in this country we always choose what we want to eat. Is that freedom evaporating, too?" he asked Pastor Warrior.

"Absolutely," said Pastor Warrior, "because of the esoteric leaders in our government. Since these schemers came into power a hundred years ago, their evil has been contrived in secret...you know...slight-of-hand. They don't think we have the brains to make decisions without Big Brother micro-managing by fear, intimidation, and force. The Bill of Rights freed us from this stuff, but after only two hundred years, tyranny has come raging back...worse than ever."

After finishing their delightful steak breakfast, they hopped into the sporty little car and turned onto a road that would take them inland. After they got to the closed air force base Pastor Warrior drove up and stopped.

Then he said, "Sean, you can tell there is activity on this closed base...right?"

"Yeah," said Sean, "it sure has a lot of activity for being closed."

"Well, let me tell you what is going on in our country... hidden in plain sight," said a disturbed Pastor Warrior.

"We have had too many treasonous people in power for one hundred years. We handed over our seaport at Commie Cove to the Communists in the 90's. We closed this base in 1992 and eventually handed it to the Communist military industrial complex to train their troops...all hush-hush. Then they purchased that property I pointed out to you and built a million square foot, twenty-unit complex to sell their cheap goods they have imported through that port. They put our citizens out of business because we can't compete. In their country they have over 30 million people in slave labor camps making these cheap goods, to whom the Communists pay not one scintilla, because the prisoners are anti-tyranny, anti-abortion, lovers of freedom and the Infinite One, dissenters, who are considered the dregs of society. Big Brother at work," summed up Pastor Warrior.

"I heard on the grapevine that they also have been bringing in arms through that port. Are they stock piling all the closed bases with arms to be used against us," asked Sean.

"Absolutely," said Pastor Warrior with urgency in his voice. "Our socialist Big Brother leaders knew they would get our corrupt congressmen to sign the global treaties, i.e. NAFTA, GATT, etc, which would de-industrialize our country, sending all the good paying jobs to third-world countries, while giant corporations get rich from slave labor. Then they caused a depression (2008), whereby retirement accounts lost at least 50% of their value, and the loss of millions of good paying jobs…never to return. None dare call it TREASON…but I do."

"In my research I found a statement by one of the leaders of the Sinister Seven banking crime families. I think it goes like this, 'They are helpless people yielding themselves to our molding hands,' referring of course to us toadies. Such audacity…the pompous pig…it's creepy!" exclaimed Sean.

"Of course," added Pastor Warrior, "if we refuse to be molded, we will be annihilated. Why else do they send their treacherous imps into every country to create war? The average family in every nation does not want war. I remember reading the warnings of Alexander Solzhenitsyn who was sentenced to a gulag and lived to tell it. He said, 'Keeping a country in a state of war serves as an excuse for domestic tyranny.' You can see how much money our current wars continue to cost, bringing our country into bankruptcy. And…they don't plan to win any war. Perpetual war accomplishes the subjugation of all the toadies of the world, under the iron fist of tyranny, confiscating more and more tax money to feed the belly of the beast, until the total world population grovels at the feet of the Sinister Seven for the crumbs fallen from their sumptuous table… government handout."

"Look, look, look, over there," shouted Sean big-eyed and disturbed, pointing to the bus station they were approaching.

"It appears the military is assisting the bus station security in shaking-down the people waiting to get on the bus," Sean observed.

"Oh…I forgot. Our protective Posse Comitatus law was overturned by our global president in 2006, permitting the military to strong-arm the citizens of our 'free' country. How awful…their luggage is being rifled through and dumped on the sidewalk. Déjà vu Nazi Germany WWII," said Sean sensing the impending doom on his country.

Pastor Warrior drove a bit closer then stopped at a safe distance to observe. There must have been three hundred people being delayed. When one man asked what was going on, he was told that this is a surprise search in order to catch a 'terrorist.' These goons found a stun gun in one lady's luggage that she kept for her protection and they confiscated it. Now she has no protection for the rest of her five hundred mile trip. It is a travesty. And…there was no terrorist. Imagine that!

"Come on Sean," said Pastor Warrior, "let's head home. I can't take much more of this. I believe that we have formed a pretty good resistance movement during the past three years. I just wish I could wake up the believers," he grumbled.

"One thing is for sure," Sean said confidently, "when the bombs hit or they are hauled off to the Civilian Inmate Labor Camp, for re-education, we will hear the shrieks of terror from the pew-warmer a mile away. Some will become stronger and join our resistance movement, while many will become turncoats to save their own skin."

"You are absolutely right my boy…absolutely right… persecution exposes what is hidden on the inside," agreed Pastor Warrior.

As soon as Pastor Warrior dropped Sean off at his home, Gilly ran out to ask the pastor to join him inside, where a few of the patriots were catching up on the latest horrors.

Julie poured coffee all around then Gilly said, "All of you know that Joe and I are leaving the agency…and Sean, too. We didn't realize that while we were doing honest covert operations, those above us were using us for evil. The Lord has shown us that our time there is ending, so we can work full time with Sound the Alarm," he explained flashing a big smile.

"But we do have a friend, an insider, who is determined to keep his position of trust in the agency, in order to trickle out to us the schemes they are plotting against the citizens of our country. I will refer to him as Elf when I reveal the info that he has provided to us."

Joe added, "You could call him a double agent. Elf serves the patriotic citizens of this great country, while steeped in the covert sins of modern-day intelligence schemes. As hard as it is for him to stay in that slime pit, he told me that he believes this is the will of the Infinite One for his life."

"One of our patriot investigative reporters, Tomiah Hito, who is also a believer, has exposed dozens of jihad terrorist camps flourishing in our country. He visited some of them to film what is going on there, reporting that these compounds are actually paramilitary training camps. Some men are even garbed in fatigues learning combat maneuvers, explosives training, as well as artillery practice. Tomiah says their training parallels our military training...but...these men are terrorists planning jihad against us," exclaimed a dismayed Gilly.

"But I thought that our government said we had to go fight the terrorists overseas, in order to prevent them from coming to our shores," protested Clarissa.

"I'm sorry Clarissa, but that is the big lie...a diversionary tactic by our government. Our going after them on their own turf humiliated them, inflaming their ire, so they would ratchet up terrorism on our soil, as well as bankrupt our country...all part of the Plan," explained Dr. Hasad.

Dr. Hasad had international experience with clandestine government maneuvers, molding the minds of their citizens to believe a lie, causing him to explain, "When your country was hit on 9/11...it was by terrorists... those in collusion with the Sinister Seven. They had to create a crisis in order to justify unconstitutional draconian laws, which were purposely designed to remove all Constitutional rights. They left the borders wide open so enemies could enter easily, unhindered, to quietly set up these jihad camps. Of course the media, which is heavily invested by Dawaism, does not report this clandestine wickedness, so their activities fly under the radar. With this evidence, you can't tell me that behind-the-scenes government gurus are not complicit in the demise of this great country."

"Yeah," said Joe, "what about those incidents on airplanes recently? Dawa religious leaders got up from their seats and began walking up and down the aisles speaking in their native tongue rather loudly, scaring the passengers and disregarding the orders from the flight personnel to sit in their seats for takeoff. When they were removed from the plane they filed a discrimination suit...and won. This emboldened them to continue this harassment and intimidation, because now the airline personnel will do nothing for fear of another lawsuit. Inch by inch they have paralyzed us by fear."

"I believe you are right Joe," confirmed Dr. Hasad. "Now they are confident they can get on a plane with an explosive hidden in a breast implant or other body parts, because no one scrutinizes them for of fear of a profiling lawsuit. The Prince of Darkness...Abbadon... is very shrewd and he certainly guides and directs their brutal political/religious ideology."

"Tomiah has told us that after he gathered together several years of facts, he put it all in a DVD and presented the evidence to the IIA. Essentially they told him to buzz off. Apparently, the 'higher-ups' told them they could not raid these camps or shut them down, because they are not on Homeland Security's terrorist watch list. He was totally blown away. Now he knows for sure that our very own 'shadow' government has a wicked plot to force the chains of slavery upon the citizens of our free country. It is unthinkable...but true," concluded Gilly.

"We must not forget what we have already learned. The Dawa creed is: immigrate, increase and eliminate... all with the blessing of our own government," Pastor Warrior reminded them.

"We have learned from Tomiah that they have been recruiting from our own prisons, seemingly with the blessing of the wardens. As soon as a recruited prisoner is released, he heads right for a jihad training camp and disappears," said Joe, his brow furrowing from concern.

"No wonder we are on the terrorist watch list. People of the Book seem to be the only ones attempting to expose their clandestine activities. Even the conservative press seems reluctant to examine all of the undeniable evidence Tomiah has offered to them," opined Pastor Warrior.

"That's because they will lose their jobs, since most of the networks are, at least partly owned by Dawa investors, so they control what is reported on their networks," Sean reminded them.

"I read a quote in Tomiah's report from a jihad leader who commands one of these compounds, who said... *we are getting ready...the day of atonement...is close at hand,"* said Sean with a concerned look.

"And...what do they mean by atonement?" asked Clarissa.

"I think they mean that we must pay (blood) for offending their god, Umma. This is what our own government thinks about 'we the people.' It is as if we offend those in power by the prosperity of the hard-working citizens of this free-enterprise country, where the individual is rewarded for the fruit of his labor. The government has the power to take from the haves, and give it to the have-nots...those who don't like to work. This is pure Marxism," explained Pastor Warrior

"What do you guys think?" he asked.

"I think that we have to prepare the best way we know how...keep having meetings to build the resistance movement, and call on our Lord for His intervention. They want our blood to run in our streets," answered Gilly.

A FEW DAYS LATER

Dr. Hasad had just gotten up and turned on his coffee pot. He glanced out the kitchen window and noticed a couple of bluebirds quietly eating at the feeder he had hung from the branch of his maple tree. It was a peaceful morning. Since it was 7:00 A.M. he thought he could catch the national news, so turned on his radio at the usual station.

"Thirty minutes ago a major jetliner with 120 passengers and 8 crew members exploded and plunged into the Atlantic Ocean just after take-off. We believe that all on board are dead. Looking at the passenger list the IIA saw a name, Ihav no Teari, who had previously been reported to the IIA by his father, as being part of a radical movement to kill all who refuse to follow Dawaism. Apparently no one paid any attention to this father's warnings, so he was not on our terrorist watch list. He had no luggage, paid cash for his one-way ticket…all red flags…totally ignored," reported the newscaster.

Dr. Hasad called Joe, "Did you hear the news?"

"Yes I did," answered Joe. "This is only going to get worse and the terrorists are laughing at our inept intelligence agencies…all of them. Of course, the Plan of the Sinister Seven is to keep our citizens in a constant state of fear, so when the big crisis rears its ugly head, and it will, we will cry out for the government to save us. We should be crying out for the Reconciler to save us."

"I noticed they wouldn't even refer him as a follower of Dawaism…just named his country. Remember last month when 54 people were gunned down at the army base by a Dawa military major? They wouldn't name his religion in their investigation report, or even call him a jihadist, because they want to protect the other jihadists in our military. All I can say…jihadists are getting bolder and bolder with the help of our Dawa-sympathizing media and President," lamented Dr. Hasad.

"Amen to that…and…because our leaders have given the jihadists freedom in our own country to destroy us… it appears that we are doomed…the end is near," agreed Joe

"This is why Chloe's case is so important. We must get a big win against them to restore our hope…and there isn't much time left," declared Dr. Hasad.

ONE WEEK LATER

On a quiet sunny Spring morning the birds were singing happily, while squirrels scampered up the tree, when Pastor Brawn arrived at his church office toting his favorite French vanilla latte, and sat down to peacefully read yesterdays mail. He checked his calendar to make sure he had no appointments. Relieved that he had the whole morning free, he flipped on his radio to catch the national news.

"It happened only minutes ago so I don't have the details," spoke the anxious newscaster.

"Wonder World, the largest amusement park that we have in this nation has been totally destroyed. Emergency crews from surrounding counties and across the state are on their way. Saturday is their biggest day for visitors, so there could be thousands dead…we don't know as yet. The earliest intelligence leak revealed they had a tip about a week ago, that jihadists could possibly attack Wonder World, but they didn't take the tip seriously. Sorry folks… this has been happening all too often with our intelligence agencies…what good are they? I think I smell a rat," declared the suspicious reporter.

Stunned by this senseless carnage, while grieving for the people who have been murdered in this cowardly attack, Pastor Brawn was not surprised by this horrific incident. He had attended the Sound the Alarm meetings, which warned about the jihad military warfare camps that were allowed to flourish in his country, by his government. So he picked up his phone and dialed Pastor Warrior to see if he had heard the news.

"All I can say…it is more urgent than ever for us prepare our people for the soon coming of the Reconciler. Funny, isn't it Pastor Brawn…our faith gave birth to tolerance, but we are no longer tolerated in our own country. Global conquest by submission to Dawaism will be achieved incrementally, through these acts of terrorism. They have done this in every country where they have infiltrated the ruling authority…compliments of the Sinister Seven. We will continue to do our best to defeat this barbaric ideology…but our hope is the Lord."

"You are absolutely right, Bob," said Pastor Brawn. "Our congregation can't thank you enough for all you do to awaken the sleeping giant."

Chapter 14

Preparing for the End

It was still dark on Sunday morning. The birds weren't awake enough to chirp, when an explosion shook Pastor Warrior's home. He awakened just in time to see a burst of bright light flash through the sky, so he jumped out of bed, quickly slipped into his jeans, while grabbing his phone. "What in the world is going on," screamed his terrified thoughts.

When he looked out the window he saw jack-booted thugs dressed in black, rushing into selected homes hauling the screaming occupants outside. Black Hawk helicopters, hovering a few feet above the sleepy city, flooded the ground with bright beams of light. He wasn't sure there was any power, but with his cell phone in hand he headed for his hidden short wave radio, hoping he had power.

Something caught his eye, causing him to look out the window once again before he left the bedroom. He was captivated by an anomaly in the dark sky, and he blinked twice because he couldn't believe what he was seeing. He had never seen into the invisible realm, but that is just what was happening to him. He was viewing images of white horses and chariots of fire moving swiftly, a spellbinding glow against the ominous sky. The glorious chariot drivers were radiant, bright as the sun angelic warriors with giant gleaming swords. There was a shimmering light shining upon this magnificent angelic army, where he could faintly see hundreds more of these dazzling angels coming out of the light with giant wings of brilliant snow-white, wielding fiery swords drawn in fight mode. He was so awed by this supernatural sight, he couldn't move or even think.

While gazing intently to absorb every bit of this wonder, he suddenly saw swooping in for the attack, the giant winged vampires of Abbadon, black as coal, blood dripping from their fangs and fire breathing out of their mouths…like dragons in fervent pursuit of dominance. Holding large fiery swords, they aggressively pursued the radiant chariots of fire…truly a clash of the titans. He literally was transfixed by this scene, not knowing what to do…but…watch and learn. Soon the colossal chariots of fire surrounded the black-winged demons, who ascended from the abyss. The clanging sound of steel during this battle between light and dark, sent chills down his spine. Then puff…all of the black-winged ghouls simply evaporated before his eyes. Within seconds, the glorious angelic warriors and golden light gradually disappeared… like a vapor in a gentle breeze.

Pastor Warrior wondered why the Infinite One was allowing him this insight, as he continued to gaze at the night sky in case the vision returned. This revelation into the operations of the invisible realm, definitely motivated him to continue to warn everyone he meets to be ready for the return of the Reconciler. After this majestic site faded, the reality of the moment came flooding back… like a bad dream.

Once he got to the kitchen he turned on the short wave radio, already set on the international channel. He couldn't believe what he was hearing, so pulled up a chair to get close to the set. He didn't want to miss a word of the shocking news.

The newscaster was speaking fast and furiously with angst in his voice, "At 3:00 A.M. a nuclear missile was launched toward Israel...b...b...but did not hit its intended target. Something miraculous took place...unbelievable. Even though we have the Nautilus anti-ballistic system to protect us, this enemy missile was supernaturally redirected. As it sped directly toward us from the East, it came dangerously close to Jerusalem, then suddenly it changed its programmed course...turned southwest... exploding in enemy territory. Friends...this is nothing less than Divine intervention," reported the excited newscaster.

After he calmed down he continued. "There is chaos at the explosion site. The dead and dying are already into the thousands. Hundreds of homes, business, many hospitals, police departments and fire departments have been blown to smithereens, while doctors, nurses and other emergency personnel have been killed...everything...just gone. Woe...woe...woe...is all I can say at this time. May the Lord have mercy on us."

"Just at minute...just a minute...word is just now coming in. The Israeli military has launched a nuclear missile due east...no...no...that is two missiles have been launched. One hit Qom nuclear reactor and the other hit the Isfahan uranium site. The world is in absolute riot mode...anarchy reigns," concluded the worried newscaster.

"Oh my," thought Pastor Warrior, "this is horrible. It appears there may be a coordinated effort between our international leaders to depopulate the planet quickly. I have to get hold of my team."

He pressed one button on his cell and Gilly instantly answered his phone. "What is going on in your part of the city Gil, it is horrific over here? At least it isn't an EMP strike...yet," whispered an anxious Pastor Warrior.

"I heard some yelling outside, but no explosion, so thought it was just some rabble-rousing kids. But now I am looking out the window and I can see at least two helicopters hovering with lights beaming upon the ground, while men dressed all in black are going into some homes. I'm already to go to our meeting place. See ya in a few," declared Gilly hurriedly, noticing the urgency provoked an adrenalin rush.

Gilly awakened Julie, who called Joe, who then called Dr. Hasad, a relay system they previously had planned for such a time as this. While Julie dressed, Gilly turned on the coffee pot so they could take a thermos of hot java with them. Within fifteen minutes Julie, Gilly and Sean grabbed the emergency backpack and coffee, and were out the door walking to the designated meeting place in the woods, careful to avoid the beams of light.

Pastor Warrior was already dressed and pouring his coffee into his thermos, when he heard a light tap on his door. It startled him because he had purposely not turned on the lights of his home in order to not draw any attention, so was maneuvering around with only a flashlight.

"Hmm," he pondered a bit suspiciously. "Why only a light tap, rather than the bam-bam-bam that I heard on other doors, though I know some homes were skipped. Besides...no one comes to my kitchen door except friends."

Cautiously, he peered through the white batiste curtain covering the door window. He thought the bright moonlight shining behind the person standing on his porch might provide a recognizable silhouette, but he still couldn't tell who was there. Carefully, he opened the door and flashed the bright beam into the face of his visitor.

"Whoa, Bob, I'm here on the QT to help," declared a startled Major Wisely. "Can I come in?"

Bob Warrior quickly turned off the bright light and hustled the Major inside his kitchen. "What are you doing here?" he asked apprehensively.

"You know that I have been to a couple of your meetings, and I have read most of the materials that Sound the Alarm distributes," confessed the Major.

"Everything the writers of your materials have been predicting, have now begun to come to pass. I am a military man because of my desire to protect my country. This is no longer possible, because the enemy has the green-light to terrorize us from inside our own military bases. I have been watching this 'tolerance code' ramped up since 9/11, rather than curtailed, causing me to realize this is the Plan of the Sinister Seven to takedown our great country," said a saddened Major Wisely.

Pastor Warrior sensed in his spirit that this wasn't a ruse, so he invited Major Wisely to go with him to the hideout. He picked up his standby emergency backpack, gave the thermos to Major Wisely, and they headed down the path that would take them to the cabin in the woods. It would be about a three mile walk into the dense forest.

Long before they got to their destination, the Infinite One had sent His powerful warrior angels to surround the little cabin in the woods with their bright shining armor, so His faithful servants could strategize unimpeded by the Prince of Darkness and his wicked, conniving imps.

When they rounded the final bend in the road to the cabin, owned by the church, they could see the lights were already on. Pastor Warrior nudged Icy with his elbow saying, "That's great...the Goldman's and Gillingham's have already arrived and probably Dr. Hasad, too. He's always an early bird."

Surprised, Major Wisely said, "Oh…are they the IIA agents that gave their testimony?"

"Yes," answered Bob. "We couldn't have rallied the troops without the inside information these men have supplied to us. Even Gilly's son Sean was being trained in intelligence, but found that most of their clandestine schemes contradicted the ethics and integrity of his Lord."

When they walked through the door they were welcomed by a warm cozy fire and smiling faces. Joe and Gilly looked a bit perplexed though, when they laid eyes on Major Wisely, but knew that Bob wouldn't endanger their secret meeting place. Coffee was poured all around as they settled in to strategize around the crackling fire, munching on the chocolate chip cookies that Clarissa had brought.

"First of all I am Major I. C. Wisely...at your service," stated the Major crisply, extending his hand to each person.

"B…but…please call me Icy, everyone does, probably because of my stoic demeanor," he said with a shy smile as he sat down.

Icy went on to tell them that he was a believer in the Reconciler, which was very unpopular in the military now, where he can no longer say the name of the Reconciler, even in prayer or he will be demoted or forced out of the military. This is because of the demands of the jihadists, who have covertly infiltrated the military in the guise of followers of the Prophet. Their religious declaration of peace is permitted to be openly respected…because of tolerance. Tolerance toward them…not by them.

"After coming to your meetings and researching your materials, I now understand why these changes have been forced into a military, I now no longer recognize. Finally it all makes sense," stated a slightly embittered

Major Wisely, who must abandon an honorable twenty-five year military career.

"When 54 of our finest young soldiers were gunned down in their own military base by an infiltrated jihadist, yelling Umma is greatest, I knew then that this was only the beginning, because the jihadists are confident they have us by the cross-hairs. This egregious act of terrorism on our own soil was played down as an isolated act of a crazy man."

"What is going to happen next, asked Gilly?"

"Well...first of all," said Icy as his eyes focused on the floor, and his voice was barely audible. "I...I...have filed my retirement papers. It was a very sad and difficult decision for me."

Then he lifted his eyes, regained his composure, and began to explain. "The military industrial complex is ruled by the Sinister Seven, who have instigated enemy infiltration of the ranks of our patriot soldiers, to bring down our nation from within our ranks. I know that it is just a matter of time before those of us who are followers of the Reconciler are either gunned down or eliminated by other means. I can be of more help to my countrymen by joining the resistance movement."

Dr. Hasad interjected, "One thing I know from history... with guns we are citizens...without them we are serfs. I know what happened in other countries. We must not surrender our guns to these goons tonight. Are yours registered?"

Gilly, Joe and Icy looked at each other, smiled confidently and said in unison, "Nope."

Just then their battery-crank radio, which had been set on the international station as soon as they arrived, suddenly spewed a terrifying report. All of them sat silently... sobered by what they were hearing. The newscaster seemed anxious and was talking fast, "It is unbelievable folks…our country is under siege. Five major cities along the eastern seaboard, including the Capitol, are under attack right now. Bombs are falling from the sky, incendiary devices set off by remote control have sabotaged our underwater subway tunnels disconnecting cities, while all passengers died in watery graves. Thousands, maybe tens of thousands, have already been killed. I don't even know how long I will be able to broadcast to you."

After a long breath then a sigh, the newscaster continued, "Th...th…the horrors of this night are indescribable! Many hospitals have been flattened, so mayors are opening their community centers to be transformed into makeshift hospitals. We truly are under siege with nuclear missiles expected any minute…we are holding our breath. We should never have signed that disarmament agreement with our enemies…dismantling our antiballistic missiles. Marshal Law has been declared in every state," reported the frazzled voice on the radio.

"Oh…that must be what is happening here in Crystal Waters," said a very nervous Chloe, as she snuggled close to her dad.

Joe put a consoling arm around her and assured her, "The Illuminator will guide and direct our steps."

Chloe looked into his kind dark blue eyes with her big, brown doe-eyes saying softly, "And we know our angelic warriors are here to help…too…huh daddy?"

Knowing that he may soon lose transmission, the newscaster threw caution to the wind speaking rapidly, "Many of you probably do not know that your congressmen and women, the Sinister Seven corrupt banking cartels, and the super-rich are at this very moment, safely hidden in grandiose underground bunkers many stories below the ground. These bunkers are abundantly placed all over this great country of ours, as well as in other nations hidden below airports, military bases, and of course, the one under the People's House with seventeen stories below the ground. Added together they have thousands of apartments with swimming pools, plenty of food with the capability of growing more, sustaining them for many months. After we toadies, the useless eaters above the ground die from the explosions and radiation, they will reappear to rebuild their Utopia with the few preserved elites. Please...friends...take care of yourselves," proclaimed the brave man on the radio.

"Wow," exclaimed Julie. "Everything Gilly and Joe have shared through Sound the Alarm is now being confirmed. It has to be close now to the return of our Lord."

"Oh my...that reminds me of what happened this morning. When I was looking out the window at the horror that descended on us today, the Lord opened my eyes to see into the spirit realm," exclaimed an excited Pastor Warrior.

He described in detail the brilliant light descending, almost like a golden stairway out of the heavens, with giant winged angels dressed in dazzling white, while many others were in chariots of fire driven by muscular white steeds. There was total silence...stunned awe was expressed on every face in the room.

"Then I saw giant black-winged vampires with fire breathing from their mouths, wielding sharp swords embroiled in a great battle against the agents of the Reconciler. Now I better understand the intense warfare that is going on in the invisible realm on our behalf," explained Pastor Warrior with a shudder, as he remembered the vicious determination of Abbadon's vampires.

"Those winged monsters from the abyss were so scary. I can't find words to adequately describe them. The Sacred Script reveals some of these things, but I never expected to see them for myself," declared Pastor Warrior with wonderment expressed on his countenance.

"Now you know how hard it was for me to describe my experience in Gehinnom, so Dr. Hasad could write my story," teased Gilly, remembering his time with Abbadon.

"It is urgent that we awaken the people to these spiritual truths...if...they will hear," he warned.

As they tried to make sense of these recent events, Pastor Warrior remembered one more thing...Israel's crisis. Everyone in the room just stared at him in disbelief...numb with the thought that...maybe...just maybe the end of the world was here, as they have been warning. It is one thing to warn...totally another thing to actually experience the predicted fiery end of the world.

Gilly got on his cell and dialed Harry, another believer, at one of the patriot hideouts across town, to see if he had heard what was happening on the east coast.

Harry had heard the news, but also told Gilly, "It is happening just north of us, Gil. I heard just a few minutes ago that incendiary bombs, set off by remote control, have decimated a mall while also destroying the only bridge to the island. This is the work of the jihadists, so we must get to their camp tonight and destroy it. You'll never guess who are the jackbooted thugs knocking down doors in our town tonight. It is those foreign troops housed at the base we're demolishing tonight."

"You've got to be kidding, Harry," screamed Gilly.

"Nope...wish I was, Gil," said a worried Harry. "The local police are working hand in hand with them. They have a list from the Homeland Security with several thousand names they call terrorists, whom we call patriot believers, and are hauling them out of their homes into military buses. Some of the buses are headed north to the air force base, although they are parked along side of the highway right now. One of my men followed one bus to the train depot, where prisoners from our town...can you imagine...are transferred to a train car that is equipped with shackles, taking them to a faraway Civilian Inmate Labor Camp."

"The worst that we planned for has come upon us," exclaimed Gilly.

"Not the worst Gil…no EMP missile has exploded yet," encouraged Harry.

"They know that this must be done as a last resort, because if the grid goes down before they hide in their elitist bunkers below the ground, they will also have communication problems causing riots in the streets. What they want Gil is for us to be incarcerated, not running loose after them until the Plan is fully implemented. They are afraid of us blue-collar tough guys, so must be safe below the ground before the worst is unleashed upon us… an EMP missile with a nuclear or biological warhead," laughed Harry.

"Yep…you are absolutely right, Harry. Let me know as soon as possible the time we are to meet. We have to get there before our citizens arrive in those buses. Talk to ya soon," said Gilly hanging up quickly.

"Well…it is time we implement our plan to blow up those buses. We strategized and practiced this only a couple of months ago," said Gilly his brow furrowing with concern, as he drew a folder out of his backpack and handed it to Joe, who had previously drawn out their plan of attack. All the men huddled together bringing Icy up to date on their strategy, asking for his input.

After carefully looking over the plan, Icy asked, "You mean you already have this place wired?" He was amazed at their efficiency.

"Oh, yeah," said Sean, with a little chuckle, "it was fun, especially since we have patriot resistance members, demolition experts, working where thousands of buses are stored."

"Not only the bus garage," said Joe with a wry smile, "but that whole despicable base will implode…flat as a pancake."

Joe answered his ringing cell, "Hey…what's up Ollie? Okay…we'll see ya there…when…about 8:00...okay."

"That was Ollie Garringer," said Joe. "He and Dave… you know…Dave Somers, have everything ready to go on the base…timers are set. He also said he has been in contact with our organization in cities across the country with closed bases, and their patriots are ready to go… time synchronized with us. He thinks the Sinister Seven may have miscalculated the knowledge, expertise, and courage of our resistance movement."

"The elites have always underestimated us toadies… well…at least we are not going down without a fight…let's go get 'em," challenged Icy flashing a confident smile.

Gilly, Joe, Sean, Icy and Pastor Warrior picked up their cells to keep in close contact with Harry and Ollie, as the 8:00 o'clock rendezvous approached. Then they picked up their AK 47's, shoulder pouch of ammo, grenades, infrared goggles, flashlights, and maps, and off they went to meet the other patriots. As they walked out the door Joe stopped and looked back, saying with determination, "The government may have forced Marshall Law upon their citizens, but we will exercise patriot law on their protected jihadists."

As soon as the military base was flattened they would head to the jihad training camp. This is another coordinated effort with the patriot members of Sound the Alarm, who will bomb all jihad camps in every state tonight.

Dr. Hasad volunteered to stay and help the women sneak back to their homes to gather together more emergency items, sleeping bags, food and medical kits, because it appears they may be at the cabin for awhile.

As they were putting on their coats, suddenly the cabin began to roll as if it was slipping off of its foundation. They all stopped and glanced at each with that, 'is this what we think it is' look on their faces, not knowing what to do. Cupboards popped open and dishes crashed to the floor. The rattling and shaking continued for fifteen seconds… but seemed like an eternity…then deathly silence.

Clarissa flipped on the radio just as the newscaster was delineating the horrifying results of the earthquake at the epicenter, about one hundred miles away. He described how twenty-story buildings have collapsed to the ground, while overpasses have collapsed onto the freeways splitting the roadway apart, creating great impassable gulfs. Their state Capitol is in shambles, so communication is difficult. All hospitals, at least the ones still standing, are using generator power.

He went on to say that he was sorry to have to report that the governor and his family were crushed to death when the roof of the Governor's Mansion fell in, collapsing all four stories to the ground. The Capitol city and surrounding counties are a total disaster. He was not able to give an accurate death count, because they don't have enough emergency personnel to get through the devastation, in order to rescue the injured or remove the dead. He ended his message saying, "It looks to me folks, like the end of the world has arrived."

Dr. Hasad and the ladies sat down around the table staring at the radio, in shock, continuing to listen for more information about this cataclysmic event.

"What are we going to do?" questioned Julie, bracing herself for the next report of carnage.

"All of these catastrophic events around the world tonight are not all perpetrated by man, although all of them are because of the sin of man," Dr. Hasad wisely declared.

"Why don't we pray before we go to town and get direction from the Infinite One?" he asked the ladies.

"Go ahead Dr. Hasad," said Julie softly, "and we will be in agreement with you."

"We humbly come before you Lord, because we love You and need Your direction and protection. Protect all of our patriots who are on dangerous missions tonight across this great country. Bombs are bursting on the east coast, north of us, and in the middle-east, while destructive earthquakes are under our own feet. If it is close to Your return...show us those who need Your help...Amen," prayed Dr. Hasad and the rest said in unison..."Amen."

While the others cleaned up the broken glass, Clarissa called her mom who was caring for Joey, to see how they are doing. Since her home is far out of town and her neighbors are part of the patriot resistance movement, she thought they would be safe, at least for awhile. Her mom was aware that Marshall Law was in force and that many citizens have been hauled off to the Civilian Inmate Labor Camps. She told Clarissa that she and Joey were fine, so far, and they have plenty of food on hand. The patriot believers are taking good care of them. Before they hung up Clarissa let her mom know they would be at the cabin until further notice.

Dr. Hasad slipped on his shoulder holster with his .357 Magnum and put his coat back on. He and the three ladies headed down the path toward town. Staying close to the forest for concealment, they found a good vantage point to view the main street of their city. Pulling out his night vision binoculars Dr. Hasad slowly surveyed the streets.

Dr. Hasad reported to the ladies, "It appears they are stopping walkers, but there is a minimum amount of military police patrolling the streets. If we are cautious, we can slip into town unnoticed. We will go the back way to our homes, get our supplies, and be out of there without being seen. I don't see a guard on the residential streets... unless they are hidden."

"Well then...let's get going," said Julie with enthusiasm. She was excited, because she was experiencing the most difficult test of her life, and wanted to be victorious in her allegiance to her Lord.

Dr. Hasad directed them down the path that appeared to be the safest. Since they already stored a few sleeping bags at the cabin, they would only need a couple more, plus food and coffee. As they sneaked quietly down the alley toward the Gillingham's they couldn't help but wonder, when seeing some homes without any lights, where their dear friends had been taken. Chloe said nothing, but her compassionate heart was overcome with sadness.

They got back to the cabin about midnight with enough supplies for a few days. The men had already returned and were anxious to share their success. After everyone hugged because they were so glad that each person was safe, Gilly exclaimed, "Wow...you should have seen those buildings implode in three seconds. We wiped them out... totally. Thousands of buses were wired to explode, flying high into the air...a sight for sore eyes...ya...hoo!"

"Yeah," chimed in Icy whose blue eyes sparkled with excitement, "and when we got to the jihad camps, we caught them totally unprepared. The fire created by our explosions wiped out the whole compound."

Then a devilish grin wreathed his face as he said, "A few hundred terrorists met their seventy-two virgins tonight...yeah!" gesturing two thumbs up.

"You mean no one is left alive? Did you have to use your AK's?" questioned Clarissa nervously.

Joe got up from where he was sitting and walked into the kitchen where Clarissa was putting away their supplies. He pulled her toward him, wrapping his strong arms snuggly around her whispering softly in her ear,

"Honey, this is war and we were successful. I know you don't want to hear the gory details…I know your heart."

"Thank you Joe, you're right," Clarissa said in a hushed tone.

"I'm just so glad you are home safely. Let's try to get some sleep," she said wearily.

They got up with the sun to see how the Illuminator would lead them today. Julie served them hot java which each one welcomed gladly, while Pastor Warrior provided a few more details about their successful evening, without the gory, bloody details. Gilly provided details regarding the success of their coordinated efforts across the nation. They certainly put a kink in the governments' evil plans to arrest and inject bio-weapons in patriot citizens. The Civilian Inmate Labor Camps had been tediously prepared for many years, but were blown to smithereens across the country in a few moments.

"I wonder what will happen to the people they already hauled out of their houses?" asked Chloe with sadness on her face, grieving their fate.

"Well…honey," said her dad, "I'm not sure. The few Civilian Inmate Labor Camps that didn't have buses were not blown up tonight, so they were probably sent there. But they won't have room for all of our patriots."

They waited until after breakfast to turn on the radio because they wanted a few moments of peace and quiet, before they heard any more bad news. As they finished up their coffee, enjoying all of the sharing and making a game-plan for the day, they heard a strange sound outside. It was a soft whirring sound, a continual…whir…whir… whir…like the sound of humming bird wings…amplified. Before they could get up to go outside to see what was producing the sound, a brilliant light penetrated the walls and roof of their cabin.

Each of them looked at each other speechless, intuitively discerning they were experiencing something... something...supernatural. It was not a fearsome sensation, but rather glorious...exhilarating. Waiting motionless, not wanting to dispel this unexplainable, but enlivening experience, spontaneously they lifted their hands and began to worship. Within moments the walls and roof of the cabin simply disappeared, and they were able to see into the spirit realm. Giant dazzling, winged angels, with shimmering light emanating from them, were flying everywhere.

"Look at us!" exclaimed Julie with a shriek of joy.

"Wow...it is happening! We are being transformed in a twinkling of an eye to welcome our King of Kings," shouted Pastor Warrior excitedly.

The angels they had been observing swirling through the air with amazing fluidity, slowly lifted up the whole room a couple of feet, so they could see fire all around them, but it could not touch them. Horrified screams and curses could be heard within the raging fire, but they could see no one. The wails and cries of the human beings revealed they must be writhing in excruciating pain. These pathetic, heart-wrenching sounds were unnerving, but not distracting.

As if with a magnet, all the people in the little cabin in the woods were involuntarily and supernaturally drawn upward, above the fire, because bright shining angels had taken the hand of each believer. An overwhelming tranquility filled the little cabin in the woods, while a billowy vapor engulfed the faithful patriot believers.

Chapter 15

The Reapers

The Land of Perpetuity is the glorious eternal City of Light which has been imagined, pondered and fantasized by writers of lore for thousands of years. The Sacred Script sheds some illumination on this invisible land of peace, a teaser, attempting to plant within the heart of man a yearning to make the City of Light his final destination. While millions of people haven't a clue what this place is all about, if asked, they say that when they die they are pretty sure the City of Light will be their final resting place. They say, "Like…uh…doesn't everyone wind up there dude?"

The answer to that question is…no! If a human being chooses to live in the darkness of sin on Earth, serving himself, why would he expect to live in the light of holiness after he dies, serving the Infinite One?

Archangels Therizo and Gasar were walking beside the River of Life on their way to the Sea of Glass. In the distance they saw a few glorified human beings building a dwelling for a soon expected arrival to this holy land. The two angels were in awe of the architectural expertise of the humans. The foundation was laid in pure translucent gold with walls formed from starlight diamonds, inlaid with blue sapphires fashioned into clusters of Chrysanthemums. The octagonal rooms were built around a beautiful garden of eternal trees blooming with delicate pink blossoms. The center of the garden was graced with an effervescent pool of living water, softly rippling praises to the Infinite One.

These two colossal angels wore golden breastplates over their white linen garments that were edged in gold lamé. Hanging from each of their hips was a sharp gleaming sword sheathed in a brilliant ruby scabbard.

Neither of them have ever been to Earth, because their assignment is not until the end of man's hey-day... self-destruction. Therizo and Gasar are known as the Reapers. For thousands of years they have watched their angelic compatriots dispatched to Earth, return to this realm for much needed R & R, then go back to Earth again. The Earth assignment is very exhausting and discouraging, nonetheless, Therizo and Gasar always wait anxiously to hear the latest report of the happenings on Earth.

After they resumed their walk along the River of Life, very soon they saw at a distance, Phileo and Eleeo, sitting on a bench crafted from translucent emerald, enjoying the gentle sounds of the rippling river. A more beautiful green could not be imagined, rich and dark, yet exhibiting the sheen of a polished mirror. This serene spot is the arrival gate for warriors returning from Earth. Here they recapture their peace and regenerate their power. It is difficult for angels, who have never been to Earth, to be able to envision the horrors of Earth because it is so unimaginable. So it is hard to find words to adequately describe this cesspool of sin and degeneracy.

From afar Therizo shouted, "Hey you guys, did you just get back from Earth?"

They both turned toward the sound of his voice and Phileo yelled back, "Yeah...come join us and we will update you."

Excited for the anticipated news, Therizo and Gasar broke out in a run toward Phileo and Eleeo, because they have been waiting so long for the word that would trigger their dispatch to Earth. They are hoping that maybe this time the news will finally send them to Earth. Since the bench was gracefully crafted into a half circle there was plenty of room for the four of them to sit comfortably, and catch up on Earth talk.

Excitedly Therizo asked, "Are you up to sharing about Earth? I know that sometimes it is difficult to immediately launch into a dissertation, because your heart is still aching from your experience."

"We have been back a few days and have revived ourselves by the River of Life. We knew you would be coming and we are ready to share with you before we have to go back," answered Phileo with a friendly smile.

"It is closer than you think for your assignment on Earth to begin. The Infinite One is reviewing Eleusis' final report as we speak. When the Reconciler was on Earth He told His followers to watch for a sign that would trigger His return," Phileo reminded them.

"'Yes...the sign of His return is the same as it was in the days of Noah's flood. The 120 years it took Noah to build the ark was a long period of time, warning the people of their impending doom. If they did not repent of their sins and return to the Infinite One, judgment for their violence, injustice, sexual perversion, murder, and paganism was inevitable...and we know their decision."

Phileo agreed, "That is correct. But worst of all was man's cozy interaction with Abbadon's demons. Since Nimrod, grandson of Noah, rejected the Infinite One choosing to worship Abbadon, Mysticism was born. The people followed, enjoying the pleasures of sin and ignoring the consequences. The imagination of their heart was evil continually. Abbadon's demons manifested themselves into angels of light (superior race) in order to have sex with humans. Their offspring became the giants of violence."

"And...this same bold manifestation of Abbadon's demons is prevalent now on Earth. Because of the high-tech information era, Abbadon is using man's worldly knowledge to trap him. When man rejects the Reconciler, he gives permission to Abbadon to order his demons to take possession of him to implement violence, war and chaos on Earth, destroying millions of human beings. Man's inhumanity to man can only be attributed to demons. Now Abbadon has ordered an influx of UFO's to appear on Earth," explained Eleeo.

"The demons on the spacecrafts have already intermingled with the humans. They are masquerading as human beings, explaining they are a superior race from a faraway galaxy. They profess peace and good intentions. And the humans have fallen for this hoax hook, line, and sinker." Eleeo revealed to his listeners.

"They are pure evil. But the humans think these beings are their friends, because they can heal the sick and accomplish other supernatural feats, beyond the natural capabilities of the humans. Multi-millions of humans, over time, have rejected the supernatural miracles demonstrated by the Reconciler when He was on Earth, as myths, but have so easily accepted the supernatural feats of these human-like demons. Go figure! Anyway the sci-fi buffs have aptly described this species of demon manifestation, as Humanoids or Reptilians, reporting that they live underground. Many have seen their spacecrafts going in and out of the center of Earth. And of course, this observation is accurate...the city of Gehinnom is in the center of Earth," explained Plileo.

Therizo asked, "Do the humans ever listen to you?"

Phileo and Eleeo looked at each other speechless... each waiting for the other one to answer. Therizo and Gasar intuitively knew the answer.

The rippling rhythm of the water was so peaceful that no one spoke for a time. Then gathering his thoughts together, Phileo spoke in a solemn whisper, "Fewer and fewer human beings listen to our message sent to them from the Infinite One. They are racing toward the alluring, deceptive supernatural power of Abbadon, welcoming his superior race propaganda with open arms. For years they have been gradually conditioned by print, audio and visual media to accept this propaganda...as truth. Now Abaddon has pulled out all stops and is boldly interacting with the humans on a daily basis."

"Since you are describing the same actions as the humans in the days just prior to the flood of Noah, are you saying that it won't be long now before Earth is destroyed with a great fire?" asked Gasar enthusiastically.

"Yes...that is what I am saying," said a sorrowful Phileo. It was obvious he was grieving, because his countenance lost its luster when confirming Gasar's observations.

Gasar suddenly realized what he had done. "Oh...I am so sorry Phileo. In my excitement for the Infinite One to have all of His family finally here with Him, I was insensitive to the centuries you have had to watch man grovel before demons, choosing to follow Abbadon and end up in his hellish Land of Abandon forever. When you have the truth that forgiveness sets men free, but no one wants to hear it, a great pain must reside within your heart."

"I know...I know...Gasar," said Phileo as he put his arm around him, "that you have no idea how hard it is to watch millions of human beings reject their glorious inheritance promised to them by their Creator, as dismissively as they discard a candy wrapper.

"You mean like when Esau sold his birthright (inheritance) for a bowl of stew, because he didn't realize the value of his inheritance?" asked Gasar.

"Yes," answered Phileo, "except Esau only lost the inheritance promised to the first born of the natural bloodline of human beings, he did not lose his eternal life. Today's human beings have not only discarded (rejected) their earthly spiritual inheritance, but also their eternal life and will not live here with us, unless they turn to the Reconciler."

"All of us with Earth duty plead with them every moment of everyday, to not go the way that seems right to them, because that self-road always leads to death," added Eleeo.

Phileo's brow furrowed, as his eyes glanced to the ground in order to gather his thoughts. "We watch in painful distress, the evil acts they do in secret right in their own homes: fathers sexually abusing their children, rapists attacking women, women murdering their own babies and men beating their wives. We must watch leaders of nations torture and starve prisoners, while the populous, worldwide, abuse their bodies in licentious activities (pornography), drunkenness and strung out on drugs, including the corporate executive in his high-rise luxury office, and the self-serving politicians just livin' it up, with no restraints on their secret sins. They were totally oblivious to the fact that we were in the room watching, when they think they are hiding their crimes. Sadly...the day finally comes when the spirit of death knocks on man's door (spirit) and drags him out of his clay shell. Once again...we have to stand by and watch...helplessly... demons drag him to his hellish fate."

Then Phileo took a deep breath, collecting himself from the trauma of recounting his Earth horrors and said breathlessly, "There is one small consolation. When we are assigned to abortuaries where little human babies are murdered at an astounding rate daily, we gather into our arms one hundred percent of them and escort these precious spirits to our heavenly nursery."

"Oh...the nursery is my favorite place to visit! exclaimed Gasar passionately. "The Nanny Angels nurture them so tenderly, and give each of them a name. Each one has a tragic story of rejection and painful death. I know that you found them in trash trucks, garbage dumps, sewage pipes, even vats of chemicals, and tenderly retrieved them. I was there when you delivered some of them to the Infinite One, who wept, as He held each one in His healing hands, assuring them they are loved and accepted in His kingdom. I love watching them mature...they are so inquisitive," he chuckled, delighting in the thought.

"When those who reject the Reconciler die, you never can erase from your memory the horror-stricken expression on their faces, as they are grabbed roughly from their bodies, only to gape at the merciless fiery eyes and smell the rotten breath of the Grim Reaper, who is laughing uproariously, as he drags them kicking and screaming to the Land of Abandon," explained Eleeo, as a chill ran down his spine with the memory.

Then Eleeo hung his head in sorrow saying in a nearly inaudible voice, "If...they...would only listen to us. They are willfully throwing away their inheritance. But...the Infinite One gives each person the privilege of choosing (free will) where he wants to spend eternity and we cannot invalidate his choice."

Sadness was about to overcome them, so thinking to change the pace Therizo piped up, "Word came to us last year that the military industrial complex has validated witchcraft as an authentic religion. Man definitely has slipped into the manacles of Abbadon."

"Well...that is because the military is a tool of the Sinister Seven. Forty years ago Stargate was a hush-hush program designed to expand the boundaries of the human potential, from which came their physic spy. The art of mind reading and remote viewing permitted them to know the plans of their enemy in advance, even attempting to predict the future. Many military agents are actually being trained in physic warfare...you know...just think 'punch,' and your opponent drops over without physically touching him," explained Phileo.

"Of course...we know that mind reading and remote viewing involves a partnership with demons. Man does not have any power of his own, but his worldly education convinces him that he is superior...god-like...just like Abbadon thinks," interjected Gasar from his wealth of spiritual knowledge.

They were so deep in their discussion they didn't see Charis and Chrestos walk up behind them until Charis added, "It all begins with a thought. If man continually thinks on that thought, he will eventually believe it. What he believes is called faith. Faith creates...good or evil. Man has a choice of two creative powers....the Infinite One...or...Abbadon. He deceives himself if he thinks otherwise."

"Yeah," confirmed Phileo, "we try all the time to persuade humans to think on the Sacred Script to renew their minds with pure thoughts...focus on His promises, so we can create those promises in their lives. If humans continue to think on pure thoughts, no spiritual (demonic) weapon formed against them shall prosper, because we have been sent to help. But...man wants to use our power for curses and revenge...which is never possible...so he unwittingly becomes a partner to the only power that delights in making his evil thoughts and words come to pass...Abbadon."

"It is written in the Sacred Script as a warning, if man follows his own way the consequences are severe, yet man still permits himself to be deceived into believing he holds the reins of his life," Chrestos lamented.

"Everywhere we go across the planet we see leaders in every nation, every city and village conjure demons (spirit guides), prostrating themselves before them seeking guidance," said Phileo.

"So it won't be long before there is no one on Earth that desires the guidance of the Infinite One. The Infinite One will know when that day arrives…but by all the signs…it is soon," he mourned.

Shaking his head in disbelief Eleeo said, "Hatred, jealousy and competition in some religious sects has reached epoch proportions, but only from those who have rejected the Sacred Script as their moral guide. Communists and adherents to Dawaism hate the Sacred Script with a passion and seek to destroy it, and the People of the Book. But if it is as they say, a book of myths and has no power, I wonder why they so passionately seek to obliterate it?"

"Hmm…seems they could simply ignore it…unless it does have power," Gasar reasoned with a knowing smile on his face.

"Abbadon, the enemy of man, has been very successful in fulfilling his motto 'divide and conquer,' because the people of Earth have been conquered and defeated," stated Charis with deep sadness revealed in his voice.

"Earth reporting is never easy for our illustrious angels, and we realize the bird's-eye view that we have, gives us a definite advantage over the murky darkness that man muddles through in the trenches of sin. But if humans would only turn to the Reconciler and the Illuminator, they would find they are so willing to shed some of their brilliant light onto his dark, blind path. Instead...man slogs along in the darkness...by choice," lamented Charis.

Eleeo explained another sign of the end. "A new Tower of Babel has been erected, confirming the esoteric prediction on the Georgia Guidestones. This new tower was completed on 1/4/2010 in the East. This tower symbolizes that man has become 'one' again, just as in the days of the original Tower of Babel, when they all spoke one language. This united effort has been produced through Globalism. The central governments of the G8 nations have united themselves into a single governing body...one mind. Also, all religions are uniting themselves through Mysticism, called spiritual contemplation in modern-day language. Mysticism declares there is no need for a mediator for sins, because man will evolve from evil to greatness through good works (social justice). The Tower of Babel symbolizes that man can communicate with the Creator on his own terms. What can I say...man has come full circle since the days of Noah...honoring himself as Deity."

"If they would only read the Sacred Script, where the Reconciler asks, *what fellowship has righteousness with unrighteousness, or what communion has light with darkness*? Man was commanded to not be unequally yoked together. Oh my...this is dreadful."

"You bet it's dreadful. That's why it is so hard for us to describe the degeneracy of man since you have never experienced unrighteousness. You have no concept of evil," stressed Eleeo.

"Globalism could not have been accomplished if the People of the Book had not lost their way, living luxuriously, lavishing upon themselves the accoutrements of the world. Evil triumphed because good people did nothing to stop it. They continually ignored the sin-convicting power of the illustrious Illuminator…heart was hardened," explained Chrestos as the reason for their defeat.

"The People of the Book kowtowing to Abbadon's demons is the most sickening sight that I must endure on Earth," added Dunamis, who had just joined them.

"While they revel in the luxuries the world throws at their feet, worshiping as pagans, their mind becomes the battlefield where Abbadon gains a foothold, polluting their minds with evil thoughts (and actions) driving them further and further away from intimacy with the Reconciler," Dunamis said with anguish in his voice.

"But the rest of the humans," he continued, "who have flat-out rejected the Reconciler, we must stand by and watch the Prince of Darkness and his wicked and disgusting imps infest their bodies, defile their spirit and pollute their mind with filthy thoughts of violence. Often I have to shut my eyes because I am so abhorred by their madness, as the demons crawl in and out of them, laughing and bragging about their great victory, thumbing their noses at us because we are not allowed to help."

"What is perplexing, outwardly these same people look beautiful, have successful careers, and even give to charity. No one seems aware of the invisible wicked demons that control their lives, because men fawn over them, honoring them with fame and fortune, as if they were gods. Apparently Abbadon makes sure he takes care of those who have sold out to him. But…it is horrifying to me!" concluded a mystified Dunamis.

Perplexed because of his innocence and heavenly purity, Therizo asked, "So you are saying people on Earth can live a successful and prosperous life without knowing the Reconciler?"

"Absolutely," Dunamis answered. "In fact…knowing the Reconciler does not guarantee success and prosperity in worldly things. It means prospering spiritually in order to arrive here successfully. In fact...believers become a target of Abbadon, who causes them grief and pain in his attempt to thwart their witness for the Reconciler."

"But to answer your question...man relinquished authority over the things of the earth when he sinned against the Infinite One. His tempter Abbadon, took ownership of the wealth of Earth. He can give this wealth to whomever he desires. As long as a human rejects the Reconciler and debunks the Sacred Script, Abbadon doesn't mind rewarding him by stroking his vanity while he lives on Earth. After all...he will have him for eternity in Gehinnom Land of Abandon. Ignoring the fact there is a place called Gehinnom, these humans are deceived into believing their good deeds will reserve for them a good home somewhere, maybe even here, after they leave Earth...at least those who even believe in an afterlife."

Still not understanding Gasar reasoned, "But I thought that all sin has consequences: sickness, disease, tragedy, trials, tribulation, rejection, failure, loss of friends and family."

"And you are correct," said Dunamis.

"Well then...if a human rejects the Reconciler, who died for their sins, yet is successful and prosperous, what consequence is this? It seems like a reward to me," Gasar rationalized.

"Oh...that's easy," Chrestos said with relief. "He may prosper on Earth because Abbadon allows it, but after he dies and leaves Earth he will face the consequences...the Creator must refuse him entrance into the City of Light. He will, with much grieving in His heart, be forced to direct him to his final destination...the Lake of Fire...forever."

"But you have told us so many stories of addictions, abuse, and tragedy in the lives of so many humans, besides all the war and chaos. Why are some people who serve Abbadon, not prospering or successful?" asked Therizo.

Dunamis tried to clear up the confusion. "Some humans prefer to complain and blame others for the tragedies that befall them, so unforgiveness, envy, and revenge eats away at them, rotting their mind and spirit. They refuse to forgive, which in turn, permits the most evil of Abbadon's demons to take charge of their lives. Once at the helm, these demons drag their complainers and haters into every imaginable wickedness and fiendish deeds. Their life on Earth is tragic…tragic is their life in Gehinnom."

"Over the past century the humans have essentially lost their praise and adoration of the Infinite One, transferring that need for worship to revering and praising celebrities…sinful man," explained Eleusis who just joined them.

"I just returned from my appraisal of the human condition on Earth and was appalled to see the abject spiritual poverty that has been accomplished by Abbadon and his demons after the days of Noah, when I was last on Earth. There are many giant stadiums filled with hundreds of thousands of people jumping up and down in excitement and praise. When I got a bit closer to see what caused all of this adulation and fervor, all I could see was a bunch of men running back and forth chasing after a pig skin ball and jumping on top of each other. It was such a shame to waste all of that praise on sinful men and his silly games. Now don't get me wrong. It is okay to have a little fun…but…save the praise and worship for the only One who deserves it…the Infinite One," declared Eleusis emphatically, still perplexed by man's irreverent actions on Earth.

"Are there stadiums filled with humans who are worshiping and praising the Infinite One?" asked Gasar hopefully.

"Let me answer that question interrupted Phileo. Two years ago the Illuminator incited revival across the planet. It was so spectacular it seemed as if the Infinite One had dumped a bombshell of supernatural revelation with signs and wonders, upon the whole planet, greater than at any time in the history of mankind. The illumination of His Son's salvation shone brightly in every nook and cranny of men's lives, awakening the sleeping giant, to do exploits across the whole planet. The revival left no doubt who is the true Creator, who represents love, and who alone offers mercy for the egregious sins of all mankind. The other gods that man has served have been publicly humiliated and shamed for their fakery."

Shalom agreed exclaiming, "This has been the most exciting time for humans, their last chance to make the right choice for eternity. Prime Time secular newscasters showed on television, the dead actually being raised back to life. They were interviewed on camera, testifying to descending into a horrifying abyss, describing in great detail about the intense fires, torment, and ghoulish creatures they experienced first-hand. They declared they were delivered from the abyss by giant dazzling angels. Their countenance still glowed with heavenly glory. The power and glory of the Illuminator was noticeably manifested, when the television crew became so wobbly they fell to the ground.

Eleeo got so excited he had to tell what he saw first-hand. "When those who were raised from the dead touched sick people, the anointing of the Illuminator appeared as liquid fire to minister to multiple needs. We saw missing limbs grow back and cancerous growths dropped off right in front of the camera. A definite line of demarcation was drawn, between the divine love of the Savior and false gods. The truth about the invisible world was undeniably obvious, and only a fool would turn down the mercy of the Infinite One."

"Are there humans who rejected this marvelous demonstration of the supernatural power of their Creator?" asked Therizo.

"Oh yeah, you see…this great revival has descended directly upon the man on the street, the unknown faithful believer and prayer warrior. Many entrenched denominational leaders decried these marvelous miracles, as the work of Abbadon. Condemnation flowed from the lips of famous religious leaders, against the unknowns who were anointed by the Illuminator. Since these miracles were not exclusively manifested through seminary elites, how could they be from the Infinite One? They are so pompous. The nobodies, those often rejected by the church elite, desire only to bring glory to their Lord, not a denomination, so He chose to anoint them to demonstrate His power to the lost in this last revival before His return. They wouldn't touch his glory," explained Phileo.

"It has been so amazing to watch. The human beings that He anointed were never accepted into the inner sanctum of the pompous progressive denominations. Some of these religious leaders are just plain cruel to ordinary believers, whom they consider unworthy of their time, let alone approval. Everyone must walk in lock-step to their interpretation of the Sacred Script, or they are not allowed to be part of their sacrosanct group. It is those who have lived in the secret place…intimacy with the Reconciler…whom the Illuminator has downloaded with the very oracles of the Infinite One, so that when they merely spoke His word it was created, be it a new heart, liver, limb or an eye. It has been simply awesome to watch," declared an enthusiastic Shalom.

Still full of excitement and enjoying the remembrance, Shalom continued. "One time when the secular television crews were in attendance, one of these humble anointed nobodies spoke, 'eyes be replaced,' and a man who was born with no eyeballs, instantly had new eyeballs...a beautiful brilliant blue...seeing the natural world for the very first time. Everyone was so ecstatic, screaming and praising the Infinite One, that I had to put my hands over my ears for some quiet...but I loved every minute of our Lord revealing His mercy," he laughed joyfully.

"Millions of miracles have been accomplished these past two years. This last great revival was promised and now has been fulfilled, in order to prepare the people on Earth for the return of the Reconciler. The line-walkers had to make a public decision for one side or the other. If they do not choose the Reconciler after this magnificent demonstration of His love...then...well...they will never come to Him," Phileo concluded sadly.

"He is absolutely right. Man's last chance to surrender to the Reconciler and save his life, has moved phenomenally and without precedent, across planet Earth. The Illuminator has left out not one human being from the opportunity to observe His supernatural demonstration of power. The sad report...the revival is over...and still billions reject the Reconciler as Savior and Lord...it is dumbfounding to us. You would expect that every human on Earth would fall down and worship him with joy and thanksgiving...but not so," said Shalom, wrapping up their sharing of this marvelous event on Earth.

Once all the excitement ebbed, Eleusis continued his Earth report. "I also attended a Rock Concert where people, mostly kids, actually swooned in front of the musicians who were swaggering to their own music (din from devils) dressed in garish demonic-looking make-up. And we certainly know what a demon looks like! The crowd was sighing, swaying, crying, worshiping, and praising, while some were screaming in ecstasy…trance-like. Fawning over mere men is incomprehensible to me."

With astute observation Gasar stated, "Well… obviously…they were worshiping demons, who were using the bodies of those musicians. How can they do that, when they have a heavenly Father who loves them with a pure and holy love? It has to be heart breaking to watch these humans wallow in such slime like slithering snakes."

Eleusis jubilantly exclaimed, while thrusting both hands into the air in high praise to the Infinite One, excited to give them the word, "We don't have to watch anymore! Since it was my appraisal report long ago that permitted the Infinite One to close the door of the Ark, we know why He requires our attendance in the Advent Amphitheatre right now! The Infinite One just sent me word that He has finished reading my global assessment report on the spiritual condition of all the humans, and He says that it is time for you to receive your Earth orders."

Therizo and Gasar just looked at each other with astonishment. It took a moment, but the announcement finally penetrated their reality and they suddenly burst into jubilant praises, grabbing each other's arms, jumping up and down shouting, "It's time…it's time...it's finally time to reap the harvest…yea!"

Eleusis said with fond remembrance, "We haven't been in that room…since…since…"

"Since…the birth of the Reconciler on Earth…the Lord and Savior of all mankind," said Dunamis finishing his sentence with enthusiasm.

"Yes, yes, yes," exclaimed Doxes. "Let us go forth and get our reaping orders."

All of the angelic warriors who were assigned to Earth for the second advent of the Reconciler, convened in the Advent Amphitheatre. Exuberant praises from this gigantic room could be heard pulsating throughout the Land of Perpetuity. Millions of glorified humans stopped their work just to listen to the resonant sound penetrating the whole realm…vibrating…alive. All knew innately that the battle on Earth was over and it was time to bring them home… the battle-weary warriors. They hugged and laughed and jumped up and down in praises to their honorable King, who has done all things well.

A holy hush fell upon the exuberant angelic reapers, when the Creator of the whole universe walked in to be seated on the Mercy Seat. The backdrop was luminous satiny platinum with pure gold etchings of cherubim throughout. The podium and grand stairway to the Mercy Seat resembled an illustrious aurora borealis… pulsating sparkling rays of colorful brilliance throughout the realm. The mighty Seraphim (burning ones) emitting brilliant streams of flaming glory, and dozens of colossal, winged cherubim beaming dazzling rays of glimmering light…ministered to Him. Then the Reconciler joined Him, sitting at His right side. A rainbow encircled them like a shimmering prism. It radiated colorful hues throughout the realm, not just in the Amphitheatre, a spectacular expression of supernatural energy.

The Infinite One stood, calling the archangel Eleusis to the front to give his report. When Eleusis came to the front he first addressed the Reconciler.

"You asked when you were on Earth, 'Will I find faith on Earth when I return?' That was two thousand years ago and the road to destruction has not only widened, but sadly, the road to life has narrowed. Gehinnom has enlarged itself."

Then Eleusis turned toward the millions of reapers, who filled the Advent Amphitheatre having already donned their mighty warrior garments and arms, ready to reap the harvest from the decayed planet. Some were assigned to reap the wicked, separating them from the righteous, while others were assigned to reap the righteous, placing them in a safe place just outside the City of Light, until after the battle of Armageddon. Armageddon is the last battle... rendezvous between Abbadon and the Infinite One.

Eleusis began his report. "There are a few wealthy banking families who have formed a consortium on Earth...the Sinister Seven partnered with the Prophet of Dawaism. Their consolidated ideology has evolved into the 8th Beast, as revealed in the Sacred Script. The Beast represents unmitigated, blatant and unstrained Paganism, now proudly practiced worldwide by degenerate humans. The humans fawn over and willingly follow after the Beast, looking for pity on their sorrowful plight. They have sold their souls to Paganism for free food, shelter, education and medicine. It is just pitiful. The great revival is now over...none are left on Earth who desire, nor ever will desire, the Reconciler and His salvation."

Eleusis then outlined some wisdom from the Sacred Script that was intended to guide human beings on Earth. "When the seeds of the gospel were sown, some fell by the wayside. These people heard the gospel, but immediately Abbadon came and took it right out of their heart. Some seed fell on rocks. These people, not only heard the gospel, but they also received the gospel with joy. When temptation came their way, even adversity, because they had no root they fell away from the truth. The seeds that fell on thorns (very wicked people) received the gospel gladly, went forth and produced fruit for the Reconciler. They built churches, radio and television networks, established publishing houses and seminaries. All of these things are good. But eventually, as they became rich from their endeavors, they became prideful, as if the world would end if they were not at the helm. Their fruit did not come to full maturity. They look very successful, according to the yardstick of the world, but not according to the yardstick of the gospel, which declares...*the first shall be last and the last shall be first*...It is through humility that spiritual maturity manifests."

A glow of radiant joy surrounded Eleusis as he proclaimed, "The seeds that fell on fertile soil, heard the gospel and kept it in their heart, glorifying only the Infinite One, not themselves. The spiritual fruit they produced was done so with patience and endurance, because the truth always brings with it much persecution from the servants of Abbadon and sadly...other believers."

"In the days of Noah's flood, the day finally came when all the people on Earth, except for only eight, rejected the Infinite One, preferring to partner with Abbadon and his demons. In those days, when I brought my appraisal report to the Infinite One, He told Noah it was time to bring onto the Ark all specified species and his family, and He would shut the door. I know all of you have been waiting for this moment...forever...it seems," shouted Eleusis exuberantly.

At that moment, every angelic reaper in the Amphitheatre could no longer restrain their enthusiasm, and jumped to their feet bursting into high praises, rocking even the walls of this great auditorium with trembling, rapturous joy. This ecstasy lasted for a very long time.

Eleusis called them to order as the Reconciler stood to talk. Immediately it became so quiet and reverent in the theatre, that you could have heard a pin drop.

"We have the final word that all who desire to receive Me as their Savior have done so. My faithful saints, who are still on Earth, are battle-weary and it is time to go get them. It is time to reap the harvest...both good and wicked. As written in the Sacred Script, Therizo will come out of the temple and shout to Me, 'Thrust in Your sickle and reap, for the harvest of Earth is ripe,' simultaneously I will begin My descent with a shout, taking with Me the saints who will be reunited with the bodies they left on Earth. Then the archangel Eleusis will blow his trumpet, which will awaken the bones in the graves prior to the great fire, while the saints who are still alive and in the thick of battle will be changed (mind & body) in a twinkling of an eye, from corruptible to incorruptible."

The Reconciler called Gasar and Therizo forward saying, "You and your army will go forth with your sharp sickle to reap from Earth all wickedness...all things that offend. Gather them together for the burn pile. One caution...be sure to take with you the special assignment cherubim from the Nanny Nursery, so they can gently retrieve all the little ones living in the wombs of the mothers who have chosen to follow Abbadon. Earth will burn with a great fire.

Then He wrapped up His instructions. "While Earth is burning, all humans will be brought to stand at the Judgment Seat, where I will separate the sheep (righteous) from the goats (unrighteous). After this is completed, you will cast the unrighteous into the Lake of Fire. There will be weeping, wailing, and clenching of teeth...for great will be their regret when they see the City of Light, as they pass by on their way to their eternal destination. The sheep, those who have been purchased by My blood, will stand before My judgment seat where their works on Earth will be judged. This judgment will determine, whether or not, they will be allowed to enter the Holy of Holies. As recorded in the Sacred Script, this is the place where the Creator of the universe dwells, which is symbolized by the wedding of the Bridegroom and His Bride in their eternal union. Many are called to the Wedding, but few will be chosen to attend."

After the Reconciler had delivered all of His instructions there was an awesome, reverential respectful silence. After a time He lifted His hands toward the Reapers and shouted, “ARE YOU READY?”

Chapter 16

Fiery Orb

Eleusis called together a few of the angelic reapers who will go with him to start the fires on Earth. The names on his roster were: Gasar, Therizo, Zelos, Stephanos, Hanan, Teleo and Ahar. None of these reapers had been to Earth, but now some will be assigned to orchestrate the gathering together of the unrighteous to be burned, while the others will call forth the righteous to receive the Lord at His return.

Then Eleusis turned to the multitude of reapers in the Advent Amphitheatre to tell them that he and these seven reapers would be back quickly for the rest of them.

These eight powerful angelic reapers soared effortlessly toward the terrestrial orb called Terra Firma (Earth), full of joy and anticipation. As they surveyed the vast universe in their descent, they couldn't help but comment to each other regarding the breathtaking galaxies, brilliant and numerous, formed into spirals and ellipses interspersed with colorful planets. This mission is exhilarating for these intrepid warrior angels on assignment to reap the harvest of Earth. As they sped toward Earth, they passed by many constellations with sparkling clusters of stars, awed by the beauty of the spectacular cosmos...created by the Infinite One.

Suddenly Gasar spotted a colorful glow in the distance, something unique, and asked Eleusis, "What is that gorgeous orb? It doesn't look like a planet because it seems hollow. That mysterious red glow seems to be exploding right out of the center," he declared with wide-eyed wonder.

"You are right," answered Eleusis, "it is not a planet. It is a Quasar...a huge cluster of divine energy in the Andromeda Galaxy. Often the energy of a Quasar exceeds the energy of the whole galaxy. The red shaft of light indicates remoteness. As the gases are released, a red glow is the result. It certainly is gorgeous. Man is unable to explain the omnipotence and omnipresence of his Creator, but the heavens declare His glory."

"Wow," exclaimed Therizo, "as his eyes focused on Earth in the Milky Way Galaxy. It appears majestic and serene, a rather stately old planet. It is so hard to imagine that it is full of wickedness and rebellion."

"Just wait until we get a bit closer," warned Eleusis, "then you will see a thick black mist surrounding this once celebrated orb."

"What is the black mist," asked Therizo?

"Do you have any guesses?" asked Eleusis, having a little fun.

"Oh...I know, I know," answered Zelos enthusiastically, "It has to be Abbadon's wicked demons of darkness."

"You are so right," confirmed Eleusis, "and we have to fight our way through his territory. But we are empowered by the Infinite One and will succeed in our mission. We have to keep in mind that Abbadon does not want Earth to burn, because his days of tormenting man will be over forever, and he will no longer be god of this world. Soon the world will be gone…puff…bye bye. This is why his imps will viciously attempt to stop us."

As they approached Earth, Abbadon's grotesque monsters took on definition. Multiple millions were packed together encircling Earth, about a half a mile above it. Some were small and slimy with beady eyes, while others were giant lumbering hairy creatures with varied freakish distortions. Some had thorns all over their bodies with fire streaming out of their mouths, as they tormented billions of humans. The giant black-winged vampires with blood dripping from their fangs were the most wicked of all of Abbadon's hordes of troublemakers.

Eleusis and his powerful reapers, brilliant as the noonday sun, drew their giant swords before penetrating this disgusting mass of evil. Immediately they were attacked by millions of these creepy ghouls from the abyss. With a shrill screeching hyena-like cry, black-shrouded vampires were observed descending to Earth attacking humans, sucking the life blood from their victims until they died. The dazzling brilliant reapers from the kingdom of the Infinite One, were horrified to see them yanking hundreds of human spirits right out of their bodies, dragging them down, down, down to the City of Gehinnom. It was a real shock for these holy servants of the City of Light to observe these grotesque demons of darkness at work.

Breathing deeply and steadily, staying focused, the eight angelic reapers successfully fought their way to Earth. Hanan was horrified as he watched these black-shrouded vampire spirits of death, wrestle with the screaming, terrified human beings who wildly resisted, unsuccessfully, being dragged to a place they did not want to go.

Needing clarity, Hanan asked, "What is happening to those human beings? From our vantage point I can see a thriving principality in the center of Earth, full of fire and foreboding. Is that Abbadon's abode…Gehinnom?"

"Yes," answered Eleusis. "I forgot…you have only heard about the place where Abbadon was condemned for sinning against the Infinite One, but you have never seen it. Pretty horrifying…huh?"

"I knew he left us aeons ago, but I had no idea that the angels, who left the light and purity of the Infinite One, would transform into such deformed grotesque creatures of darkness. Th…th...that would have happened to us, too, if we had gone with them," concluded Hanan, as he mulled over the horrifying thought.

"Absolutely," answered Eleusis. "You have very astute observations, Hanan. When one lives close to the Infinite One he exudes: light, honesty, love, patience, forgiveness, hope, gentleness, joy or endurance. When one lives close to Abbadon he exudes: darkness, lying, unforgiveness, hatred, murder, revenge, thievery, impatience, strife, envy or jealousy.

"So those humans that are being dragged to the center of Earth to the City of Gehinnom lived for Abbadon, rather than for the Infinite One," reasoned Hannan, wrinkling his brow with consternation.

"Right again, Hanan. Unimaginable…I know," answered Eleusis.

"B…b…but how can the humans ever have victory over this constant bombardment of evil overwhelming them 24/7?" asked a concerned Teleo.

"It does appear that the humans are at a disadvantage. And…the facts are…they can't in their natural strength and human wisdom obtain victory over Abbadon and his cruel, unrelenting temptations," answered Eleusis.

"But that isn't fair," opined Zelos.

"Oh…you are so right, Zelos. There is nothing fair about Abbadon. He has declared all out war on mankind to get back at the Infinite One," declared Eleusis.

"Wow! Now I understand why the Son of the Infinite One had to come to Earth and pay the ransom for sin," exclaimed Zelos, excited with his sudden revelation.

Adam and Eve were kidnapped from the Infinite One by Abbadon, when they fell into his temptation to disobey their Creator. The Reconciler paid the ransom price to redeem man from this sin, by dying on a bloody cross of shame and humiliation. He rose from death to reconcile man to his Creator. He didn't do away with Abbadon's ability to do evil…yet. His light penetrated the darkness of sin providing man a way to overcome sin. If man chooses the Reconciler, he can live in the midst of this evil and overcome it by the power and strength of the Lord."

"Bingo…you got it, Zelos," confirmed Eleusis.

"Never having seen Abbadon at his worst…like here on Earth, it was difficult to imagine the horror chamber he had made of Earth and the human inhabitants," Ahar commented.

"Hatred and revenge are ugly liabilities. It is obvious that Abbadon has pulled out all stops to plunder the land and kidnap the humans from the Infinite One," observed Zelos with great sadness.

"In His wisdom, the Infinite One devised a plan to get them back from Abbadon. He was well aware of the fact the human beings had no choice in being born into the natural realm…they didn't ask to be born. Since sin kidnapped them from Him, He decided they would have to choose to come back to Him…He would not force them. The choice to be redeemed from their sin…to become born again into His spiritual world…would be His gift to them. His instructions on how to choose Him or how to choose Abbadon are clearly defined in the Sacred Script," said Eleusis, awed about the grand plan of salvation.

"With what we are seeing, it is clear that billions of humans have made the choice to follow Abbadon," affirmed Hanan sorrowfully.

With a puzzled look he asked, "But my only question is...why?"

With the wisdom of the ages Eleusis answered, "Remember...Abbadon is god of this world. He lured humans to him by tempting them with money, success, and fame...an...an...and. Eleusis couldn't finish his statement because a great grief suddenly came over him. When he regained his composure he proceeded.

"And...the price man pays for Abbadon's generosity..." Eleusis still couldn't complete his thought, because grief stifled his words.

So Hanan, who was always so intuitive ventured to guess what Eleusis could not allow to pass through his lips...the thought was so horrifying to him. "The price man will pay for his allegiance to Abbadon is, never living in the presence of the Infinite One in the City of Light. He condemns himself to the Lake of Fire with Abbadon... forever."

A holy hush fell upon these awesome powerful angelic reapers, who knew that the Illuminator had worked diligently for centuries, trying to persuade man to follow the Infinite One, so there is no satisfaction, no 'you made your bed, now lie in it' like humans do...only grief and sorrow because too many humans have made the wrong choice.

Once they reached Earth, Eleusis took them on a tour of the perimeter of the whole planet. After he pointed out the seven continents, filling them in on the details of centuries of spiritual degeneration and depravity, all of the reapers could easily see that anarchy reigned in every nation on the old, once glorious and vibrant globe. The reapers were observing thousands of human beings killed by bombs exploding airplanes and train tunnels. In some nations radical religious bigots were invading villages and gunning down or beheading the occupants, then setting fire to everything. It was a horrific sight. Because of global anarchy, they clearly understood why it was time for the return of the Reconciler...humans are annihilating their own species. After their tour, Eleusis began to distribute the assignments to his reapers.

"Hanan and Zelos...you are assigned to earthquakes. In the depths of Earth thousands of earthquakes have rumbled over the centuries, surfacing occasionally to create great devastation, warning man of his fallibility. When you speak the command, strategically placed fault lines will ignite a great rolling, rocking and shaking to the surface of the whole planet. The giant skyscrapers, built by the ingenuity of man and the grand cathedrals of apostasy, will collapse on the underground cities of the elites, clever hideouts, where they have escaped for protection from the wrath of the Infinite One on paganism. The majestic mountains in every nation, which men conquered to exploit their bravado, will crack and crumble burying the pagans beneath the mammoth boulders."

"Teleo and Ahar...you are assigned to fiery volcanoes, both land and sea. As you can see from our vantage point that a majority of these volcanoes are entrances to Gehinnom, so they are filled with angry raging magma desiring to spew upon mankind. The Infinite One has essentially kept them in check over the centuries, limiting the will of Abbadon...but no longer. You will work in conjunction with Hanan and Zelos, since earthquakes set off volcanoes. There will not be one spot on Earth where the ground will not be rolling and reeling, until everything that man has built to the god of self completely collapses upon him. The tempestuous oceans will slosh and swirl tossing everything in them and on them to their death. The volcanoes will erupt to their full intensity, spewing molten lava one mile into the sky, then return to cover every portion of the globe burning up every living thing...global Pompeii. Nothing living will be left on this old planet."

"Now...Gasar and Therizo," instructed Eleusis, "you will be responsible for gathering together all of the wicked workers of unrighteousness. As we now peruse Earth I believe you can spot them.

Gasar quickly surveyed man's kingdom and exclaimed, "Oh yeah, absolutely. Piece a cake. They ooze moral decay and corruption from their spirit like a growing fungus, revealing to whom they have surrendered their allegiance. In contrast look over there, that human reflects the light of the Reconciler from his spirit. From our vantage point he appears to be encased in liquid light. Wow... all over this planet the righteous ones twinkle like stars, sharply distinct against the backdrop of ominous darkness generated by wicked demons," he assessed accurately

"Once you and Therizo have collected the wicked into strategic areas all over the planet, you will instruct the Nanny Angels to remove the babies from the wombs of the mothers, who have chosen to follow Abbadon. They will immediately carry them to the infant nursery in the City of Light. Of course, all of this will happen in a nanosecond," instructed Eleusis.

"Stephanos and I, with multitudes of angelic reapers, will be responsible for the bones of the dead saints to rise from the grave transformed, and unite them with their spirits appearing in the heavenly with the Reconciler. After I blow the trumpet the battle-weary saints, who are still alive will transform from an earthly man to a heavenly man. We will usher them to their Lord, who is returning for them as He promised. Then we will escort them to a safe place until after the Battle of Armageddon. After the righteous are safe, Teleo and Ahar will intensify the fire, until Earth and the works of men will melt from the fiery fervent heat."

"Any questions?" asked Eleusis.

"Well then...let's ignite the volcanoes, allowing a few to blow now in strategic locations as a warning...the end is upon them."

Arriving back to the Advent Amphitheatre, the eight returning angelic reapers found the other reaper warriors milling around and chatting excitedly about the most anticipated event in two thousand years. So they quickly headed for the temple to finalize the plans of the Reconciler.

Soon Therizo came out of the temple. Throughout this glorious heavenly realm his words could be clearly heard, "Thrust in Your sickle and reap, for the harvest of Earth is ripe."

At the sound of his shout, suddenly multiplied millions of saints living all over the great City of Light, stopped their joyous work and headed to the temple of the Reconciler. As the crowds of saints moved toward the temple they were hugging each other, crying and shouting exuberantly, "The day has finally arrived...our joy will now be complete, as we welcome our loved ones home."

As soon as they arrived at the temple, the Reconciler headed toward them with outstretched arms. On his head was a bright shining, pure gold crown, while in His hand was the Reapers sickle, which symbolizes He will release His saints from Earth's gravitational hold, so they can soar effortlessly toward Him, before His wrath burns Earth with hungry flames. The mass of redeemed human beings, wearing gowns of brightest snow-white, appeared as one gigantic cloud in the form of a body, while the Reconciler formed the head. They were preparing to descend toward Terra Firma (Earth).

Just before they departed, Gasar rushed out of the temple of the Infinite One in the City of Light, and shouted to his end-time reapers who had power over fire, Teleo and Ahar, to be ready to thrust in their sickles. The time to harvest the wicked has arrived. They hastily went forth to Earth to gather together the unrighteous, those who hated the Reconciler, to be burned in the great fire of the wrath of the Infinite One.

As soon as they arrived to Earth they went right to work, spreading out over every nation, wherever there was a human being who serves Abbadon. As they moved across Earth with flawless agility...liquid lights of majestic beauty...they commanded all volcanoes to intensify the fullness of their ferocity. Earthquakes rolled, reeled, moaned and groaned from the depths of Earth to the surface in every sector. From their vantage point, the reapers could see the tallest buildings waver and reel, then crumble into dust. Gas lines, oil wells, and chemical drums exploded creating a terrifying blaze in strategic areas.

Men, women and children were shrieking in terror unable to protect themselves from this cataclysmic end of times event. There was no government, no politician, no celebrity, no bishop/pastor/priest/imam to come and rescue them from the wrath of the Infinite One...because... the wrath of the Infinite One is a global experience. Thousands could be seen falling from amusement rides, climbers fell from mountain pinnacles, while others fell from their magnificent architectural structures (high-rise apartments, condos and offices). Giant war ships in the ocean turned over as effortlessly as a toy boat in a bathtub, while thousands of airplanes in the sky found no landing strips. Flashing through their mind was an image of their final destination, invoking profanity and blasphemy to flow from their lips against any god that came to remembrance. Yet arrogantly, some continued to believe they were still in control, and somehow they will get out of this mess. But... there was no doctor, no nurse, no EMT, no hospital, no policeman, no fireman...simply no one to rescue them. They were deceived right up to the end...just like in the days of Noah.

As they died by the millions, Gasar and his mighty angelic reapers gathered together those who had been burned up in the global fire, and took their spirits to the Judgment Seat of the Reconciler. The Nanny Angels safely transported millions of babies to the nursery in the City of Light, though Abbadon's wicked fire-breathing vampire demons attempted unsuccessfully, to disrupt their transportation to the safety of their nursery in Paradise.

Simultaneously, Eleusis awakened the bones of believers from their earthly graves by blowing his trumpet. This same blast transformed the battle-weary saints who were alive on Earth from...an earthly man...to a heavenly man. Stephanos directed each of his angelic reapers to take the hand of a heavenly man, and escort millions of them to their returning Savior. As they were freed from Earth's gravity...they moved up, up, up...closer and closer to the returning Redeemer, who was moving closer and closer, drawing them like a magnet until they could embrace. Joyful crying and trembling was their first response, as they laid eyes on their bright and shining glorified Lord, because it was unbelievable that the time had actually arrived. When they nearly reached Him, shouts of joy and ecstasy catapulted them into His arms. After this great reunion in the heavenly realm, time was of the essence. So the Reconciler quickly instructed His angelic reapers to take His redeemed to the Camp of the Saints for their safety, until after His rendezvous with Abbadon…Armageddon….the last battle.

When Abbadon sinned against the Infinite One aeons ago, he still was allowed to join the angels of the Infinite One, when they walked with Him daily around the outskirts of His vast kingdom. Once the Savior rose from the dead and returned to the Land of Perpetuity, Abbadon lost even this privilege and was cast to Earth like a lightning bolt. The angels were so grateful they no longer had to endure the arrogance of Abbadon, who had brought sin into their pure and holy home.

Once he was cast to Earth he was only allowed movement, between his abode in Gehinnom to the area surrounding Earth. He could never again enter the Land of Perpetuity, even the outskirts, until the last battle. The Infinite One had bound him to these parameters a long time ago.

Now…centuries later…the end has arrived. The fires of Gehinnom have swallowed Earth, so the archangel Eleusis loosed Abbadon from his limited boundaries. He was free to go anywhere in the universe. Enraged for having his power, to hold man in bondage to the fear of death, bound (limited) for two thousand years, he wasn't a happy camper even with his new found freedom. He snarled and cursed Eleusis, as he set out faster than the speed of light, to gather together his hordes of dragon monsters and serpent slayers from every part of the cosmos.

Once he was free to rant and rave in front of all of his compatriots, Abbadon immediately began to strategize their offensive attack on the Infinite One. He had been planning this day and night for centuries, thinking, plotting and imagining his final victory over his most hated enemy. He was not satisfied that he had kidnapped literally billions of human beings, out from under the nose of the Infinite

One…no…he wanted much more. Abbadon plans to usurp the throne of the Infinite One, so he will be revered and worshiped as the only God of the whole universe… yes…that is what he has dreamed about all of these centuries.

Abbadon had lived so many centuries away from the regenerating power of the River of Life his mind had deteriorated, causing his common sense and spiritual reasoning to become eroded through the practice of depravity. Because the transformation happened slowly, he had adjusted to his mental and spiritual degeneration, deluded into thinking he was still as powerful, as when he lived with honor in the Land of Perpetuity.

Meanwhile…at the Great White Throne of the Reconciler…Gasar, Therizo and their holy angelic reapers had deposited every follower of Abbadon from Terra Firma, as well as those who had been held in Gehinnom for millennia. Then the reapers took a strategic position, where they could clearly observe this massive gathering of human souls for the judgment of the sins of the nations. They waited for their next assignment from the Throne.

Abbadon had taken all of his wicked demonic hordes to advance on the Camp of the Saints and the City of Light. Millions upon millions of grotesque creatures from the darkness of the abyss, the fire-breathing vampires black as coal, mustered the power of their most evil expertise, and charged the Camp of the Saints. They expected a vicious battle because their swords and spears were thrust offensively against the angelic army of the Lord, boldly attempting to kidnap the saints from their haven.

But no such protracted engagement ensued. Upon their arrival they were met with, suddenly and without warning, a colossal burst of furious fire (glory of the Infinite One) showered upon the Prince of Darkness and his whole army of wicked demons…instantly vaporizing them. Earth and Gehinnom were in the process of dissolving in the furious fire, so there was no place left for Abbadon and his followers except the Lake of Fire...their final destination.

When the battle of Armageddon concluded, the saints were escorted from their safe haven by the angels, to the Great White Throne of the Reconciler, joining the human followers of Abbadon who were waiting for the Book of Life to be opened.

"Look at them," exclaimed Gasar, pointing to a specific section of Abbadon's followers, "the terror on each face reveals they really didn't believe there was judgment for their sins. Oh my...now it is too late...how sad."

Eleeo walked up and pointed to a group close by, whispering, "Those are the great leaders of Globalism... the Sinister Seven and their fawning entourage. Because they were possessed by Abbadon's demons of darkness, they were greatly feared while they ruled with an iron fist of corruption on Earth. Now they are simply cringing toadies. It is amazing how all members of the CFS, IIA and all secret societies, witches and vampires still surround them...even in judgment."

"Do they think the Sinister Seven still has power?" asked Gasar naively.

"No," answered Eleeo, "these servants of Paganism were so blinded by the demons that possessed them while they ruled on Earth, the fact there was a Land of Perpetuity never entered their minds. Truth has shocked their sensibilities, so congregating together gives them temporary solace."

"Shh," said Therizo putting his finger to his lips, "The Savior has arrived at the Judgment Seat."

In front of the Great White Throne Judgment, the archangel Eleusis was assigned to search the Book of Life for names written in it. A name will be found in the Book if he/she has accepted the Reconciler as Savior.

Stephanos called out the name of each person appearing before the Throne. If Eleusis found that name in the Book of Life that person, referred to symbolically in the Sacred Script as a sheep (easily led), was ushered to the right side of the Savior's throne. If a name was not in the Book of Life that person, referred to symbolically in the Sacred Script as a goat (self-willed), was ushered to the left side of the Savior's throne.

The long procession of billions of human spirits appearing before the One, who shed His blood for their sins...was finally over. Eleusis waved his hand and snapped his fingers, indicating to Gasar and Therizo, they were needed at the throne for their next assignment.

Just as they arrived at the Judgment Seat, they saw the Savior stand and turn to His left side. Sorrow transformed His countenance, while large teardrops rolled down His cheeks, as He addressed the goats on His left side.

His soulful eyes, deep and penetrating, gazed longingly at those who had rebuffed His longsuffering toward them. Billows of love emanated from His entire being onto this mass of humanity...liquid love...causing them to collapse into pitiful wailing and regretful lamentations, knowing now they made the wrong choice when they lived on Earth.

Then the Reconciler spoke tenderly, "When you were conceived in your mother's womb, your name was written in My Book," while moving His hands gently and lovingly across the Book of Life.

"I claimed you as My own, so I'm sorry that you scoffed when you heard there was a Book of Life. There is only one way your name could ever be blotted out of My Book," He explained, casting His eyes down briefly to regain His composure, but when He looked up, tears had welled again in His eyes.

"What happens now is not My will. While you were on Earth I longed to gather you to Myself, as a mother hen gathers her chicks under her wings for protection...but you would not have Me. Mourning is in My heart today and forever...because you did not choose My unconditional love offered to you. By rejecting Me, your name was blotted out of the Book of Life."

Still standing, though the grief He was experiencing could not be hidden, He pointed toward their final destination saying, "Depart from Me you workers of iniquity (disobedient, lawless)...to the Lake of Fire prepared for Abbadon and his angels...everlasting punishment."

Gasar and Therizo and their mighty angelic reapers gathered together billions of condemned human spirits and led them toward the Lake of Fire. The path they would take allowed them a clear view of the Land of Perpetuity. Loud wailing and mournful sobs could be heard from this mass of humanity, as each one for the first time, gazed upon the City of Light. Breathless awes of regret pervaded the whole crowd, when they saw the shimmering hues of colorful light pulsate throughout the heavenly realm... alive...thrilling. Everyone could feel eternal peace radiate from the holy city...the peace they tried to obtain by allegiance to Abbadon and his worldly sensual pleasure, while they were on Earth.

With sorrow in their hearts, Gasar and Therizo led this mass of humanity to the Lake of Fire, where they will be tormented day and night forever. This torment is the degeneration depicted by Abbadon and his grotesque demons, who have lived for aeons separated from the regenerating power of the Infinite One. And...the destructive flames will eat away their spiritual beauty. Allegiance to Abbadon...mark of the beast...had brought them to eternal damnation.

Along with these followers of the 8th Beast (Paganism/ Globalism) was the Prophet of Dawaism. He had proclaimed himself to be greater than the Reconciler, trumpeting that he was the divine chosen savior of the world, attempting to claim the divinity bestowed only upon the Son, by His Father, the Infinite One. He now has received his reward for his arrogance and presumption...the Lake of Fire.

The beast-world system of Paganism, the human followers of Paganism (goats), and the Prophet were delivered by the powerful luminescent angels of the Infinite One to the Lake of Fire. After the battle of Armageddon was lost by Abbadon, the Infinite One personally escorted him to the Lake of Fire along with his wicked agents, where they will be tormented day and night...forever.

Back at the Great White Throne Judgment, the Reconciler called for the other books to be brought forth, so His angels scurried to situate the books before Him. Then He stood to address the redeemed saints. He could see on their faces, which were bright and shining, exuberant joy and anticipation. He knew very well that a large percentage of those standing before Him, did not understand what was recorded in the Sacred Script regarding the judgment of the works of the saints...and He sorrowed.

"Each of you standing here today were kidnapped by sin, yet My blood paid your ransom, which allowed you to stand before Me today to judge the works you accomplished on Earth...in My name. Each of you were born with specific gifts or talents that were meant to be used to glorify Me and My eternal kingdom. At the time of your conception you were assigned a guardian angel, who had the mission to guard you from Abbadon, according to the words from your lips. Your words bound your angel from helping you, or your words loosed him to help you. The Illuminator convicted you of your sins and once you repented and accepted My ransom, He resided in your spirit to comfort you and guide you all your days on Earth, so you could arrive here safely."

Then a serious look dimmed His brilliant countenance, as He waved His hand gently across the many books. "In these books your guardian angels have recorded, the good deeds and evil deeds you accomplished, resulting from the gifts and talents that you received from Me. In the Sacred Script I promised, at My return I would bring you a reward. Inside these books before Me will reveal whether or not you will receive My reward. Because of My blood all of you here today will be joyfully welcomed into Paradise, but not all of you will receive My reward. For this I will be eternally grieved."

There was a buzz of discussion among the waiting saints, as they whispered to one another to see if someone understood what He was talking about.

One saint whispered, "I thought that my judgment was finished when I accepted the Reconciler as my Savior. So am I to be judged again?"

"Yeah," said a man on his right side. "I know I never shared the gospel with anyone, but after all, I wasn't a preacher, so I'm sure He didn't expect that of me. I worked fourteen hours a day and it was really hard to do anything else. I'm sure I will get his reward," he said assuredly.

A lady close by said, "I was at church every time the doors opened, taught Sunday school, cooked for our banquets, and visited the sick, so I was so busy doing good works for Him, to spend time with Him. My pastor said that the blood was all I needed to get His reward... and I have that," she concluded with confidence.

The conversation sounded like a low continuous hum, as the mass of humanity discussed with the ones around them what He meant. After self-assessment, most of them concluded that their good deeds (works) would definitely receive His reward...and why not?

The Reconciler waited patiently for the chatter to ebb. "When Stephanos calls your name your guardian angel, your life-long advocate will escort you before Me," explained the Reconciler.

"Pure motives of your heart that glorified Me...My character...will provide for you My reward. Nothing else is allowed to enter the Holy of Holies. Deeds of the flesh that defiled your earthly temple will burn up attempting to enter," He explained.

"Written in the Sacred Script was My invitation to you to participate in My wedding in the great Wedding Hall here in the Land of Perpetuity," He said, with a wave of His arm spanning the sparkling brilliance, pulsating throughout the glorious realm behind Him.

"In order to attend My wedding you must receive my promised reward...your Wedding Garment. The wedding symbolizes the Holy of Holies, the inner chamber where the Infinite One resides, where His glory is released in its fullest. Only the human beings, whose spirit, mind, and body have been purged of any semblance of sin, could tolerate the powerful glory of the Creator of the universe, released without measure in the Holy of Holies. In this chamber He has thrones for those wearing the Wedding Garment, from which they will rule over the new heavens and new earth...along side of Him."

"You may remember the prophetic parable, if you studied the Sacred Script, where the Infinite One came to the Wedding Hall to see who had come to His Son's wedding. The wedding was ready to take place, when He noticed that a man had sauntered into the Wedding Hall who was not wearing a Wedding Garment. The Infinite One asked the man how he got in the Wedding Hall without a Wedding Garment? The man was speechless... astonished...to be asked such a question. Why was he astonished? He had been taught by religious leaders, that every human being who enters the Land of Perpetuity, automatically participates in My wedding. They were very wrong. So the Infinite One had no choice, but to bind the man hand and foot (symbolizing error), and cast him out of the Wedding Hall into outer darkness. Outer darkness means a place where His glory is measured...less intense. All of you here today have been invited to My wedding, but few of you will be chosen to attend."

The Reconciler continued His explanation. "Multiplied millions of you standing here today believed that all you had to do was avoid Gehinnom, by accepting Me as your Savior. Although this action did pay your entrance fee to the Land of perpetuity, you thought that nothing more was required of you. You did not take the time to read in the Sacred Script, where I recorded that your moral and excellent works (character traits), fruits of the spirit, would weave for you your Robe of Righteousness...the Wedding Garment. I realize that many of you formed your character by reading the writings of revered theologians, rather than searching the Sacred Script for yourselves. Nonetheless, the Groom cannot receive His Bride unless she is wearing the Wedding Garment. This garment is clean and pure, unspotted by works of the flesh that honor men, in order to enjoy eternal spiritual intimacy with their Creator...where no sin of any kind has ever entered.

He was getting no pleasure in having to explain to His saints, at this late date, what they should have known on Earth, so they would have been better prepared. "The majority of you standing here today will not receive your Wedding Garment, because you are already shrouded in a garment...a cloak...called 'darkness of error.' Your cloak was woven for you on Earth with numerous threads of pride, rebellion, arrogance, selfishness, unforgiveness, greed, jealousy, envy, dishonesty, anger, strife, criticism, impatience, impure thoughts (motives), uncompassionate toward the needy, gossip, slander, hatred, rudeness, revenge and lasciviousness. You thought you were kept holy by church membership, strict adherence to man-made religious laws, or a denominational name, which only divided My body…the church."

"Many of you thought that your works of great missionary excursions, preaching in giant stadiums to tens of thousands, radio and television ministries, and publishing dozens of books proved that you were not only called to do great works, but you were greater than those who received your message. This is not so. I said in My Book that if anyone receives the message of the prophet, the reward is the same for both."

"It is true…many of you I did call to do great works… which some of you accomplished. But in time, they became great works of the flesh, glorifying you, rather than Me and My kingdom. You winked at abortion (murder) and euthanasia (murder), because you did not prevent the laws that legalized these horrors…and you could have with My help. But you did not ask. You chose not to get involved in governing yourselves, but rather allowed the heathens to govern you. All of these works of the flesh are the 'darkness of error' that defiled your human temple, where the Illuminator resided. This defilement created the shroud you wear this day before Me. The talents or gifts I gave to you did not create this garment," He explained, exhibiting a grieving countenance.

"You are probably asking yourself about now, how was the Robe of Righteousness…the Wedding Garment… woven?" and I will answer your question.

"Again…you may have built great cathedrals, you may have preached to tens of thousands and enjoyed radio and television ministries which are commendable, but these works do not provide threads to weave your Wedding Garment. Most of you did not take seriously the words of John the Baptist, who said that he must decrease, while I must increase."

"The Wedding Garment is woven by innumerable threads of forgiveness, humility, mercy, love, honesty, peace, patience, long-suffering, kindness, gentleness, joy, food for the hungry, water for the thirsty, clothes for the naked (relieving suffering), godly governing, and all moral excellence personified and exemplified by Me when I was on Earth...and...allegiance to Me only. Each of these spiritual attributes...fruits of the spirit...represent a thread that wove together your Wedding Garment. Remember...many are called to the Holy of Holies...the Wedding Chamber...but few are chosen to enter. You personally chose the threads that were used to weave your own garment. Sadly...I am well aware this concept was not preached from your pulpits...but it was written in the Sacred Script," He said lowering His voice to a dispirited whisper.

After his detailed explanation was complete, the time to give His reward had finally arrived. After Stephanos called out a name, one by one Eleusis read from the books the works of each person. Then it was finally time for the Bride to receive her Wedding Garment. With great joy in His heart, as tears welled in His eyes the Savior handed the fine linen, white as the driven snow, Wedding Garment to each saint who did not become a friend of the world. Then each one was led by his/her guardian angel to the great Wedding Hall in the center of His Kingdom... to wait for Him.

While walking down a golden path to the Wedding Hall, cobbled with brilliant diamonds and sparkling red rubies, they couldn't help but recollect how much they suffered on Earth...the rejection, humiliation, false accusations, media condemnation and chastening, torment and torture by government tyrants and imprisonment. Multiple-millions had been martyred (murdered) for their bold witness of salvation, while others suffered many indignities, often at the hands of other believers.

"But…now…it was worth it all," they joyously whispered.

Then the Reconciler addressed the saints who were left behind. "Those of you left here today arrived wearing a garment…'darkness of error.' You may be asking yourselves how you arrived in this pure and holy place, since you were told on Earth that only pure and holy people could do so," he declared with sorrow in His voice.

"By now you know that My blood sacrifice was payment for your sins, which reconciled you to My Father, after the disobedience (sin) of Adam and Eve severed that relationship. But you gave little thought while on Earth, about the works that you produced in your body. You chose not to renew your mind to righteous thoughts. This was your responsibility. An unrenewed mind produces works of the flesh, which glorified you," He explained with no joy on His face. He was deeply moved by grief, as His eyes slowly and silently surveyed the masses of now glorified humanity.

After all their secrets were revealed from the books, the Reconciler gazed intently…His compassion flowing upon them like liquid healing love, while the multitude of precious saints sobbed, inconsolable sorrow, struggling to calculate their great loss.

The crackling of intense flames instantly brought their attention once again to the Throne. They were thunderstruck, when suddenly and without warning, the books that recorded centuries of fleshly works, spontaneously ignited into a raging blaze…puff… disintegrated and disappeared.

After a time of contemplation, the Reconciler spoke very tenderly, "I wish you had studied the Sacred Script where it described this day, so you would have been prepared. I wish you had not chosen to build kingdoms, ministries, networks and businesses in My name, yet took all the glory. I wish that you had not disparaged My humble servants and prayer warriors, who distained the limelight because they desired to honor only Me. Many were poor in material things, yet you mocked them because they were not 'prosperity minded.' All who are in the Holy of Holies (Wedding Hall) waiting for Me right now suffered willingly, rather than selling their reward for worldly accolades. You judged the motives of their heart...now your motives are being judged accordingly. Yet...I take no pleasure in revealing these things. My heart mourns grievously."

"Since you are shrouded in 'darkness of error' you would be overwhelmed by Our unmeasured glory that dwells in the Holy of Holies...the Wedding Chamber...the eternal union of the Groom and His Bride. You cannot enter the Wedding Hall without the proper clothing... the glory conductive garment...enabling you to dwell in Our unmeasured glory. On the exterior (outer darkness) portion of this vast and glorious realm, there is a suitable place for you to live and mature in your knowledge of Our Kingdom."

Then He motioned to Eleusis and Stephanos to escort them to their eternal living quarters saying, "There are several communities in this portion of the Land of Perpetuity filled with various degrees of Our glory, depending on your level of purity to comprehend the glory." Several angels assisted Eleusis and Stephanos in directing them to their particular communities.

While being led to their new home in this spectacular spiritual realm, loud cries and sobs of regret could be heard throughout the multitude of redeemed souls, because of their great loss...not participating in the Wedding Supper...a loss they had not anticipated.

When they arrived to their new communities they were overjoyed to see that their homes were a million times more glorious than on Earth, and dropped to their knees to worship Him with grateful hearts. They were acutely aware they barely made it into the Land of Perpetuity, because they really deserved to be in the Lake of Fire. Yet…His marvelous grace (unmerited favor) allowed them to be part of His kingdom…all because they accepted His blood sacrifice for their sins. The spiritual body they received from Him was more magnificent than they could have ever imagined, and they were so grateful to be in the Land of Perpetuity with their Lord…forever. Joy unspeakable and full of glory filled their spirits with ecstasy.

As they settled into their eternal homes, their eyes surveyed their new surroundings. The vibrant colors of the flowers were otherworldly…pulsating eternal energy. The giant trees swayed with the rhythmic songs of worship that echoed continually throughout the glorious realm. The birds in these trees sang a new song of everlasting joy. Wonder and awe filled the hearts of these saints, as they perused this majestic land of grandeur…there was so much to see and explore.

Then they noticed a great brilliance in the center of the realm that was so spectacular, it captivated them all at the same time. One of the saints asked an angel walking by, "What is that spectacular site in the middle of this wondrous realm? It looks like a rotating prism streaming colorful light into infinity?"

Another saint exclaimed breathlessly, "It appears to be a magnificent display of fireworks, shooting stars of dazzling shimmering light."

Looking toward the place they were pointing, Shalom answered joyfully, "Oh yes, I see where you're looking. That is the Holy of Holies…the Wedding Hall…the Bride is now being joined to her Groom…never to be parted again…no more sorrow, no more tears, no more pain, nor more war and no more death…forever.

The Beginning

ABOUT THE AUTHOR

Mary Ann Gillispie has taught the Bible for 35 years...children, teens, and adults. Concerned about the spiritual degeneration of her beloved country and the distain for the Constitution and Bill of Rights by those in power, prompted her to write Terra Firma Angelicus, in order to provide spiritual truths to her generation.

She prays for the hearts and minds of the young people to find hope in the pages of this book.

She has two grown daughters and six grandchildren. Nestled in a mountainside in Montana, where wild rabbits , squirrels, and deer have befriended her, the Holy Spirit in this serene setting provides the inspiration for her writing.

Her past entrepreneurial endeavors include: a Christian bookstore; a Christian nursery school; a Christian radio program and a health-food dessert shop.

<u>Other Books by Author</u>

Endtime Reapers